I0688435

to Dream in Daylight

candace j. thomas

Published by Shadesilk Press
All rights reserved.
Edited by Talysa Sainz
Cover Art by Ben Villanueva

Cover Design by Monika MacFarlane

Ampersands Book Covers

Library of Congress: 2020913377

ISBN: 978-1-7352331-0-9

BISAC: Young Romance, Dreaming, Romantic Comedy, Fantasy

For my brother Josh and Humphrey Bear

"And no, his name cannot be Joe."

One

"What are you doing?"

The boy looks up from the tree and smiles. "Scratching."

The girl runs forward across the grass. "You can't scratch on the tree. You're hurting it."

The boy completely ignores her.

The girl looks around at the grassy meadow. "This is my tree. My own tree. No one ever comes to this tree. It's mine, and you're hurting my tree." She marches right up to him and shoves him hard on the shoulder.

The boy barely moves and laughs at her little attempt to stop him. "Ha. Right. I found the tree first."

"No, you didn't." Her hands fall on her hips. "I come here all the time. I have since I was six."

"And how old are you now?"

"Eight."

The boy smirks. "Well, I'm nine. Technically, I have seniority."

The smirk turns into a big toothy grin. He enjoys watching her temper raise.

The girl huffs. "Are you teasing me?"

"I might be."

"Who are you?"

"Who are you? Queen of the Tree?"

"Protector, thank you." She squares her jaw, sending her ponytail swinging around her shoulder.

The boy's eyes narrow as he looks her over. "Well, do you have a name?"

"I'm Adrianna."

"Adri-awna . . ." he drawls.

"Stop it. It's Adri. Don't call me that."

"Okay. Adri Paydrey. Adri Paydrey." He sings and returns to scratching. "Adri, who's eighty."

"Stop!" She swipes at his hand. The boy laughs. "I'm not eighty. I'll be nine in July."

"I'm already nine. My birthday's in May. You lose."

"Fine. You'll always be older. You'll be forty and I'll still be thirty-nine. So, nyah." The girl sticks out her tongue. "Okay, spill it. Who are you?"

The boy takes his stick away from the tree and flips it around his hand. "Not tellin'."

The girl reaches for his stick and he swings it behind his back.

"Gimme it."

He smiles, dodging her every effort. He starts to run.

The girl chases him around the meadow attempting to grab the stick. She stops mid-stride and stares. "Simon?"

The boy smiles. "You like that?"

She runs to the tree evaluating the damage. "You carved your name on the tree?"

"Yep. Now it's mine." He laughs harder than before. "Doesn't have your name on it."

"Trees feel pain."

"No, they don't."

The girl presses her palm on the sad scratched name. "I'm not leaving this tree. It's my favorite. It's where I come when I imagine."

"Well, you'll have company." The boy swings the stick toward the grass, nipping the tops.

"You won't be back. This is my dream."

The boy laughs. "Is it?"

"Done." I hammered the enter key on my keyboard, sending the last round of apology emails. I stared blankly at the absence of numbers in my inbox before putting my head on my desk. I rolled my head to look at the time visible on the corner of the computer screen. It was two hours past my time. I sighed deeply. "I'm logging off." I slowly raised my head and went back to the keyboard to sign off. I stretched out my cramped arms as the screens went to sleep. "Do you think we could ask for double the pay next time the server crashes?"

"Yeah, right, Sy. Not super likely." Adam took another handful of chips, wiped the collective salt from his fingers onto his pants and continued typing away.

The small corner room lay strung with collected gadgets and parts, where old keyboards and mismatched circuitry came to die. My co-worker Adam had a good set-up, four monitors; three displaying different system operations, the fourth one had a paused co-op game he hadn't touched in a few hours.

My own set up was not as cluttered—modest with only two screens—but the papers and drawings from my idea notebook fell loose-leaf from the pile. My monster sketch stared right in my eyes, taunting me.

I glanced once again at the clock, gaging the next train coming. "If I leave now, I can catch the Red. You cool if I head?"

Adam's fast fingers kept typing. "Yeah, not much more we can do tonight." His hand went in for another chip. "I may have to work some hours tomorrow. Make sure it's still running."

"I hope not." I quickly straightened my pile and shoved it back into my backpack, along with my phone, charger, water bottle, and all the other things I had randomly pulled out during the day. "These late nights are killing me. I'm beat."

"Know what you mean." Adam didn't look up from his screen, continuing typing. "Lisa is sick of me coming home late. The kids are already in bed. Think they're forgetting what I look like."

"Doubt it." I threw on my jacket one sleeve at a time. "They all look just like you."

Adam coughed a laugh. "Yep. No need for a DNA test there." He swiveled in his chair and held out his fist. I gave him a well-deserved fist bump. "Later, dude. I'm gonna look at the server one more time and make sure everything's working. Don't get mugged on the train."

"Got it." I flipped out my collar and prepared for the rain. "Good luck with On Call this weekend."

Adam waved his fingers shooing me out the door. "Yeah, yeah. See ya Monday."

I pushed out of our little office, down the scarce hallway, and out of the building into the rain.

Rain. I needed the rain. The smell of the wet sidewalk renewed my steps and fueled my energy. I felt the air return to my lungs. The week had been long and miserable, soul-sucking to the very end, and now I needed this rain. The smell in my nostrils, the soaking splatter cooling my temper. It tapped the ground lighter than I wished, but it was enough. Not many things are as miraculous a healer as rain.

The train wasn't far from my building, but I still needed to skidder around the puddles in order to catch the right one. I usually enjoyed the walk through downtown Portland, but I wasn't in the mood. I could hop on the Green line rather quickly and wanted, or more needed home, a bed, everything better than sitting in a poorly circulating office space, crammed with sweat and frustration. I ached to close my eyes and dream.

I ran up the platform and scanned my pass. The door opened and I plopped comfortably into my usual spot, the quiet corner near the back. I unzipped my bag and pulled open my laptop, the story still eating at me. The half-dragon creature still needed a name—Albert wouldn't work anymore.

A few more people came in. I briefly raised my head at the noise. A woman came with her hood held up. I caught the slight auburn color escaping her braid from under her jacket. A sudden jolt tightened my chest and my breath halted. The hood hovered like a Final Fantasy character, in a perfect mold keeping the face hidden and mysterious. I searched for more information as she took a seat.

"Well, hello, Simon."

I didn't register the voice at first, still somehow willing the girl to take down her hood. Simon. Someone said my name. I glanced over to see a pair of wise brown eyes staring at me. "Oh. Margaret. Hey."

The older lady had two filled sacks of groceries. We often rode the same train to our own particular destination. She stopped at Holgate Blvd and walked out of my life, until the next ride home. She laughed heartily at my startled response. "What? See a ghost?"

My eyes roved back to the hooded girl and let my heart quiet at the lack of a button nose. "Feels like it sometimes. This train is a little late for you."

"Well, I stopped to get some things on the way home." Margaret sat on the bench a corner away, pressing the sacks gently by her feet. She eyed my laptop propped on my knees. "Writing your story again? Did you get much farther? You said you'd write into the night."

"Yeah, about that." I ran my hand through my slightly damp hair, drying it a bit. "Didn't happen, unfortunately. Life, you know."

"Life," she smiled back. "Keeps us from our dreams sometimes."

I sighed, deeper than I intended. "Yeah." I couldn't keep the exhaustion from my voice. Dreaming felt like the only thing I was any good at. Adulting sucked every moment of creativity dry. Even when my roommate wasn't around, I still had to face the reality of him being with my ex-girlfriend. The contract on my lease didn't harbor much comfort. June needed to be here, still two months away. The rain pelted the train distracting me from counting the days.

"To be honest, Margaret," I returned to her original response. The woman sidled back from her wandering. "Dreaming is all I do to stay sane. If I didn't have dreams, I would've lost all hope." The girl in the black hood distracted me as she pressed her head to the glass like a child. An endearing gesture I recognized. "Dreams are keeping me going."

"Ah." Margaret's gentle laugh mixed with the rumble on the tracks. "You're soundin' like my daughter, always with her head in the clouds."

"My head's firmly planted. I promise." I sat forward, closer to her. "But here I am, you know, *adulting.* I have my degree. I have a job that pays fine. I'm living exactly what was expected of me to do. This is the dream life I figured out back in high school. I *am* the guy they told me to become." I sat back in my thoughts. "My teachers never told me it was joyless. My job completely infuriates me daily and makes me more miserable than it should. They never mentioned the cage I'd live in outside of college. I'm finding out I'm not that guy. I didn't find out who I wanted to be until after."

"You probably didn't know yourself." Margaret grabbed the rail as the train slowed for the next stop, holding steady. "Not many people do."

"I mean, I knew I was good with computers, and it felt like an obvious choice."

"What it sounds like, it was the easiest choice."

My shoulders sagged at her words. "Uh, yeah. Probably right." I sat back in my seat, considering.

"Listen, kid." Margaret's face took a turn. "I've bounced from job to job trying to find myself and didn't find nothin' until I had purpose. What you need is purpose. I mean, I didn't expect raising a daughter by myself, but I had no choice. And the decisions came at me, because it mattered now to someone else." She stared hard at me. I felt the sadness crack under her always calm face. "What I see for you is opportunity. That's something I didn't have until later."

"Opportunity?" I nearly scoffed but composed myself.

A few passengers came on the train but chose not to sit by us. The hooded girl still sat pressed near the window, now looking at her phone.

"I'd give anything to have the freedom you have." Margaret reached to secure her bag when the train jolted forward again. "Don't waste your dreams on doing what's expected. Life is the mechanics to keep dreams alive."

The words hung around and rolled in my head, but I wasn't sold. "I don't think I get it."

"I think you do," Margaret winked. "If you had your dreams, you wouldn't be on this train with me. You wouldn't be clutching your laptop right there." She leaned forward. "Or staring at someone on the train."

I straightened, knowing Margaret caught me. "Yes, but having my dreams would be nice. It would make me happy."

"Would it?" Margaret laughed again. It was hearty and made those around us nervous. "Happiness is not handed to us when we reach our dreams. There is always a morning after." She leaned forward. "Have you ever been kissed?"

"What?" I fidgeted a little. "Of course I have."

Margaret leaned back in some kind of memory. "Before I was ever kissed, I dreamed when our lips touched, I would forget myself and would be whisked away to a dream-state fairyland. Right?" She pointed a finger at me. "You see what I mean? When you kiss, your brain still works. It's actually working fast, preparing for what's next."

I looked around. Some overhearing young girl was blushing. The hooded girl was looking out the window. "I think I'm missing the analogy."

"When you reach your dream, you still need your brain. That's what I mean. We still need to eat and sleep and breathe in and out. And then we go out and reach for another dream."

"One dream is all I need right now. One win, you know? I'll worry about my brain afterward."

Her bright toothy grin lit up the dark night. "One will do." She laughed again. "For now."

My laptop screen went dark. I wiped the track pad with my finger and my manuscript returned. The cursor blinked again and again on the last sentence I wrote, each blink regulating my heartrate. I closed the laptop, not having any desire to write, and placed it back in my backpack.

The train slowed again for Holgate Boulevard. Margaret carefully snatched up her sacks again getting ready for her stop. "Dreaming is a good thing, Simon. Dreams can bring us happiness, sure they can, but try to find happiness where you are, in something real."

"Something real." I sighed and grinned back at her. "I'll try."

"Take care of yourself." The doors opened and Margaret walked out onto the wet platform and back into wherever her life led.

The "fifteen-minute wisdom from Margaret" sessions I usually smiled away, this one though, this one needled me. She poked an already deep soreness I was grappling with. She wouldn't have known anything about my struggling writing, my daylight dreaming, or my never-ending fight with what's real and what's not.

"Something real." I leaned my head against the glass, watching the rain pelt the window. I closed my eyes quick.

A face flashed through my mind and I opened my eyes again. The hooded girl was gone.

A dream was all I wanted.

My mind numbed as I stared at the screen, the stupid ellipsis glaring at me like it shouldn't be there. I read the whole sentence again. Fine. I clicked and dragged over the sentence and hit delete. Looked again and panicked. I found the back arrow and returned the sentence.

"This is the lamest thing I've ever . . . argh." My hand went to my face as I exhaled in complete frustration.

"Adri!"

My own name startled me and I shot up. Pauline leaned on the doorframe to my bedroom with an exasperated sigh.

"Girl, you told me you'd be dressed a half hour ago."

"I did." *Shoot.* I muted the music still playing on my computer. "Sorry. I thought if I just finished this sentence—"

"You're still on *that* sentence?" Pauline came and sat next to me on my bed, tapping her nails disapprovingly. Her bouncy dark hair tickled my arm as she leaned over looking at the screen. "Emily gazed deep into Joshua's eyes, knowing how dangerously close he stood to her, how tempted she was to reach once more and do something she shouldn't . . ." Pauline glared back at me. "The sentence is fine," she stated, snapping my laptop together.

"Wait! I haven't saved it."

"It's fine." She dismissed, yanking on my arm. "Come on. The party started an hour ago and you promised to come."

Pauline pulled me upright off my bed. I quickly got a glimpse of my current state in the full-length mirror. My black frame glasses were smudged on the corners, turning the whole world fuzzy around the edges. My hair was still in the make-shift bun I had stuffed it into after my shower. I could only *fix* it now, being too kinked to do anything down.

Pauline darted over to the closet and rifled through my things. "Seriously. We need to get you shopping. You only own two *decent* dresses."

I shrugged, still contemplating my hair. "I have a bunch of skirts."

"Something fun," Pauline snapped back. "Not boring librarian clothes."

I knew what she meant. I liked looking smart, like scholarly smart. I didn't owe leggy dresses that would show me off at some party in Andersonville. Pauline disapproved of everything I owned. She hated my completely adorable thrift shop finds. Chicago had many niche shops. When I found something unique and interesting, something with history and a story to tell, it breathed life into the clothes, someone else's life and making it my own. I'd go with Pauline to Magnificent Mile if she liked, but it lacked the personality I liked in my clothes.

Pauline threw the green dress on my bed, still on the hanger. I eyed the skimpy, skin-tight creation with a sour taste in my mouth. "Not this dress."

Pauline flicked her head from my cluster of shoes. "What's wrong with it?"

"Well, nothing." I picked it up and turned it around viewing the plunging back. "I'd only bought it with the idea of looking completely stunning in front of Miah." Of course, it was beautiful, but I wasn't interested in wearing the dress I wore to my ex's wedding. It was an impulse buy, something I regretted. Miah married Lydia anyway. It had been a good three months since the ceremony, and a year and change when we split. "Fine," I said and stripped off my yoga pants and tee. I slipped the dress off the hanger and pulled it over my head.

"Wait, uh-oh." Pauline waggled her finger at me. "You can't wear that bra." She snapped my boring white, very sensible bra strap.

"Stop." I peeked helplessly through the top. "Now I have to change my underwear?"

"The dress demands it." Pauline went back to my closet. "It's a crime to wear cotton with that dress. And besides, nothing feels better than beautiful, sexy underwear."

"That ride up," I said under my breath. I pulled the dress from around my shoulders. "No one's going to see it."

Pauline stuck her head up from my shoes. "You shouldn't plan your evening around what panties you're wearing. You never know."

"Cotton makes me safe."

"And dull." She stuck a shoe out at me. "But it's not about showing them off. It's about making you feel good. Sexy panties make you feel good."

"Ugh. Fine." I grunted and went to the top drawer of my dresser. Inside were all sorts of lacey creations I was too timid to wear. I ran my finger across a set I bought not too long ago on a vulnerable impulsive shopping trip.

I stepped behind my dresser and changed my underthings, letting the black lace hug what little curves I had. I walked back to the bed and grabbed the crumbled dress.

"See how much sexier you feel?" Pauline reappeared with strappy black heels, another impulse buy, and placed them right on top of my closed laptop, like a dagger into my manuscript. "We'll have fun."

"You said that last time," I grunted, struggling with the zipper in the back.

Pauline stepped in and helped. "Not my fault you got wasted."

"I had no idea what I was drinking." I grabbed the heels and sighed. "I'll kill myself in these."

"It'll be worth it." Pauline smirked. The grin on her face was something to admire, making her dark eyes big and shiny. "I'll text Danny and tell him we're on our way."

Pauline nearly skipped out of my room leaving me to evaluate myself in the full-length mirror. It was true, the strappy heels made my legs look awesome, but it wasn't like me to wear heels, even if I wanted to look taller. The dress— a creamy, dark green chiffon—would look rather stunning on anyone else, but memories were trapped in the fabric, and I resented still having it.

I pulled my hair out from the bun and shook it loose, combing it through with my fingers. The lump rose in the back and pushed my hair out like a mushroom. I shook it again like a dog, making it poof out more. "Fine," I conceded and carefully re-twisted it back into a neater bun, pinning some of the random stray strands into place like I had always meant for them to be there. Not half bad, I thought. A little make-up and mascara and I felt rather decent.

"Not your glasses." Pauline stared from the door. "Where are your contacts?"

I picked up my cat-eye frames. "I like my glasses."

"It doesn't match." Pauline rummaged through my make-up bag. "You look too smart with those things on."

"Too smart?"

"Yeah, it's intimidating. Guys won't talk to you if you're too smart."

"How absurd," I retorted, placing my glasses back on my face. "Guys like smart girls."

A bubbling laugh stuck in Pauline's throat. She cleared it and handed me a pack of the disposable lens. "You'll intimidate Dan's friends with the glasses. They're lively and funny, but they tend to date the superficial, big-boobed type."

I glanced down at what little God gave me. "Why am I going again?"

Pauline came behind me and considered my lack of enthusiasm in the mirror. I looked like a pasty ghost next to her beautiful dark skin. "You promised me, that's why. And you need to get out of the house. Meet people." She fluffed up my bun trying to tame it. "Let *Joshua and Emily* figure out their problems. You need to get away from your computer sometimes."

Pauline pulled me up straight and checked me up and down. She grabbed a bottle and I assumed the position. She quickly sprayed me with her fancy pink mist which smelled like cotton candy and handed over some chapstick. "Now, get in those contacts. Oh, and don't forget a jacket."

"I don't have a jacket that matches this." I complained.

"My tan one is in the closet," Pauline yelled from the other room.

After fumbling with my contacts so much I wished I could redo my eye make-up, I glamorously left with my roommate to catch the Brown Line.

Two

Adri brushes her hand down the bright, red rail. Her nail chips the exposed paint and flicks it in the air. She feels a bump on her hip, which pushes her sideways. Adri whips around to wild, dark hair. "Hey, Simon!" She shoves him playfully.

Simon starts laughing, walking in stride next to her. "Not my fault you're a featherweight."

Adri readjusts and slugs him in the arm. "Where are we?"

"Six Flags." Simon responds. "I went with my buddies on Saturday. I guess my subconscious is still living here."

"I'm not much for roller coasters. Even Cedar Point couldn't hold my interest."

Simon turns his head away from the double-looped dragon ride with sadness and focuses again on her. "Well, what do you like?"

"I never dream about flying. I'm always being catapulted or flipped like a pancake." Adri looks at the twirling swings near the small duck pond. "I like those things—the swings."

"The Tilt-A-Whirl?" Simon grabs her hand. "Wanna go?"

Adri blushes at the touch. "Well, yeah!"

Simon laughs. "Come on, then."

They run forward.

Adri's hand slips from his as they reach a railing before the ride. She laughs.

"What?" Simon replies, bouncing on his heels as he grips the rail.

Adri runs her fingers through her loose ponytail. "I'm glad I'm here. That's all."

"Yeah. Me too."

"This is fun. Not like the last dream where we met."

Simon grimaces. "I know. School dreams are the worst." He extends his palms in front of her in a 'you gotta believe me' manner. "I was wearing pants, though. Lucky that I've always worn pants when you visit."

Adri giggles. "You have pantsless dreams?"

"Of course." Simon waves his hands. "I mean, I'm usually in my boxers or something. My anxiety, I guess."

Adri lifts her head back to hear the echoes of excited squeals coming from the riders. "Do you ever think about big stuff?"

Simon sends her a side glance. "Big stuff? Like the size of the universe?"

Adri starts walking forward toward the entrance. "No, not like that. Like jobs, life, who you marry? Big life stuff?"

"What? No." Simon skips ahead of her and turns around. "You've already asked me this."

"Maybe it's something worth thinking about."

"We're teenagers." Simon holds his hands in the air as he approaches the turnstile. "Why do you keep asking?" He waits for her to reach it and lets her go first.

Adri enters and gets in line behind a few others. "My older sister is getting married. It's on my mind." She gestures toward the sky. "And she's marrying this really stupid guy."

Simon smirks. "Is he really stupid or does he just look stupid?" He bumps her side again. "Or maybe he's stupid because he's changing the way things are."

"Well, I don't know." Adri rubs her hands together, awkwardly. "Maybe I don't like him because he's stealing away my sister."

Simon makes a low whistle. "Sisters are overrated."

Adri cocks her head. "Don't you have a sister?"

Simon places his hands in his pockets and continues whistling without answering.

Adri waits, but he stays silent. She wraps her arms around herself. "So, there isn't a girl?"

"A girl? Like my sister?"

Adri gives an eyeroll. "A girl you like at school or something."

Simon scoffs. "Why? Jealous?"

Adri feels heat in her cheeks. "No. Of course not."

"You are." Simon's eyes brighten.

The line starts to move forward. Adri walks past and up the stairs. "And why in the world would I be jealous? I only see you in my imagination, in theme parks like this. You're not even real." She reaches the top where all the swings lay quietly dangling. She starts to dodge through them.

Simon feels her energy and sneaks to chase her around. "You always say I'm not real, but I think you're the one who's not real."

Adri laughs until she finds a red swing and sits, buckling herself in. A painted tree rests at the base of the ride, discolored and flaking from years of weather.

Simon buckles next to her. "No one gets under my skin like you. You have a plethora of opinions—"

"A plethora?"

"Yes. A plethora. And a ton of things to say about life. All stuff I don't know, or ever remember hearing."

Adri grabs onto the chains. "Well, I like to talk."

Simon finishes buckling. "And I like to tease."

Adri finds herself blushing again. "So, truth." Adri inches toward him before the Tilt-A-Whirl begins. "There isn't another girl?"

Simon twists her chair. "No. Not in dreams or at any different tree that I carved my name on. What about you? Ignoring your own question? Is there a guy out there, not imaginary, that you like? You're the one who's always carrying on about these things."

They both feel the jolt as the ride begins to lift.

Adri looks over. "Not really."

"Not really?" Simon returns.

Adri's side of her mouth turns up. "Not anyone not imaginary."

Simon narrows his gaze. "Not imaginary?"

Adri laughs and looks forward, feeling the rush of air as the Tilt-A-Whirl begins to spin. She lifts her arms and begins to fly.

Andersonville, IL

My ankle wobbled as my heel found a crack in the sidewalk.

"Why did I let you talk me into these shoes?"

Pauline didn't answer. She just kept dragging me onward, never mentioning once how far the house was from the train. My ankles were killing me. The shoes bunched up my toes and made me walk differently than usual, like a model sauntering back and forth. I was not used to wearing heals. I didn't have the muscle strength to pull it off.

The house sat in the middle of Catalpa. I knew the area somewhat because it wasn't far from the bookstore, but never had any reason to venture farther. It was nice to see the quaint, older houses stacked close together. I got distracted by the little neighborhood library nailed to a post outside one of the houses. I stopped to look what rested in there.

"Come on." Pauline yanked on my sleeve.

"Little Women," I said before she dragged me away. "I love that book."

"It will still be there when we leave." Pauline started to skip. "Come on. We are so late."

I let her haul me forward.

Did it matter where I was going and what I was doing? I was following Pauline to her boyfriend's friend's party. I wouldn't know anyone anyway.

The house was a brick dream, classic old red and fading white trim. I liked the divided subletted charm Andersonville offered, though too pricey for what I could afford.

Pauline pushed me through the door, and I immediately encountered the gentle smell of crisp, old house. Our apartment sat below a foodie brunch house, where the smell of garlic and brie permeated everything. This house smelled fresh and clean of old Chicago. Appreciation bubbled inside me, like it did when handling an old, well-worn book. I had expected loud booming music like in a 90s rom-com, but the sweet hum of chatter covered the unidentifiable music in the background.

I shed my borrowed jacket, letting my bare shoulders say hello to all the house strangers, and hung it next to Pauline's black knit sweater on the coat rack.

"Come on." Pauline pinched my arm pulling me across the room and into the kitchen.

"Oh, hey. There you are." Danny stepped over and kissed Pauline on the cheek before wrapping her in a sweet bear hug. I liked Danny. He was a little goofy for Pauline, but he made her happy. His tiny, light brown curls stuck tight to his head like spicy ramen noodles. Tonight, it had a slight part on the side and stuck up in certain places, but he never cared much about what other people thought—another part of his charm. "Pleasure to see you, Adri. Looking great. How did Pauline talk you into those heels?"

"Ha ha," I joked. "The same way she talked me into coming. Being scary and demanding."

Pauline reached up and kissed Danny again. "I know how to get what I want."

"This is my buddy Greg's place." Danny turned his head around. "I'll try and find him. Get a drink, will ya?"

He and Pauline headed out of the kitchen, and I was left with a bunch of different bottles in front of me. The last time I had worn the green chiffon, I got, as Pauline put it, "wasted" on whatever was available at Miah's wedding. The dress had a history I was not about to repeat. I grabbed a glass of what looked like lemonade and went back to the living room.

I hoped I might know someone here, but I scoped through the hipster socialites and didn't know a soul.

Perfect.

An old couch lined a corner wall, covered with long legs and teasing smiles. Corners crowded with college grads fairly entertained with each other. The chatter was a cool addition to a background music I didn't recognize. Watching people was fascinating. I pressed myself to the back wall and tried as hard as I could to disappear.

I took a gentle sip of the drink and felt the quick burn down my throat. Definitely not only lemonade.

"Hey." Someone was talking to me. I turned to find a guy leaning on the wall. He seemed slightly familiar, but a lot of people looked familiar to me in the city.

"Do I know you?" I buttoned my lip. "Sorry. That came out way ruder than I intended. I should have said, 'Do we know each other?' or something friendlier."

The man couldn't tell if I was joking or not. "Don't think I know you," he stated halfway yawning. "Name's Lincoln."

I raised my eyebrow. "Like the president?"

"Sure. But more like the city."

"Okay." I took another sip, not because I wanted more, but to keep my mouth busy. "Oh. Can I call you Link? You know, like the video game?"

Lincoln squinted his eyes at me. I took the gesture as a no. "And your name?"

I choked a little before I spoke, trying to hide the burn in my throat. "I'm Adri."

"Adri? Not a common name."

"Short for Adrianna." I smoothed out the condensation left from my lips on the glass.

"Adrianna." He rolled my name out like an expert. "So, how do you know Greg?"

"I don't. I'm here with a friend."

"Oh." He shifted a little. "Who's your friend?"

"Uh . . ." I thought of lying, but there was no point to it. "Pauline Williams."

Lincoln perked up. "Dan's girl? She's fantastic. I'm surprised I've never met you."

I laughed. "Don't be surprised. Pauline's my roommate. She likes dressing me up and forcing me out of the house. I don't come to parties often."

"Well, what do you do?"

The conversation had turned from small talk to getting to know someone. We had surpassed the general, awkward air fillers. He was changing the atmosphere and if I ignored it, he would know I was deliberately avoiding getting to know him. I wasn't in the mood to talk, but I didn't have an inner bitch to scare him away. I angled toward this stranger.

Lincoln had dark, fuzzy hair haloed by the living room lamp light. The sharpness of his nose amused me, like Jack Frost, set before eyes so dark I couldn't see a color. There was a geek charm to him, the kind I tended to be attracted to, but I felt too out-of-place to comfortably feel anything.

I cocked my head. "I work in a bookstore."

I could tell Lincoln was thinking of how to respond. "Okay, cool. But, I meant if you don't go to parties, what do you do instead? Just work?"

"I read."

His head went back to nodding, and I went back to pretending to sip.

I figured Lincoln was catching on how boring I was, but he started up again.

"I never have time to read." Lincoln's head rested on the wall, his weird curls flattening on the surface. "I read mostly science books anyway, science journals. No fiction or anything."

My heart snapped a little. "You don't read fiction?"

"Nah." He twisted again facing forward. "It doesn't interest me. Especially fantasy. I don't know why people like it."

Any attraction I had felt for Lincoln vanished as quick as it came. I forced myself away from the wall. "I love fiction. I'm a writer as well. I've written a few things. Last summer, I published a short story on Zagmag."

"Oh." Lincoln was taken aback by my sudden urge to share. "That's cool. It takes a lot to publish something, right?"

"Yeah, sure." An awkward silence came between us. Luckily, at the same moment, the door opened. A couple came hand-in-hand through the door.

"Hey, Lydia! Miah!" Lincoln hailed the people and walked forward.

My head shot up as I took in the figures.

There, standing no more than ten feet away from me, stood my ex-boyfriend Miah and his striking new bride.

I downed the drink in one huge gulp.

Portland, OR

The rain beat fast on my hood as I stepped from the train. The zipper on my backpack kept getting caught in the fabric, but I tugged it closed. It was still a hike to my apartment, and I didn't want my laptop getting ruined.

I liked rain, speaking in its pounding rhythm, numbing every feeling and emotion I had. I liked wearing a jacket and pulling the hood up around my head, like an RPG character. It was one of the only things I liked about living in Portland. Rain provided the perfect environment for a would-be writer with the dark, brooding doldrums an overcast sky can provide. I took the job here because of the seasons. It didn't rain much in Colorado, and I supposed with how boring the job sounded, I could get more writing in. The tired ache in my chest from such a horrible week told me otherwise. I lifted my head and felt the rain drip on my face.

I didn't, however, like the hike to my apartment.

The rain pelted from the east, slashing my face and limiting my vision. I tucked my chin down, staring at my shoes. I nearly missed the sight of the little red beetle parked on the street. A pang ripped in my chest, the same pang I felt every time I glimpsed the bright paint job.

Jessica.

The swear formed in my mouth. The wound named 'Jessica' hadn't healed properly, since she was at my apartment all the time. I seriously saw her *all the time*. Why did they have to hang out at my place instead of her place? She had a great apartment, bigger and nicer than mine. I considered maybe she was deliberately torturing me, but in truth, I think she just didn't care.

I wasn't even mad, honestly. I wasn't ever in love with her. I didn't like how everything ended, though.

I briefly contemplated kicking the bumper of the little red car, or maybe cracking her window letting the rain get everything inside wet, but I sighed and climbed the stairs to my apartment.

Vapid yelling emanated through the door. Maybe they wouldn't notice me come in.

I turned the knob and pushed the door open. The rage of rapid gunfire filled my ears. It was surprising the neighbors didn't complain about the daily disturbance, but they were never around anyway. I snuck in, quietly closing the door behind me.

"Yo! Sy!" Nate yelled his greeting without looking up from the screen.

He sat on the beat-up couch by himself. No Jessica. I felt a mix of panic and relief looking at the empty spot by him. Her car was definitely outside, its black kitty sticker slapped unmistakably on the back window. No, Jessica was here, and a nervous energy swept through me, worried about where she was currently hiding in my apartment.

"Hey." I returned the greeting as I flung my backpack on the square card table crammed in the corner of the dining area.

I slipped off my rain-soaked jacket and hung it on the back of the matching folding chair. "Where's Jess?" I had to ask.

"She's taking a nap," Nate stated between the muttering in his headset as he took another kill shot.

"Oh." Relief. She could sleep and I could sneak to my bedroom, shut the door, and not even see her. I quickly rummaged in the fridge, made a sandwich, and grabbed a cold Dr. Pepper. I tried to balance the plate and the can in one hand while grabbing my laptop to head into my room.

"Whoa, Sy," Nate called over. "Come see this. Found online a way to kill the zoigets without completely unloading on their asses. Check this out."

I stepped closer, evaluating the violent eruption of gunfire to satisfy Nate's vulgarity spewing freely at the flat screen.

"Yeah, see that?"

"Very cool." My laptop tottered in my other hand as I worked to get a better grip. "So, I'm gonna head to my room. You got the place."

Nate's mouth curled. "Okay. cool." I couldn't read his expression, a slight disappointment possibly. I don't hang out with him much anymore, not since he and Jessica started dating.

Jessica did the typical move you see in all the movies. We had met in a coffee shop by my work. I immediately liked her because she was different from other girls I had known. She wasn't ordinary, though ordinary for Portland still leaves a lot of room. We had similar tastes in music and liked to game, which I found rather sexy. A girl who could talk gamer was a keeper. But she lost interest in me and liked Nate better. I wouldn't put her as the top of my priorities, because honestly, she wasn't. I still didn't like seeing her at my house all the time. Memories are the cruelest form of torture.

My finger flipped in the direction of my room. "Yeah, I'm gonna head over . . ."

My phone buzzed in my pocket. I couldn't reach it with my hands full. It continued to buzz; someone was calling me. No one ever called me. I slid my laptop between my arm and my chest to reach it.

Liane.

I slightly smiled. I swiped it open.

"Hey, hold on." I answered.

"Oh . . . kay?" came through the speaker.

I nodded to Nate and left for my room.

Once I shut the door and placed my stuff on the bed, I picked my phone back up.

"Hey, sorry about that. My hands were full. What's up?"

"Well, hello to you too." The sweet voice of Liane filled the room. It was good to hear my sister's voice. "Listen to this." There was rustling around and I could hear the gentle jabber of my niece. "Okay. Who's your favorite uncle?"

More gentle jabber.

"Oh, come on. You were just saying it." A few more times and more noise. I could hear the outward frustration from my sister and laughed. "I swear. Sorry. I wanted you to hear it. She can't say 'Simon', but she says 'mon mon.' It's so cute."

"I'll be Uncle Mon Mon." I laughed again.

Liane had a way of making everything brighter. Listening to her light conversation about her tiny human made all the heaviness of my current situation feel better. Liane made it a point to call just to hear my voice. She could always tell from my tone when something was wrong. My little sister, the one I was supposed to protect, went off and got herself married and started a life without me. Only the slightest bit of jealousy twinged in my chest. Marriage and family were the furthest thing away from me right now.

"You sound miserable, Sy."

I stretched out on my bed. "I'm not too bad." My voice sounded more tired than I felt. "When my lease is up, I'll think about what to do."

"And come home?" Liane's optimism was still cute. I could hear her grin.

"I wouldn't go that far. Portland's good to me."

"No, it's not," she bantered. "It was a place to run away."

I hated when she hit the nail on the head. "Well, maybe, but I have a good job here."

"No, you don't. You have a job."

Stop being right all the time. I sighed at the truth of everything. "It's not that easy, sis."

"It can be. Oh, hold on." I could hear her struggle for a moment to keep the phone away from her toddler. Finally, I could hear quiet. She must have given little Lily a cracker to munch on. She came back, her voice solemn. "It can be, Simon. I know you have a job and an apartment and everything, but it can be as simple as packing up one day and flying back. People do it all the time."

A cool silence settled over me as I pondered what to say. "I have responsibilities."

She sighed again. "Think about it. That's all. I didn't call to make you feel bad. There isn't anything keeping you there, really. You aren't dating anyone, and you haven't many friends."

"I have friends."

"Land dwellers, not those gremlins that live in the basement."

I knew she meant my RP Gaming friends. "They're good people. And stop worrying about me. I'm the older one."

"Right. Right." She laughed. Liane had always been more responsible. "Is the girl still around?"

She knew everything that went down. "Yeah. She's here taking a nap right now."

"Well," she quieted down. "Don't get caught up in it. Let her go. You always fall for the redheads."

The image of the hooded girl from the train flashed in the back of my mind. It wasn't her I imagined under the hood, but she was close. I was soul sick, but I couldn't let Liane know. "Trying, promise."

I swiped my phone closed and rested it on my chest. A door in the hallway creaked. I could hear the little footsteps of Jessica making her way out of Nate's room and into the front of the apartment. I gawped half-heartedly at my sandwich but was now glad I had it. I could stay in this room for a while.

I opened up my laptop, took out my headphones, turned on my writing station, and stared at the last few lines I had written.

Three

"Are you okay?" Adri asks, launching her airplane. It dives but doesn't come close to the cliff edge. "You don't seem okay."

Simon rests his head on the orange rock, staring off into the settling sun. The quiet canyon casts long shadows down the steep ravine. His paper airplane remains unfolded. "I'm not very creative right now."

Adri creeps through the dusty rock to pick hers up. "You're always creative. Come on. Finish your plane." She walks back and rests against the rock next to him.

Simon folds his plane meticulously into a tight dart.

Adri scoffs. "That's cheating."

"No, it's strategy." Simon launches his airplane, traveling twice as far as Adri's had until it plants itself on a cactus.

Adri throws hers again. It takes a quick nosedive two feet away.

"You threw it too hard." Simon stands. He leans forward and grabs Adri's plane.

Adri flips her hair. "I threw it just as hard as you did."

"Yeah, but yours isn't made like mine." Simon takes Adri's plane and tosses it up. It catches the canyon wind and glides softly near his plane.

Adri blushes. "How did you do that?"

Simon walks to retrieve the two planes. "It's called patience, something you don't have."

"You're one to talk." Adri stands next to him, dusting off her pants. "You okay?"

The wind picks up near the cliff face.

Simon holds both planes. He hesitates to give Adri hers. "My mom's sick."

Adri stares. "What kind of sick?"

Simon still stares at the planes. "Not a sick that goes away with ibuprofen."

Adri stumbles for words. "Oh." She takes her plane from his hands. "Do you think she'll get better?"

Simon shrugs. "Probably. It's still early. She just told us."

Adri stiffens. "Are you talking cancer?"

Simon lifts his head and stares at the sun. "Yeah, something like that."

Adri touches Simon's elbow, unsure what to do. "I'm really sorry."

Simon doesn't flinch. He holds up his plane and smiles. "She taught me to cheat at making paper airplanes."

Adri laughs. "I thought it was strategy?"

Simon laughs too. "Well, let's see." He holds up his plane. "The sun's going down."

Adri bumps his arm. "You know, your voice echoes from here. Try it?"

Simon grins. "Okay!" he yells. A clear echo rings "okay."

Adri matches his position. "Ready!"

"Together." Simon says.

"One!" "One!"

"Two!" "Two!"

"Three!"

Chicago, IL

The headache was there way before I could open my eyes. I felt the pillow over my face like a lead weight, pushing with such gravity, I worried the pressure would suffocate me.

"Oh, you're awake." Pauline's muffled voice called far from somewhere in the room.

I groaned and rolled over. I was not in my bed. I could feel the scratchy stitching from the homemade quilt Pauline kept on our couch. I was home, but I had no recollection of how I had gotten here.

"I'll make coffee!" Pauline shouted, the sound ringing in my ears.

A muffled "Yeah" exited my lips.

I felt Pauline sit next to me, setting the steaming mug on the coffee table. The husky aroma filled my nostrils, tempting me. She always made great coffee.

I finally opened my eyes. The sun hitting our bottom apartment window was past its usual morning appearance. It had to be around 11 AM. I peeked over at Pauline. Her wide smile hid something behind it.

I sat up a little straighter, my muscles aching with every stretch, especially my side. I still wore the green dress, though it was crumpled around my body, creasing the delicate pleats. I smoothed it out and saw a little tear near the bottom. "Oh, darn."

Pauline grabbed the mug and handed it to me. "Come on, drink up. I need to hear all the details."

I took the warm cup and sipped. The deep flavor filled my mouth and coated down my throat like some lifeline heading straight to my heart to keep it beating. The wicked sensation of caffeine jolted around in my bloodstream, like a superpower surging. It was heaven. I took another sip.

"Girl, stop messing with me."

My head hurt too much to think. "Messing with you? What do you mean?"

Pauline's jaw jutted out in a weird 'don't you know' kind of way. "Are you telling me you don't remember?"

I put a hand to my temple, rubbing it gently. "I don't know. Maybe?" The night was fuzzy. After my third shot of the lemon drink, whatever it was, the details disappeared. "Miah showed up with Lydia. Lincoln kept close to me all night. I remember complaining a bit." The coffee helped clear my mind. "Hey, where were you all night?"

"We were playing billiards in the back. I didn't come up until I heard the shouting."

"Shouting?" The jigsaw slid into place. "Oh, gosh." My hand covered my eyes and I could feel my face was more tender than just the hangover. I set down the mug so I could touch my cheek a little bit. "Is it bad?"

Pauline examined my face. "I've seen worse."

"I've never had a black eye before." I slowly stood and checked my reflection in the small mirror by the door. The dark ring ran below my eye and up my temple. A small scrape shaped like a star appeared right along my cheekbone. "Lydia's left-handed," I commented lightly deducting the ring mark.

"Please, girl," Pauline pleaded. "I've been waiting all morning to hear this story."

"Ah, geez." I sighed and slumped back on the couch. "So, let me see what I remember."

I took two long draws of the steaming coffee, and it felt warm all the way to my stomach. Pauline's eyes could not get any wider.

"Let me start from the beginning." My knees wrapped up on the couch toward her. I fumbled with the fabric of my dress as I told her what happened:

Miah and Lydia, the most celebrated couple of the moment, arrived in splendid fashion. The waft of his cologne hit me first. He always smelled incredible. The scent brought so many memories flooding back: our first date, the Halloween party, making out on his sofa—little things like that. But there was Lydia, and it was painfully obvious why we didn't work out. Her legs were way too long for her black skirt and killer heels. I spent years with the guy. We break up and six months later he's engaged.

Miah spotted me quick, his funny half-smile smeared on his smug face. I knew he didn't like seeing me there, but he came over and greeted me fine. Actually, asked how I was doing.

There were little things I was still hanging on to, memories I couldn't shake. And that's the hardest thing about falling out of a relationship—the good times. There were many good times, hardly any bad times. I didn't see it when he had fallen out of love with me and fallen in with someone else. It stung, and I guess that's why I clung on to things. Two years of my memories were filled with this guy. I couldn't easily erase it.

Lydia, however, knew she had taken this guy from me. And I didn't like how she glared at me—like I was the biggest loser. A firm, contemptable gaze lit under those voluminous false lashes.

I stayed away for the most part. Downed a few more drinks. Talked boring stuff with Lincoln. Turned out he was an okay guy, but I wasn't listening. At some point I went to find you, but things started to get fuzzy. When I get a few drinks in me, I feel like the funniest person in the world. I thought I was being charming.

After not finding you, I stumbled into the kitchen.

Miah was there. Just Miah. He was grabbing a drink.

"I thought you didn't drink?"

Miah squared at me. "I usually don't."

"But, tonight. Tonight is different. Because I'm here and a drink might help this painful situation."

Miah surveyed at me. "Are you okay?"

"Yep. Perfectly fine." I grabbed a carrot stick but didn't eat it. I used it like a sword in my hand. "Still sucks, ya know. You and Miss Perfect. Sorry, Mrs. Perfect." I drawled out misses like a hissing snake.

Miah levelled. "Lydia's not perfect. There are things I'm learning. It's fun, but it's far from perfect."

"Yeah, but does she make you laugh?" I put the carrot stick between my nose and my lips and held it there like a mustache. The words "like this?" were muffled as I squeezed my mouth together not wanting to drop the carrot.

He laughed. And it was good to hear him laugh. "Never like you."

And the hurt was there quickly, but so was his charm, and I dropped the carrot to the ground and kissed him really hard, it surprised him. But he kissed back. I could feel that. I pulled away right before I felt the liquid splash all over me.

Pauline interrupted my story. "You kissed him?" She slapped my arm, more out of surprise than horror. "Oh, sorry." She immediately started rubbing it better.

"Ugh. I know." I grew defensive, as if I needed to justify it, like it was right. "It felt like we were hanging out. Like old times. I just lost it. I mean, he's married now."

I sank back into the couch.

"Oh, so, you kissed him. And then?"

"Well, but he kissed back."

Pauline's face went slack. "That's not the point."

I sighed. "And it's not like I'm still in love with him. I'm not." I kept saying it as if I needed to believe it. "I felt like the old me, the one that was loved by someone, not this scarred version of me, the one no one loves."

"You're not the first to find themselves in front of their ex, ya know." Pauline took a sip of my coffee that I wasn't drinking. "But your story doesn't explain the fight."

My head still hurt on all the details.

For the smallest second my heart spiked, and a face appeared in the back of my mind. And a field. And a tree. I closed my eyes to see him.

"Hey." Pauline pushed me back awake. "You're not finished. What happened after?"

I pressed on my temples. "I'm not positive. Lydia splashed her drink on me, called me a bunch of names. I remember her punching me because I remember the hurt. It doesn't matter, besides the 'I completely screwed up' part."

I curled back into a ball and closed my eyes again. The field was there, but empty. I sighed. "Do you ever wish dreams were real?"

There was no answer. I glanced over at Pauline. She was on her phone reading a message she'd received. I guess she didn't care that much about my story anymore. I went back to closing my eyes, mentally massaging my head.

"Oh my—" Pauline exclaimed a good few seconds later. She laughed but again started swearing. She nudged me. "You're gonna die."

My eyes flitted open. Daylight was not being kind.

Pauline's face spoke volumes. Her bemused but mortified face told me enough. "What is it?"

"Someone caught the fight last night on their phone. Danny just sent it to me." She laughed again. "Are you kidding? You lunged on her back?"

"I did what?" I sat up and stared at her phone. The display on her screen made me want to hide my head like an ostrich. "I don't remember doing that."

"Whoa." Pauline busted up laughing. "Wow. That had to hurt."

I lifted my skirt to see the big bruise purpling my thigh, accompanied with a few scrapes from the bush. "I do remember that part, at least the landing."

Pauline scrolled back. "Oh, let's re-watch it."

"No. Please." I tried to take the phone but started watching it from the beginning. Everything from right after the water splash to the crazy ninja spin to me toppling over the railing.

I lay back on the couch and smothered the pillow over my head.

The apartment lay still in the hazy morning light. Even though I felt trapped in my own apartment, we only had one bathroom. I quietly crept out to relieve myself. There was no sign of anyone attempting to wake, so after I washed up, I went to the kitchen to make coffee.

I enjoyed Portland mornings. It was different from where I grew up, surrounded by mountains, where the sun had to climb and crest the peaks before shining. Here the skies simply lightened. The trees absorbed the light and eventually made it through the branches. I sipped my coffee, watching the world awaken, and didn't hear the soft pad of feet behind me.

"Have any creamer?" Jessica asked from behind me.

I didn't turn around, not yet. "No, but there's almond milk in the fridge."

"Nice." The fridge opened and shut. I felt her walk closer until she brushed next to me, looking out the window to my view of the street below. "Mmm, thank you."

"Sure." I glanced over at Jessica's morning self. Her auburn hair twisted around in a messy bun, like some artist on Pioneer Square, and she wore Nate's shirt like a robe. It was sexy and distracting, and I wanted to retreat back into my room. But I didn't. I instead studied my outer world.

"What are you staring at?"

"I'm not staring at anything," I corrected. "I'm observing."

"Observing what?"

"The shadows from the sun through the trees."

"You never stop being the writer." She took another sip of coffee and slipped back to the table.

I turned around. I didn't know how to respond, not sure if it was a compliment. Probably not, but I took it as one. "I guess I don't," I finally stated. "Is there something wrong with that?"

Jessica didn't answer. She put down her mug and stared at me. Her makeup was smeared a little around her eyes, giving a gaunt, hollow expression I assumed meant she was pissed.

"What do you have against writers?" I sat down across from her, my mug still warming my hands.

Her head cocked to one side. She bit her lip as the words came to her. "It's not anything against writers, but you know why we would never work out?"

"Lots of reasons." I laughed. "You hate my aspirations. You think they're unrealistic."

"You're half-right." She swept a falling piece of hair from her face. "I liked your aspirations at first. It was fun. Ah, a writer." Her hands shook like a crowd cheering. She sighed and leveled her eyes. "You slowly disappeared. It was about time. You spent more time with your made-up girlfriend than you did with your real one."

I pieced together my thoughts logically and slowly. "So, watching my roommate play videogames is better spent time. Because you can, you know, sit by him."

Jessica took a contemplative sip and peered out the window.

"Sounds like you were jealous of my made-up girlfriend." I smiled at the idea.

"Totally not true. But it . . ." She stopped.

"It what?"

"Come on, a redhead?" Her stare was point blank. "You're obviously writing this story about me. That's kinda creepy."

"What?" My jaw dropped.

"Writing fantasy about me is—"

"Seriously? I've been writing this story for years. We dated for what, six months?" I didn't feel like sitting anymore. "Your red hair isn't even natural." Why did I feel I needed to justify my work to her? "The story is about the dragons, not the girl."

"Simon, come on. Admit it. The way you describe this person is too real not to be based on someone."

"She is," I blurted, regretting it. Jessica folded her arms waiting for an explanation. "Someone I met a long time ago. I . . ."

Jessica snickered. "There's no girl. I've never heard about her. You're writing about me or your subconscious created this girl from every girl you've ever dated."

"Believe what you want to believe." I picked up my coffee and refilled it. I grabbed some pieces of bread and an apple ready to head back into my room. I spun back toward Jessica. "Even if you did make it into my book, wouldn't that be a compliment?"

Jessica swung her head back from the table. "It's about time, Simon. You didn't have time for me, but you have time for this girl, this fantasy girl. I don't find it a compliment when

I was ignored. It has to do with time. Your novels haven't gotten you anywhere anyway. Why even try?"

I walked into my room without answering the question.

Four

"Brandon asked me to Prom."

Simon continues to write, not looking up from his desk. "Who's Brandon?" He glances up. "Why are you pointing this out?"

Adri fumbles through the pages. "Brandon is in my science class. He's okay. You misspelled misspell. It has two s's."

Simon looks at the paper and snatches it back, shaking the old desk lamp.

"Hey." Adri examines her empty hand.

"There. Another s for you," and hands it back.

Adri doesn't take it back, but instead stands and looks around Simon's bedroom, admiring the fantasy posters and notebook pages taped in a cluster by his bed. "You asked me to look over your essay. I'm helping, like you asked me to."

Simon chews on the end of his pencil. "I do need your help. It's sneaky having my subconscious look at my writing."

Adri snickers. "You probably fell asleep writing it. Right there." She gestures back to the well-used hand-me-down desk.

"Ding!" Simon points with his pencil.

"Thanks for asking for my help."

"I trust you." Simon went back to scribbling. "So far everything I pass by you has done well."

Adri let her shoulders dance in smugness. "You're not a bad writer. It just needs a little tweaking."

Simon thumbs through his papers. "I'm not interested in the rules of grammar as much as I should be."

Adri plopped down on his bed, noticing a dark shape in the corner. "You never told me you played guitar?"

"There's a reason." Simon continued without looking up.

"Why would you say so?"

Simon eyes her. "Because I knew how you'd act." He spreads his hands out in front of him. "Exactly like that. Expecting me to be good. I planned on telling you when I felt I was good enough to play something for you."

Adri crinkles her mouth. "Meaning you're not going to play for me tonight."

"Does Brandon play guitar?"

"Brandon?" Adri looks confused.

An incredulous expression passes Simon's face. "The prom guy."

Adri feels her own stupidity wash over her. "Right. I have no idea."

Simon turns in his swivel chair. "Are you gonna go?"

"Hmm?" Adri answers while reading some of the papers on his wall.

"With Science Class Brandon?"

Adri semi-ignores him. "Oh, to Prom? Oh, sure. It should be fun, probably."

Simon's eyes shift. "Do you have a dress and everything?"

Adri mumbles. "No. Not yet. He asked yesterday." She peels one of the papers off the wall. "Did you write these?"

"Some of them. Which one is that?"

Adri holds it out and he snatches it away.

"Yeah, but this one's old. It's one of my first songs." Simon moves closer to the wall. "This one here." He points to blue-penned scribbling on the wall. "This one I really like. I wrote it last summer."

Adri's eyes rove over it. "Is it about our tree?"

"Sort of." Simon sits next to her. "I mean, the tree inspired it."

"And you won't play this for me?" Adri's mouth turned up at the question. "I may never get a chance to be in your bedroom again."

"What would Science Class Brandon think?" Simon mocks.

Adri laughs. "What. Jealous?"

"No." Simon stands. "Well, not really. I shouldn't be jealous. I mean though, why bring him up if you didn't want me to know and feel jealous about it? I know I'm dreaming so I shouldn't feel things."

Adri reaches for his hand. "It doesn't mean the feelings aren't real."

Simon keeps still until he places his hand over hers. "I don't dream of you often enough."

"Only when you need help with your homework." Adri teases and squeezes his fingers. "But I know what you mean. Everything feels real. And when I wake, the feelings are still there."

"See this?" Simon holds up Adri's hand and evaluates it. "How's this not real? I can see your little veins."

"Stop." Adri pulls her hand back and rubs it. "That tickles."

Simon moves back to his desk. "Well," he sighs, "I hope you and Science Brandon have a nice time." He drawls out his name.

Adri looks at her hand, missing where he had touched it. "Did you ever go to Prom?"

"Nah," Simon dismisses. "What's the point if my dream girl won't be there?"

Adri giggles. "Dream girl? You need to stop. I'm distracting."

"So what?" Simon tosses the papers in the air. "I don't care about the essay anymore."

Adri watches the papers scatter around the room in a beautiful paper dance. "Okay. So, what do you care about?"

Simon walks to the corner and opens his guitar case. "It's only fair that you hear the song you helped inspire."

Adri sinks back to the bed, resting her hands on her knees. "I inspired it?"

"Helped," Simon clarifies. He pulls the strap over his head and tunes the strings. "And remember, I'm still not very good."

Adri places her head in her hands. "I wouldn't even know. Right now, it's amazing."

"But I haven't even started playing yet?"

"Doesn't matter."

Simon laughs as his first notes strike the air.

I plugged in my noise-canceling headphones and turned on some soundtrack I had queued. I typed a while, reread certain parts, and typed more. The manuscript looked good. It was nearly complete. It wasn't until my stomach hurt from lack of food did I notice the time.

I took down my headphones. All was quiet. I glanced out my window and didn't see the red beetle. Jessica had left.

I quickly saved my progress and shut my laptop.

My phone chimed with some notification. *Game*, it read on my calendar. There was another text from James about picking up some Doritos.

"Sure," I replied back.

The game didn't start until five, I had plenty of time.

I showered, tidied around the place, grabbed some food, packed up my computer and some other things in my backpack, and left before anyone came home.

My friend James had started a deep world RPG campaign. We started the game before he got married and it's been a good nine months. James was lucky he found a girl who liked gaming as much as he did, and Steph made dynamite game guacamole. Our campaign consisted of Maria, Katelynn, Leo, Pete, and sometimes Pete's special guest we referred to as "The Game Crasher." It was usually someone who knew nothing about role playing games. Nate didn't come anymore, not since his ridiculously-high-level wizard was killed off. I knew James was out to kill him. It wasn't fair to have anyone so advanced in the party. Nate was still sore about it.

James and Steph didn't live far, and I enjoyed the nice walk. I stopped at the closest convenience store by their place and grabbed the Doritos, plus some impulse goodies. Ten minutes later I rang the doorbell.

"Simon!" Steph greeted me with a hug. Her belly pressed awkwardly into me.

"Hey, Steph. Who's here?"

"Just Leo. Maria and Katelynn are about fifteen minutes away. I haven't heard from Pete."

I walked in. James had his screen set up before the coffee table in their small living room, the player's board displayed as we had left it a week ago. James waved slightly as I walked in, but went back to scribbling behind his screen, making some last-minute decisions on the campaign. I tossed him his Doritos. He caught the bag without even looking.

"Hey Leo." I hailed my friend already seated on the couch. His long mane of hair slicked back into a tight man bun.

"Yo, Sy!" He stood and slapped me on the back. "Glad you could make it. By how you sounded yesterday, I didn't think you'd come."

"Nah. Adam's on call this weekend. The whole upgrade was a mess. Things are running again, for now, but there is still some repairing. I needed time away."

"Hear ya." Leo sat back down and propped his foot on the edge of the table. He continued to rant about his work, similar enough to mine. I wasn't interested in talking work though. My blood pressure rose just thinking about the amount I had to fix on Monday.

Maria and Katelynn arrived with pizza, and the gloomy work-talk atmosphere changed.

"I know, you've missed us." Maria plopped the pizzas right down in the middle of the board.

"Hey, be careful." James straightened some of the pieces back to where they were and went back to his notepad.

"Yeah, you guys. No grease on the board." Katelynn hopped down next to me and opened the fresh, steaming box. She grabbed a slice, the cheese stringing away from the rest of the pizza.

"Did you get a veggie?" Leo asked.

"Of course." Maria lifted the second box. "Just for you, big guy."

I smiled at her banter and grabbed my own slice.

Both Maria and Katelynn carried a vibrancy and zest I rarely felt other places, both exciting and dreadful, like the moment before you entered a nightclub. I never knew what to expect, making me like them even more. Where I tended to stay reserved, both of them were loud and silly—a perfect mirror in personality. I had to admit, it was refreshing.

"You want some, Steph?" Katelynn shouted to the kitchen with her mouth full of food.

"No, thank you." Steph walked in with paper plates and some napkins. "Cheese is making me nauseous right now."

"And that's why I could never have kids," Maria added. "A world without cheese. Sad."

"And you are a wuss when it comes to pain," Katelynn added. "It's like a bowling ball coming between your legs."

"Hey, don't scare Steph," James mumbled from behind the screen. "She's going to have to face the inevitable." He smiled dryly at his wife.

"Ha," Steph added. "Like this was my fault."

"It was," James rebutted. "If you would stop being so sexy—"

Steph threw something at him and missed badly.

"Is Pete coming?" I asked, finishing my slice.

"Don't know," Leo returned. "He never answered my texts."

Katelynn sneered. "Can't we kill off his stupid bard?"

"His character is so disruptive." Maria grabbed a Red Vine from the bag. "Seriously. And whatever girl he brings never knows how to play, or watches while she plays with his hair."

James' mouth slipped sideways, not quite smiling, like he had considered the idea already.

"Well," I said. "You have to admit, Pete's got great hair." I received a giggle out of a few people in the room. But my statement was true. Pete's hair was Prince Charming worthy.

"We already lost one member of our campaign to suicide," James' serious tone came out as he mentioned Nate's character. Tempt fate with a dragon, yeah, you're gonna die in its belly. "But I have some ideas."

I went to the kitchen to grab a glass of water. James and Steph's place was inviting, and I felt comfortable grabbing a glass and fetching the pitcher from the fridge. Steph came in. She looked exhausted.

"Are you doing okay?" I asked.

"I've been better." She stretched strangely with her hips, working out some cramp in her legs. "I'm starting to eat better though. How about you? How's your story?"

"The same." I leaned forward on the counter, glad to talk about something other than work. Steph majored in Creative Writing, so we often talked about creative stuff. She feigns interest, which is enough for me. "I don't think I can write when I'm under stress. I haven't felt inspired. Everything I'm writing sounds like utter garbage. I do think I figured out my ending, or at least for this book."

Steph stretched more. "You've got a very unique idea. Sometimes you need to write garbage to understand where the character plot goes. It's just a draft after all. Don't try to make it your best work. That comes in revision."

"You're completely right." I took a sip. "I hate what I'm writing though. It's hard to see the good stuff."

"You'll find your voice in there." She patted my shoulder. "You got this."

The doorbell rang.

"Probably Pete." Steph straightened up to answer the door. "Blonde or Brunette? What do you guess?"

"He brought a blonde last time. I'm going with a wild idea and say pink."

Steph laughed. "Daring choice. Let's see if you're right." She stepped out of the room.

I remained in the kitchen finishing off my glass. The room filled with cheers and groans as Pete arrived with the mystery girl. I had tipped the last gulp on my mouth when I heard, "Everyone. This is Adri."

I spit, choking on the last bit stuck in my throat. A deep ache came from my stomach and ran up my throat tightening everything. I quickly wiped the water from my mouth. My breath quickened. I set down my glass and took a quick glance into the room.

Pete stood next to a tall brunette with bronzed skin and fake, sculpted eyebrows. In my mind, I understood the person in the room was not what I expected when I heard the name, but my pulse still whipped around my body like a ghost had entered the room—a ghost of an imaginary girl.

I went back to the sink, turned on the faucet, and splashed some cool water on my face. I let it drip from my nose before I ran my wet hands through my hair.

"You okay?" It was James. I would recognize his deep bass anywhere.

"Yep." I flipped off the faucet and rubbed the rest of the water from my face and chin. I stared at my friend's concerned expression. "Have you ever felt like you've seen a ghost?"

James' eyes shifted around. "Seriously?"

I searched for a towel near me. "I'm fine. Needed to cool down. Is everything ready?"

"Yeah, I think so." James reached the cupboard for a glass. "Pete is here. His girl isn't interested in playing."

"Of course." I wrung my hands on a small dish towel by the sink.

"You, uh, sure you're okay?"

I slapped James on the shoulder. "Never better."

Chicago, IL

The gentle bell rung as the door opened. Someone came into the bookstore near closing. I wouldn't mind normally, but my day had been exhausting, and hot ginger spice and a good book, curled up on my sofa called to me. I had to clean up a few books and organize the drawers. Annette left early, the poor lady wasn't feeling well, leaving Brody and I closing.

The quaint little store of Moonstone Books nestled near other adorable shops in the Andersonville area. It held several reclaimed titles and rare oddities, but it also stocked newer things when we could get them. I loved the smell of old books, the dust and paper mixed with memories. So many hands had handled some of these treasures. Salvaging books became as much a passion as reading itself.

I examined the stack of newly acquired old books needing pricing and placement in inventory. Some were old fantasy paperbacks but popular titles I recognized. Life was full of books and adventures. As much as I loved them, it had to take a really good series in order for me to keep with it. I had so many that I sampled throughout my life, sampling books here and there. I was the ultimate taster of books.

I thumbed through one for fun and found myself sucked in the little bit I snagged. I laughed.

"You're laughing." The voice startled me and I bolted up right. Brody stood over me, a big smile on his face. "I haven't seen you smile all day."

"Have you ever read this book?"

"Oh, yeah." Brody grabbed another one from the stack. "Pratchett's a genius. You've never read him?"

"I think it was on the list." I admitted. "I have a long list."

"This one is great, but it's the third in the series. You gotta start with one." He rifled through the stack and found the most beat up of the collection. "This is it. Start here." Brody handed it over.

I liked Brody. He was on a sophisticated nerd level when it came to reading, grades higher than me. I called him an intellectual reservoir, always thinking and reading. I found his opinions marvelous and refreshing. I could ask him any question and he would know something about it, and if he didn't, he would come back the next day and have read up on it and would share. We had a fantastic friendship.

"You want to head out to Cloverleaf after this?"

I shook my head, still reading the back of the book. "I drank enough last night. I'm not in the mood. But thank you." I glanced up at him and smiled sincerely.

"I told you not to go. Remember?"

I waved my hand, dismissing the topic completely. He got the hint. "Who's left in the store? Maybe we could close a few minutes early."

"A couple of teens were back in Young Adult. I'll sweep around and check."

Brody walked toward the back and I quickly checked the till, organizing and counting as the two teens came up to the counter—a boy and a girl, clearly a cute couple.

"Hello, you find what you were looking for?"

"Oh, sure." The boy placed the book on the counter, a Dune title I hadn't reached in my reading.

I flipped through the cover to find the price and felt the eyes on me.

I looked up briefly. The girl was staring at me with these huge eyes, which darted back to her phone.

I continued with the purchase, minding my own business when I glanced up again, and both the boy and the girl were whispering. She showed him something on her phone and he eyeballed me.

"It's seven dollars," I recited.

The boy fumbled in his pocket, searching for money or his card. Whatever she had shown him had made him forget about the book.

He handed over a wadded up ten. The folds were deep. I knew he had been holding on to this money for a while. Maybe this book was something special, something he had been searching for. I glanced again at the title. Maybe I should pick up the series again, like so many other series I never finished.

I grabbed his change and handed it to him. The look he gave me in return was completely perplexing, nothing like the warm smile he had first graced me with. "Ah, thanks?" Was that a question?

"Let me get you a bag." I leaned over to our supply of paper goods.

"Nah, I got it." He waved it away with his hands and headed to leave. His girlfriend kept staring at me. She whispered something else to him before they exited.

"Is that everyone?" I yelled, hoping everyone was gone.

"Yep!" Brody's voice answered from the back storeroom.

Phew. For whatever reason, this day felt longer than others. I counted out and uploaded the receipts. Brody and I worked through the closing activities rather quickly. The brief tidy and organizing never took very long with him. When I closed with Annette, she liked to be thorough. The store was Annette's life, and I respected the care she put into it. Brody and I knew how to get on with our lives.

I reached for my bag and jacket as Brody went to turn off the lights. Everything went dark as I waited for him near the back door. Soon he was there jangling the store key.

"All closed," he said locking the door. "You want a lift?"

"Yes, please. I'm not in the mood to wait for the train."

I felt a slight vibration from my phone and turned the screen on.

I had twenty-eight missed calls. My stomach hit the floor. Something had happened. Something was wrong. My head and heart went to my parents. I knew I hadn't been back to Michigan for a while, but I had talked to my mother on Wednesday. Nothing felt out of the ordinary.

I scrolled through the calls. Most were from Pauline.

I opened my messages. Pauline only sent one.

"Don't get on Facebook," I read aloud.

"Why not?" Brody heard me as he was putting on his jacket.

"No idea. Which is only going to make me want to get on Facebook."

Brody opened his phone and within a few clicks he froze. "No way."

"What?" I went to see his phone. What in the world could be happening? The fine hairs on my neck stood on end, like the strange feeling you get when others know something you don't. "What is it?"

Brody turned his phone to a video streaming on his page. "Looks like it went viral."

I peered over again closer than I had.

And there it was, the video someone recorded of me at the party the previous night, bottom up in the flower bed as I fell over the railing. My lace panties leaving nothing, or rather everything to the imagination.

The nausea took over. Brody reacted to the wave and quickly pointed me to a grassy place where I could be sick.

Five

Adri empties her mind of all thoughts. A blank canvas. "Is this what you mean?"

Simon smiles wide at the lack of anything. "Yes, perfect."

"So I need to pretend to be someone else?" Adri asks, looking at the completely white room. She evaluates her very plain pajamas and takes in Simons appearance. "What are you supposed to be? Robin Hood?"

Simon swishes his dark green cloak. "I'm a rogue. This is my character, Torian."

Adri frowns. "Not very fanciful."

"What?" Simon gives an incredulous stare. "Fanciful? I don't pick fanciful names. Torian is fine. It's mystical."

"Okay, Torian. How do I win?"

Simon eyes her. "You don't win, you just play."

"And no winning?"

Simon faces her. "No. You can't beat me this time."

Adri tips her head back and forth. "Gotcha. Okay. So, it's like in a play with no script."

"Kind of." Simon grows more animated in his explanation. "It's like playing pretend but with rules. You create a character and give him," he glances at Adri, "or her . . . them strengths and weaknesses. You have to keep those strengths and weaknesses and play them up."

"Do a lot of girls play?"

"Sure, but not many I'm around." Simon twists the satchel about his waist. "I think it's cool if girls play."

"So, it's basic character development, like in my creative writing class."

"Well, yeah." Simon grows impatient. "But it does have a few more rules than just playing the character."

Adri looks around the empty room. "Okay. You got me to clear my mind."

Simon rubs his hands together. "I didn't know it would work so well." He turns to her with a manic, excited look. "Now, this is your story. I want you to tell me about your world."

Adri's mouth goes up in concentration. "A fantasy world?"

"Sure. Whatever you like."

Adri closes her eyes.

Nothing happens.

"I think I might need help." Adri opens one eye and looks at him. "Is anything happening?"

"Nope." Simon squints. "How 'bout a tavern?" He raises his hands palm up in suggestion.

Suddenly, the room goes dark. Little fragments of building appear, the lines of wood ridges and iron hinges. Cobblestone paves the street beneath their feet.

"Adri. Adri." Simon shakes her to open her eyes.

A few torch lights pop into flame. Men march about and horses clop across the stone.

"This is amazing."

Adri smiles. "Thanks. I couldn't think of a real tavern. It's the best I could do."

Simon looks around. "What do you mean?" He walks forward to read the swinging sign at the entrance. "The Prancing Pony?"

Adri presses her hand to her chest. "Yeah, is that okay?"

"You've read Lord of the Rings?"

"Of course." Adri holds out her plain pajamas. Her eyes light up. "Can I be an elf?"

Simon straightens. "Like Arwen or Galadriel?"

"Like Eowyn, because she was the tough one. The others didn't do anything."

"She wasn't an elf," Simon clarifies. "And we still have to roll."

Adri puts her hands on her hips. "You're still going to make me roll?"

"That's the game, the fate of the dice."

"But I think I want to be an elf anyway, regardless of how I roll."

Simon laughs. "Why?"

Adri's smile changes to a smirk. "Because elves are ethereal and pretty—"

"Says Tolkien," Simon interrupts. "They don't have to be. Look at the Keebler Elves. They are fat and goofy."

"They are more like gnomes than elves."

Simon feels the charm. "Fine. You can be an elf. Anything else?"

"A beautiful elf."

"Why?"

Adri's shoulders shrug. "Maybe I like the idea of being beautiful. If I'm pretending, I might as well be beautiful."

Simon looks at her more intensely. "In the game it doesn't matter if you're beautiful or not. No one will care."

Adri's face falls. "But I will."

"Wait." Simon looks deeper. "Are you okay?"

Adri shrugs. "I guess."

Simon taps the sign. "We are in Bree, in Lord of the Rings. Do you know how long I've ached for this moment?"

Adri takes in the night sky. "Should it be raining?"

Thunder crashes.

"Wait, no." Simon pulls her under the overhang. "You aren't an elf yet."

Adri shakes her head. "Elf was the first pretty magic thing I could think of."

Simon touches her shoulder, a gentle touch. "If there's something wrong, you know you can talk to me."

Adri nods. "I sometimes wish I was someone else. That I had a different life."

"It's a very normal feeling." The rain starts and Simon pulls Adri closer to the building. "Teens aren't supposed to feel like they don't belong anywhere. We aren't kids, we aren't adults. We all feel like this. My life isn't a picnic. I don't think it's supposed to be easy."

Adri hesitates. "I . . . don't feel very pretty."

"That's absurd."

Adri grins slightly. "Nice word."

Simons stares blankly feeling the rain tap his cloak. "I'm serious. How could you think that?"

Adri shrugs again. "There are reasons. Someone might say you're pretty, but they do something that hurts you."

Simon turns her toward him. "If anyone hurt you, I swear, I will hurt them."

Adri's sad eyes glance away. "I know you would, but it's hard to defend me when I only know you here. You know, in Middle Earth."

Simon leans back against the wood. "It's not fair, you know."

"What's not fair?"

Simon collects his thoughts before he speaks. "The girl of my dreams is only in my dreams."

Adri feels her face get hot. "You say dream girl a lot."

"You know you are." Simon gives a smirk. "But, you know, metaphorically speaking."

"So, I can be an elf?"

Simon exhales. "Yes. Of course. Make yourself an elf. Please."

Adri closes her eyes again as a midnight blue gown wraps around her, gold thread quickly stiches the seams and laces up the back. Her hair springs curls naturally around a thin, gold crown centered with a dark, blue sapphire.

Simon can't stop staring. "And royalty?"

Adri winks. "If I'm playing, I'm playing right." She looks at his appearance. "You know, grow a beard and you'd make a perfect Strider."

The tears came fast. How humiliating.

"I'm never drinking again."

Brody helped me back up. "Let's get you home, Lightweight."

Brody had a car, a cute little Beetle, which I was very grateful for right now. I wasn't interesting in catching the Brown line home. He helped me in on the passenger side as another wave of nausea came over me. I forced my stomach to calm, to kept it down while I was in his immaculately clean Volkswagen. Brody was on the phone. I listened until I understood he had called Pauline.

"When did it go online? That's fast. Well, but I'm watching her now and I don't think it's as funny as you think it is."

The one-way conversation was very clear what he was talking about and how Pauline was handling it. I'd never heard Brody angry before. He was always so calm.

"No. It's not amazing. She's physically ill by this . . . But how big? Over four hours? There is nothing to gain here. What can we do? Well, can't we get it taken down? Why not? Are you serious? Paid per hit?"

That's about when I stopped listening and pressed my head to the car window.

Chicago, from the quiet view of a window, told a rich but sad story. The old brick of times gone by was beautiful. The aged, sometimes blackened stonework still stood despite the years of battering and change of scene or occupants. The different streetlights streamed past my eyes and blurred the colors.

Brody was off the phone. "Are you okay?"

I didn't answer at first. "Sure."

"Really? I wouldn't be."

"Well," I collected my thoughts. "I don't know the damage, do I. I'm kinda numb. I mean, it's just an embarrassing moment. I have those all the time. The fact that someone caught it on their phone and posted on YouTube?" I felt like I was drifting. My hands came to my mouth in shock. "It's a new experience in my already humiliating life that I've never had to deal with."

Brody didn't say anything. He turned down my street and grabbed an empty parking spot around the corner from my place. Parking was impossible in this neighborhood. I was grateful for the lucky spot he found.

I opened my side and stumbled out, tripping over the curb. "It's cool. I'm fine." I pretended it didn't hurt and continued to my house. The nausea was mostly gone. Humiliation tugged me forward as I hurried to my stairs. Brody followed—I felt him lingering like a horse being led. He finally caught up and grabbed my arm.

"You don't seem okay."

Brody's face filled with shadows from the streetlight, like a no-face anime creature. "Did Pauline have something to do with the video?" I asked quietly.

"It was some person at the party. She might know who it was but doesn't think it's important."

I lifted the iron latch to my walkway. "Okay." I believed him. I liked Pauline, but she was only my roommate. We had a very convenient friendship. As awful as I felt, I didn't want this to come between us. "You wanna come in for a minute?"

Brody rolled on his heels with his hands in his pocket. "Yes, for a minute."

I opened the gate and walked down the stairs of my bottom dweller. I checked the door. Open. Pauline must be home.

As I walked in Pauline poked her head out from the kitchen and headed toward me. "You okay?"

"Sure," I repeated numbly. I flung my stuff on the floor and sunk into the old couch. Brody followed in and shut the door.

All went quiet. I looked at the two people staring down at me. I held up my finger, stopping any advice spewing out of their mouths. "Wait, don't tell me yet."

I walked into my bedroom, slipped on pajama pants, and found my favorite Star Wars tee. Even though it was technically dirty, I grabbed it from the laundry pile and threw it on anyway. I needed it right now. I glanced in my mirror. Those kids had recognized me even with my glasses on. I guess Clark Kent *really* is Superman.

When I exited my room, pulling my hair up in a lose bun, Pauline and Brody were talking on the couch. They stopped when I came out.

"Nah, it's okay, keep talking." I went to the cupboard to get what I needed for some cocoa and toast.

Pauline and Brody followed me to the kitchen.

I filled the teapot. "So, spill it. How bad is it?"

Pauline pulled herself up on the counter. "Seriously. I never imagined how far it would go on YouTube. I promise." She was apologizing without apologizing, like it wasn't important. "I mean, I've put crap on YouTube. No one cares about it. I think it's on TikTok as well."

I put the kettle on the stove and rummaged for my Winnie the Pooh mug. "Just tell me the damage. How did it all happen?"

Brody inquired on his phone. "On Facebook," he scratched the back of his head. "It's around five thousand likes."

"Five thousand?" I became so frazzled I lost track of how many scoops of cocoa I had put in the mug. "But how did it get around so fast? I mean, Pauline, you messaged me, what, around eleven and told me it was around two hundred and I thought that was big."

Pauline flipped through her phone. "It was uploaded last night, not long after the party."

My toast popped and I began to butter it trying to calm down. "It's just a video. It will disappear eventually. It's a brief moment in time when everyone could see my butt and laugh." I took a bite from my toast. "An- thann gaaw I wah woo e-en my cutte wlack l-acey ones," I said through my chewing.

"They were from Your Secret's collection," Pauline interjected.

I swallowed a little. "Well, yay. Thank goodness for small miracles. And you, Pauline. For telling me I should always be prepared just in case, right? In case someone beats me up." I pointed with the toast. "Or in this case, get filmed falling over a railing." My bruises ached at the memory.

I poured the warm water and took my dinner to the table, slamming my elbows down in a hunch.

Pauline slid closer. "Danny doesn't know who shot the movie. All he knows is that a link was sent to him by a co-worker because Danny is in it. He's in the back at the beginning. I didn't know many people at the party, so I couldn't say who it was."

"But why are you guys all secretive?" I darted my eyes between Pauline and Brody.

"Because someone tagged you in the Facebook link. Someone recognized it was you."

I dropped the toast. It tumbled off the table and landed butter-side down. "Wait. What? They can't do that."

Pauline held up the Facebook feed. It was the exact video she showed me before and it was shared on her feed. I peered in closer. The video was shared by a person she didn't know.

"This is crazy." I bent down and picked up my toast, wishing I had swept, and tossed the piece in the garbage. It hit the wall and we all watched it as it slowly slid again to the floor.

Pauline turned to Brody. "If whoever sold it to a site, is there anything we can do?"

"But my name is in there," I interrupted. "Can I untag myself? It has to be someone that knows me who tagged it, right? Facebook is all about friends."

"I don't know your privacy settings," Pauline answered.

"I don't know the YouTube account either," Brody mentioned, still scrolling through his phone. "I think it's bogus."

"But I'm the nicest person. Why would anyone do this?" And the moment it came out of my mouth, I thought of the ring scraping my face laying on Miah's new wife Lydia's finger.

Maybe it was a way to get back at me for kissing her husband. "Well, that's fair," I said out loud. The others stared at my weird outburst. I cocked my head to Pauline. "Oh, come on. It's Lydia. It's a perfect revenge for me kissing Miah."

I took my remaining piece of toast, my steaming mug, and went onto the couch. The two followed me, but kept a distance, like I was some ignited firecracker ready to explode. I wasn't going to explode. I wasn't even smoldering. I was numb.

I sighed through my words. "I can't do anything. There's nothing we can do about it." I went for the remote but didn't pick it up. "On second thought," I glanced up at the two. "I think I'll go to bed." I took my stuff to the room and closed the door behind me.

I sank on my bed, my face on my pillow, and cried until I fell asleep.

"Hey, Pete." I walked in the room, after catching my breath.

"Hey, man." Pete shook my hand and we did our regular guy hug, slapping him on the shoulder.

"Good to see you." I knew I had to say something, so I stuck out my hand to the newcomer. "I'm Simon."

Pete straightened. "Yeah, Simon. This is Andie."

The air hitched in my throat. "Oh, what? I'm sorry."

The tall brunette, not anything like the girl I had envisioned, grabbed my hand and shook it. "I'm Andie."

I blinked. "Andie. Andie? I thought I heard . . ."

"Short for Andrea."

"Right." Not being rude, I shook her hand once more and smiled. "Yeah, Andie, glad you could come."

Pete could see my hesitation. "Are you all right there?"

"Oh, yeah." I looked squarely at him with a big grin. "Yep, totally fine. Come have a seat."

I made it back to my place on the couch by Katelynn. The girl was laughing about something on her phone.

The noise and chatter in the room silenced in my ears to a relaxing, unnerving hum. For the briefest moment I was not in the room at all. I transported to somewhere else—a grassy field with a lonely tree, a tree with two names on it, mine and...

The girl who visited me there I had always known as a figment of my imagination. But in so many ways she felt real. I could smell her skin in warm sun. I remember walking into a department store and smelling her. Instantly, her memory hit me. I could see the little goosebumps on her skin when a breeze would come along the trees or hills or wherever we were. She was goofy and clumsy and charming. I would know her anywhere, and if she had walked in with Pete, as I imagined she had, I would have wrapped my arms around her without hesitation.

But they don't create people like her in the real world. My dream self needed her so my awake self could cope. She was my best friend, my invisible confidante, and she didn't even exist here.

The tightness in my chest came back, a feeling of crazy love and impossible dreaming, mixed with the hurt of crushing reality. *Snap out of it, Simon. Adri was a dream, a beautiful dream, a ghost to haunt me forever.*

"Whoa, where'd you go?" I felt a nudge next to me. Maria's knee.

I studied her dark curls and composed myself. "Somewhere magical, apparently."

She shoved me again. "Well, I'm taken, space cadet."

I laughed. "I'll remember that next time I daydream."

Both her and Katelynn bumped my leg for my comment.

James handed out our player sheets. The pizza boxes were removed from the coffee table, and everyone set out to grab their dice and calculate where they were in the game. The party members recapped the long battle we had finished last time. Several of our characters were still hurt and recovering from the orc slaughter.

I absently spun my dice, my headspace completely occupied by other things. I watched the ten-sided die wobble like a top on the surface.

I glanced to the corner where Pete and his girl Andie sat. She looked slightly interested, but mostly bored, switching back and forth to her phone. James sat forward explaining the delicacies of the role-playing game, trying to convince her it wasn't just about playing Lord of the Rings. My mind drifted to Adri again. I had taught her a little, a conversation from years ago, when I was first excited about it. She liked the vision of the game but insisted on being pretty.

I made an audible huff, thinking about the memory—*no, the dream.*

"Seriously, Sy. What are you smiling about?" Maria, now sitting cross-legged on the floor, stared at me with curious brown eyes. "Still daydreaming?"

"Was I smiling?" I instinctively put my hand to my mouth. The corners were definitely curled up.

"Yeah, like you have a secret you are dying to tell us."

Katelynn bumped my shoulder. "Spill it. You have a secret."

I eyed the girls, collecting myself. "No. Really. I don't." Neither of them believed me. I repositioned myself on the couch. "It's like when you have a memory of something."

"Oh, like Déjà vu?" Katelynn sat up straight. "I've had that. I get Déjà vu all the time."

"But doesn't that happen from your *previous lives*." Maria said the last words in a spooky, Halloween voice.

"Maybe." Katelynn smacked Maria's shoulder gently. "Don't make fun."

I wasn't following what they were kidding about. Maria caught on.

"Katelynn believes in mystic reincarnation stuff, heartlines, palm reading."

"Are you not a subscriber?" I asked Maria.

"Ugh, no. I don't ever want to live again. Kate can have all my lives." She winked.

Katelynn positioned herself toward me on the couch, propping both of her bare feet next to my leg, her toes nesting under my thigh in a playful way. "There are so many things we don't understand about life and the world. I'm on a spiritual quest to discover myself and understand my world. Here."

She grabbed my hand away for the dice-spinning and placed it in both of her hands. The touch was rather intimate, and I wasn't sure how to respond.

Katelynn drew an invisible line from my middle finger and down my palm to my wrist. She evaluated it closer. I grew a bit self-conscious at what she was doing. But it was silly. It didn't mean anything, so I indulged her.

"You have a good heart." Katelynn's eyes grew wider and turned my palm over, glancing at the top of my hand. "Look at this vein." She traced it with her thumb. "This is very strong, leading right to your heart." She turned it back around and pointed at where two of my creases met. "Right here. So, you have two different paths. Right here and here. But here is the intersection of both lives. Would you like to know what it means?"

I admitted Katelynn was a cute girl, like a pixie lost from the forest. I knew the flirt well, so I went with it. "Sure, why not."

Her mouth quirked. "There are a couple of things." She pointed at a line running up to my knuckle. "This is your heart line. Everything looks good. Looks like you've had a bunch of relationships."

Maria elbowed her. "Stop charming him, river siren."

Katelynn glared at her and continued. "But this is what's interesting is this line here." She traced the center of my palm with her fingernail. It tickled. "This is your fate line. Not everyone has one, you know. But look how it curves up and crosses the heart. It usually doesn't reach that far."

"Kay?" I didn't mean it as a question, but it came out as one.

"Someone from your past is about to meet you."

"You mean see me again?"

Katelynn looked again. "No. This is where you meet." Her finger rubbed the folds in my palm. "Do you have a pen pal or anything?"

I glanced between both of them. "Ah, geez." I snagged my hand back, knowing I had been played. "You guys set me up just to get me to tell my secret."

"Aha!" Maria sat up. "He admitted he has a secret."

"Of course there is a secret. There is always a secret." I grabbed my die and spun it again. "Doesn't mean I'll share it."

Both of the girls laughed at my expense, disrupting whatever James was explaining to Pete and Leo.

Katelynn straightened up on the couch and grabbed her character sheet. "I was being honest though. Maybe there is a girl from your past."

Maria laughed. "Yeah, like an ex-girlfriend." Both the girls laughed harder. I didn't get the reference.

"I have a few of those," I admitted. "But not as many as everyone thinks."

"Any that would fight for you?" Maria said, snacking on her licorice.

I sighed, thinking of my freshest encounter from the night before. "I don't think any of my girlfriends liked me."

Katelynn put her hand on my shoulder. "You're *too* likable, Sy. Too nice."

"Being a gentleman is a problem?" Girls stupefied me.

"Speaking of fighting," a voice from the other side of the room interrupted our little conversation. It was Andie, Pete's girl. "Did you guys see that video?"

"Oh. Oh." Maria pointed right at her like they spoke the same language. "Are you talking about the girl who ended up in the flowerbed?" Her mouth still chewing.

Andie nodded, gesturing with expressive hands, waving her phone in a little dance.

"What are you talking about?" Pete crowded in.

Katelynn whipped out her phone. A few swipes in. "Oh, this poor girl."

Maria was already laughing. "It's one of the funniest things I have ever seen."

It took Katelynn about fifteen seconds to scroll through her feed to find a video.

Maria climbed up to see it again. "Wait, watch right there." And in a few seconds Pete, Maria, and Katelynn were all laughing.

Pete grabbed it. "Wait. Back that up again."

I shook my head, having no stomach to watch another girl's already public humiliation get placed on feeds around the world. But Katelynn placed it right in front of me anyway.

"You gotta see this." And she pushed play.

I rolled my eyes but watched. I couldn't comprehend what was happening. What I could make out at first was an argument between two girls. It accelerated unto a jumble of arms and limbs and chaos.

I froze. "Wait. Back it up."

"No, wait," Katelynn tried to explain. "That wasn't the good part. It's when—"

I grabbed the phone and swiped back. It started over. I leaned in to look at the details. I didn't care what was really happening. I watched closely the girl in green. And paused it.

. . . and stared at the ghost that haunted me.

My chest tightened. I didn't understand.

"You okay?"

The room was silent. I could only hear the thumping of my own heartbeat accelerating in my ears. Everyone in the room had stopped in time, all staring straight back at me.

I couldn't breathe.

"Dude, seriously." Leo sat forward.

What was I seeing? I gaped back at the face of the girl frozen on the screen.

"Umm . . ." I didn't know what to do. I needed more answers and they weren't here. "I'll be back."

I stood and searched for my backpack.

"What are you doing?" James stood. "We're about to start."

"Just, put my character to sleep or something. I'll be back. I just . . ." What was I going to do? "I need to make a phone call, and . . ." I didn't finish.

I heard a few voices of protest, but I put my jacket on and put my stuff back in my bag.

"Thanks," I said to Steph, who was close to the door.

"Are you sure you're okay?"

"I don't know anymore," I answered honestly. "I think I know that girl. I need to find out."

Six

"What are you doing?"

Adri is kneeling near the tree. She looks at Simon. "Well, it's about time. Where have you been?"

Simon runs his hands through his hair. "I haven't been sleeping well."

Adri glances back at the uneven letters on the tree. "Well, I got bored."

Simon reads the first few letters. "The tree doesn't have room for your whole name."

Adri looks at it. "I'll stop with the i then."

Simon brushes his hand against the newly carved name. "You struggled with the knife."

"I didn't want to cut myself."

"Here, let me help you." Simon takes the small pocketknife and examines it. "This is what you used?"

Adri scowls at him. "I didn't know what else to use. I don't have any brothers and my sister is six years older than me. It's the only thing I could think of."

Simon sits down by Adri and starts carving more of the 'A'. "Brothers aren't all you would think they should be. I'm smack in the middle of my family. The only one I get along with is my sister."

Adri watches as his hands work the knife, gently picking away the bark as he fixes her name in the tree. "Why aren't you sleeping?" The question sounds warm coming from her mouth.

Simon thinks about her question. "There"—he sighs—"There are a bunch of reasons."

"You can talk to me, you know."

"I know." Simon fiddles with the pocketknife, flicking his thumb against the dull blade. "You're the only one I want to talk to."

Adri remains silent for a moment. She rests on the back of the tree. "So, what's stopping you?"

"Your tree-carving abilities." Simon looks at his own name carved above. "It's been years since I carved this. Look, it's all worn and stretched. I thought you were against mutilating trees. Don't they have feelings?"

"So do I." Adri avoids his eyes. "I figured the tree could handle it."

Simon crouches next to her. "So, you need to talk too."

"Yes." Adri sits up and slugs him in the arm. "Where have you been?"

Simon stops. The knife in his hand shakes. "My . . . ah . . . mom."

Adri claps her hands to her mouth. "Oh no . . . oh my goodness. I am so selfish." Simon sits back in the grass. His face shows the grief he feels. "She died last Sunday."

Tears emerge from Adri's eyes. "I can't believe I didn't think about that. You weren't around. I worried you wouldn't show up again."

"We've been meeting for years, Adrianna. Of course I'll be here. My restless tossing won't stop me from coming here."

"What . . . I mean, I don't know what to say."

"Don't say anything." Simon absently picks at his shoe with the blade. "I don't want any advice. That's all I've been getting all week. But now the funeral is over, and the house is weird and quiet. My dad's been sleeping on the couch. He doesn't want to go in the bedroom. My sister won't stop crying. I want some peace."

Simon reaches for Adri's hand. "It's nice being back at the tree. I'm so glad we're here right now. I need this."

Adri reaches out and pulls him close.

Simon accepts the embrace and cries quietly on her shoulder.

Fresh air rushed my lungs as I stepped out of the stuffy house and into the night again. My mind scrambled with what to do. I pulled out my phone and paced the sidewalk.

"What do I do?" I said to no one. I stared at the screen until some idea came to me.

I hadn't logged into Facebook for a while. I didn't have an app on my phone for it. I first clicked on the internet, but it rerouted me back to the app store for download.

So, fine. I downloaded it.

I tried several times to log in, not remembering what email I had used.

"Argh." I swore big, hairy swears with every failed attempt.

I went again to the internet, typing in "drunk party girl fight" to see what was trending.

I scrolled down and found something. I clicked it and it sent me to YouTube.

It wasn't it.

I clicked on a lot of the links.

It wasn't there.

I had to find her. This was not possible. The mass of embarrassing videos you find typing in Drunk Girl Fight was appalling. YouTube was sending me down a rabbit hole I did not wish to enter.

I went back to Facebook. I breathed in and tried calming my nerves when logging in. On the third try I was in. Because it had been so long since I had been on, I had to do a security screen before getting onto the nightmarish slew of information it spewed at me. My notifications were off the charts.

I typed in Adri and stopped. I didn't know her last name. Or did I? The frustration gnawed at me as I erased her name and stared blankly.

"I cannot *believe* this." An old couple walking the street glared at me as they continued their evening stroll. I waved and stared back to my screen.

"What do I do? What do I do? What do I do?" I mumbled with my fingers dancing in the air.

I clicked on my friends list and I found Katelynn. Her profile picture had her dressed as a kitty, which I completely understood. I scrolled down, searching to see if she posted it on her Facebook wall. It wasn't there.

I clicked on Maria's profile from our mutual friends. Her profile had art on it, a dark black and white sketch of something I didn't recognize.

Bingo! It was the first thing posted on her wall.

I found it. My trembling fingers pushed play.

I sat down on the stone steps outside James' apartment and watched the video play out the entire thing. I watched it three times, each time my heartrate increasing. Was it her? It was her, definitely her. Or was it? The clumsy, funny personality, the endearing manner. Even when she fell over the railing I was charmed. It was her. It was most definitely Adri.

The words hit me like a punch in the face. "She's real. I knew it."

I ran down the street. I didn't know where I was running. All the time spilling the words, "She's real. Holy shit, she's real."

On a street corner sat a Starbucks. I ran over and went inside. There were only two people working and no one inside. I felt bad for just using their Wi-Fi, so I ordered a regular cup of black coffee. The barista dully poured me a cup, glad it wouldn't take long.

I took out my laptop, and within a few more minutes I had located the video and played it again. And again. I made it take up my whole screen. Then I played it again. And again.

My phone buzzed. James messaged me. I promised to go back to the game, but my mind was nowhere near ready to fight giant orcs. I couldn't concentrate on gaming right now. I didn't know what to think or do. It didn't seem real. None of it.

Dots started connecting. Every conversation, every experience, though in a dream setting, was somehow connected with her. We had real conversations, real experiences we alone shared. I was so cavalier in the dreams because they didn't mean anything. They were just dreams, right? I was a better self in dreams: the dream guy, the guy I pretended to be. But now they all meant something. It was no longer pretend. Everything happened. And if everything happened for me . . .

My hands fingered through my hair until it was crazy.

I had to call Liane.

"Hey there," she answered. "What ya doing calling me? We talked last night. Aren't you sick of me?"

I didn't immediately say anything.

"Hello? Did you butt-dial me?"

"Hey," I said.

There was an intake of breath. "Ah crap, what's happened?" She knew me too well.

How the hell do I start? My mind scrambled. "Okay, so remember a long time ago. Like a long, long time ago I told you about a girl I met in my dreams?"

"Wait. What?" Liane laughed. "Are you having the girl dream again?" More laughing. "Geez, Sy. I thought someone had died—"

"Liane." My tone couldn't be more serious. "You do remember."

"Well, sure. I mean, you talked about her for a while. I called her your imaginary friend. Aaron totally made fun of you."

"That's why I stopped talking about her. I didn't want to get picked on anymore." I tapped my finger against the coffee cup.

"What, are you still dreaming about her?"

I considered my words. "Liane. You know me better than anyone. You know I trust you more than any other person in the world. You know I'm honest and that I'd never lie to you, right?"

"Of course." Liane's reply was genuine.

"So, if I told you that I've been meeting the same girl in my dreams for sixteen years, you would believe me?"

There was a quiet moment before she answered. "Have you?"

My hand clenched in triumph. I knew I had her. "Yes."

"You haven't told me anything about this."

"Because I thought you would think I was crazy."

"I think it is sweet that you made up a girl in your dreams and—"

"No," I stopped her and stopped my absent-minded tapping. "You don't understand. I didn't make her up."

"So, wait. Is she someone I know? Someone you've been thinking about? I'm not understanding why this is such a big thing. You called me to talk about dreams?"

Crap. I was losing her. I had to tell her. Would she believe me? Did it matter? I looked back over to the baristas, but they were quietly in their own conversation. "I've never physically met this girl. She started appearing in my dreams. I don't know how. It just happened. I thought I made her up." I took a deep breath. "Liane. She's real."

There was a pause. "She's real." It came out matter of fact.

"Yes. She is real, a real human, not made up."

"So, you've been fantasizing about someone—"

"No. Not fantasizing—"

"I'm trying to understand, big brother. Honest. I mean, I think I remember you telling me about it. It was after mom died."

I had her again. "Exactly. I don't know how it happened, but it did."

Liane was quiet, too quiet for her house. My niece Lily must be asleep. "Did she age at all? Or it is some creepy ten-year-old girl haunting your dreams?"

"No," I laughed. "No, nothing like that. She did age with me. We grew up together. Next to you, Adri's my best friend."

"So, somehow you were on the same subconscious plane together and met in your deep cerebrals of your brain?"

"Well, when you say it like that, I sound crazy."

"Yes, you do sound crazy."

I sighed. "But, you believe me, don't you?"

"I always believe you. You aren't the kidding type—well, not when it's important. Even when you joke, people don't know you're joking."

There was silence between us.

"So, this dream girl is real."

"Yes." I paused, waking my computer and I pulled open my tabs. "Here. Go to Facebook."

"You were on Facebook?" She scoffed. "Did you see any of the embarrassing photos I tagged you in?"

"I haven't dug deep. I posted a link to your wall."

"Wait, hold on. I'm on my phone and Ian is finishing up his paper. Give me a minute."

I listened to the movement in their apartment and her gently persuading her husband to let her use the computer to look at this link I had sent.

"Okay. I'm logging on. What's this link about?"

"She's in it. She *IS* it."

"She what? Oh!" Laugher erupted from both Liane and Ian. "Oh, that poor girl. Oh. Oh, crap. This is funny." More laughter. "Which is the girl? The one in black or the one in green?"

"Green."

"Oh, good. Because the other girl looks snotty to me."

I grew fidgety. "You do believe me."

"I told you I did. What's to doubt?"

I took a sip of the cooling coffee. I wasn't losing my mind. "Making sure."

"So, what are you going to do now?"

Good question. "Find her."

"Find her?"

I sat up straight. "Yes. Help me find her."

"Wow. That's stalker-ish of you."

Yes, it was. But she didn't know I existed either. I had to try and find her. "I've been in love with this girl for years, Liane. That's right. In love. Please! Help me find her."

I didn't plan on falling asleep, so when I woke around midnight, I felt disoriented. My bladder ached incredibly, and I got up to use the bathroom. My place was a peaceful quiet. I figured Pauline wasn't here, maybe staying at Danny's or still out dancing or whatever she did to occupy her time. It was Saturday night after all. She chose a more party lifestyle than I did. I enjoyed my books and my writing, my quiet existence.

I glanced in the bathroom mirror. The black eye wasn't bad. It was purple in places, but it wasn't on my eye, more my cheek. The ring mark was the ugly part. The scrape could leave a scar, a humiliating reminder of what an idiot I made of myself.

I splashed my face and looked again. Yep. Still me. I sighed and headed for the kitchen.

I didn't feel like sleeping, though dreams helped me when I felt blue. Still I wasn't sure this was something I should share, not even in my dreams.

I slept but hadn't dreamt. Chances were slim he would be there to talk anyway. I grabbed some Oreos and milk and sat on the couch.

I snagged my laptop from the side of the couch and turned on the TV.

My story opened to where I left it. It lay blinking at me, waiting for some action to take place. I reread where I had left off and rewrote some lines. I wasn't happy with it and inwardly threatened to delete the whole thing again but continued on for a paragraph hoping it might help.

Truth was, I didn't feel like writing either. I didn't feel like doing anything, besides disappearing. A strange thought came to me that I should call my mother. I hadn't thought about including my parents. I never liked to bother them with such petty things, and my mother would only turn the conversation around and make me feel bad somehow, like she always did. My mother knew very little about social media. She liked her old flip phone which worked perfectly well in her opinion. My dad was more tech savvy, as he had to work on computers for his job. Where my mother, the practical crafter, beekeeper, and avid reader, liked her quiet simple lifestyle. My only sister, Viv, lived too far to care about my troubles, but it was only past ten in California. Maybe my nephews were asleep by now and she could relax and chat with her sister for a while. She never had much time to talk with her busy mothering schedule. I decided against it. Her lectures were sometimes as bad as Mom's. I didn't want to bother any of them with my trivial media melodrama.

The internet icon on my laptop kept taunting me to click it. Usually, I couldn't wait to enter the world of cyberspace, but tonight I worried. I was afraid what I would find on the other side of that button. I kept going back and forth, but eventually I clicked it. It was the logic in me. I would eventually click and see everything. I wouldn't stay away forever.

I clicked it open. When I daringly opened Facebook, I was bombarded. Not only was the link on multiple pages, and people spreading it like herpes, but it had made some serious circulation.

I stared unblinking at the Likes. "Thirty-two thousand?"

My palms grew instantly sweaty, and my vision grew fuzzy around the edges.

"Swallow me, please," I said to no one. "This is *not* happening."

I looked at my friend requests. I didn't know any of these people. How could they find me? I started deleting requests. "Nah. Forget it."

I went to my settings and without any remorse, I deleted my profile.

"There. Try to 'friend' me now, people." My laugh was rather evil, but it felt good to laugh.

I continued removing myself from every social media I could think of, changing my names, setting up security, blocking people, all with a satisfied impish smile. I grabbed my phone and did the same, deleting apps that upset me.

When I had finished, I sat back and checked out the mess I made. My poor computer, serving quietly as the chopping block to my axe. I promised not to drink, but whiskey sounded like the perfect accomplice.

The door handle jiggled as a key was pressed in the knob and turned. Pauline walked in and stopped, seeing my computer and phone strewn about me like discarded leftovers. "Hey," she said, rather confused. "What are you doing up?"

"All the things." I took a deep swig of milk. "I got rid of all my social media."

"You what?" Pauline hung her jacket on the hook. "Why would you do that?"

I gave Pauline a very dry look. "My media is exploding. I had over thirty new friend requests. Several were creepy guys."

"No kidding. You're becoming cyber-famous."

"Thirty-two thousand on Facebook." The words drawled out.

"No way." Pauline went to her phone. Within a minute she found it. "On YouTube, there's way more likes."

I sank in the couch a little deflated. "Well, I can't delete YouTube. Let them have their fun."

Pauline came over and rubbed my head, like I was a little kid. "You'll get through this."

"Thanks." I flipped on the TV and scrolled through all the BBC English dramas saved on my list. I felt very Bronte-esque, something both romantic and tragic.

Pauline went to the kitchen and returned with some water. "It's one in the morning. Aren't you tired?"

"You would think," I answered. "I'm having a hard time relaxing."

"Don't you have work tomorrow?"

"Brody's covering for me. So I have plans to stay around here all day." I jingled the remote in my hand. "I've got a date with this guy right here."

Pauline quietly sipped from her glass. "Well, I think I'll head to bed."

"Did you have a good evening?"

"Sure. Danny and I are trying to finish Skinstalkers."

"Yeah, no thanks. That's the last thing I want to watch, some paranormal show about stalkers."

Pauline headed to her room but stopped in the doorway. "It's gonna blow over, you know. No one will remember this."

I sighed. "In some ways I feel that's true, but it's still a consequence of my actions. That's the hardest part. If I would've left Miah alone, everything would be fine. But I didn't. It's out of character for me to do something so reckless. Now I feel like it's all people will know about me, the drunken, jealous ex. That's not me at all."

I felt the welling of tears. I wiped each eye and brushed my nose on my sleeve. Pauline came over and gave me a side hug from the couch. It was brief, but nice.

"You'll be fine," she encouraged from my shoulder. "You'll be stronger."

"Okay."

Pauline got up and went into her room, leaving me alone with Jane and Mr. Rochester.

Seven

Simon flicks a stone into the river. "Well, I read it."

Adri straightens, the dandelion dropping in her hand. "And what did you think?"

Simon smiles and doesn't respond. He picks through more stones near the shore. "Where are we anyway?"

"The Hundred Acre Wood," Adri says nonplused. "So, come on." Adri bumps his hip. "You tell me you finished it, but you don't tell me anything else?"

Simon shrugs. "You asked me to read it and I did." He throws a stick into the water and watches it disappear under the surface.

Adri sits on a rock closer to him. "You didn't like it."

Simon stops mid-throw. "I didn't say that. You're assuming when you shouldn't."

"Well, what else should I think if you don't answer?"

"I promised to read it and I did. If I make a promise, I keep it."

Adri grabs around her own knees, the dandelion falling apart in her hand. "But I wanted to talk about it. That's the reason I asked you to read it in the first place. It's the best part about reading books, sharing the adventure with others."

"Like the Hundred Acre Woods?" Simon gestures to the scenery.

"Absolutely." Adri breathes deep. "I had to read A. A. Milne for my poetry class. It's still fresh in my mind."

Simon spins the rock into the water and sighs. "Did you ask me to read it so you could get my take of Rochester?" Simon makes little guns with his hands and shoots them her way.

Adri looks confused. "Ugh, no. It's not about Mr. Rochester; it's the journey Jane took."

"Man, the guy was a creep."

Adri's mouth drops open. "What?"

Simon crinkles his eyebrows. "He was old enough to be her dad. And he's the first guy she's ever had an intelligent conversation with." Simon throws another stone. "See? You got me talking about it."

Adri gently brushes the dandelion wishes from her pants. "Whoa, you're spilling out a bunch of things here." Adri lowers the dandelion and points it at him. "First, Rochester is not a creep."

"Yes, he is."

"Wait, no. Hear me out." Adri adjusts her posture and sits right in front of him. "You can't help who you fall in love with."

Simon shakes his head. "He shouldn't have fallen in love with her."

"He didn't expect to fall for her. He was starved for company, and this strange girl interrupts everything."

"You don't think the age difference is a big deal?"

"Well, when you put it that way, it's a little weird, but she is eighteen. It's not a teen romance. And things were different back then. At eighteen, she was old."

"He was older."

"Guys married young women because women died in childbirth and stuff like that." Adri playfully throws the dandelion at him. A few wishes escape and fly in the air. She watches for a moment before she speaks. "It's about the heart being connected. Get it? That's what I like about it, what I want you to share with you. How Jane could hear him cry for her across hundreds of miles away. When two hearts understand each other so well, when one needs the other, it knows."

Simon turn his head to her displaying an impish grin. "Well, I guess I like that idea."

Adri blushes and looks back down the river.

Simon picks up a stick. "Someday read Ender's Game. My favorite book."

Adri nods her head. "Deal. Does it have wistful romance?"

"Not at all." Simon sees the wishes still floating about. "What did you wish for?"

Adri's breath catches. "What do you mean?"

"You stopped." Simon points toward the wishes. "You made a wish on those dandelion seeds."

"How do you know that?"

Simon picks up the fallen dandelion she threw at him and blows the rest. They fly up, catch a sweet wind, and dance in the air before disappearing. "I make wishes too."

I felt better after talking with Liane, like the weight of this secret had lifted from me. I debated going back to the game. My mind was still occupied, I couldn't concentrate on our campaign. But James counted on me to help lead everyone and keep the campaign going. I packed up my computer and drained the last of my coffee.

Everyone welcomed me back. Both Maria and Katelynn must have had a conversation about me, because when I returned, both were more flirtatious than before, each trying to pry secrets from me. We ran our adventure. I made some bonehead decisions that almost triggered our campaign's demise and an early ending to the evening, but the others were determined and we kept plowing through.

I fidgeted all night. I kept looking at my phone. I texted Liane a few times to see if she had found out anything, but she never responded. She probably crashed on the couch as she often did. I hated pretending like things were normal when they weren't. I daydreamed seeing her in my head: our first meeting, how I wanted to feel her skin, what color her hair really was—red, or auburn, or strawberry blonde. My mind was anywhere but in the game.

I thought more clearly about the possibility of finding her on Facebook. If I researched, I could find out where the video was shot and track her down. Social media made connecting easy. I could send her a friend request. She would know it was me. Well, I should replace my picture with a real picture of me and not a doodle I made at work. But she would know it was me. Simon.

It's Simon.

Yes, *that* Simon.

What would I even say to her? *Hey. I'm real. This is cosmic and insane, but let's meet. I live in Portland. Where the hell have you been all my life?*

No. I'd probably just say, "Hey."

I said this out loud. Everyone in the game fixed their eyes on me. Leo laughed. "Hey, yourself."

I scanned around at the others, who were packing up. I glanced at my watch. It was one in the morning. "Sorry. Are we done?"

"Yeah, you're still in the prison," Leo complained. "We will have to go get your sorry ass out of there next time."

"I'm in prison?"

James laughed. "I threw you in there when you spaced out."

"Geez. I'm sorry."

"What is with you?"

I didn't know what to say. "Leo, do you think I could catch a ride with you?"

"Sure."

I packed up my dice and notebooks. I made quick conversation with everyone, wished them luck, and headed out the door with Leo.

"Man, what is with you?" He asked once we got out to the car.

I couldn't hold the secret anymore. "I know that girl."

"What girl?"

"The one in the video everyone was laughing at, the one who toppled over the railing."

Leo laughed. "No way. Seriously?" He laughed even harder. "Poor girl. Did you call her or something?"

"No, it's not like that," I said. I wanted to explain but went with the simplified version. "We met when we were young. I wasn't sure if it was her or not. I've been trying to find her for a long time."

"Oh, okay." The car started up and Leo moved out into the street. "So, you don't know where this girl is?"

"No, not really."

"Do you even have a Facebook account?"

"Yeah, I do, but Facebook irritates me."

"Dude, are we even friends on there?"

"I have no idea." I placed my forehead on the window of the passenger side watching the shops and streetlamps brighten and pass.

"Well, if you need any help, I could mess around and see if I can find anything. I have super hacking skills."

Leo pulled up to my apartment. There was no red beetle parked at the bottom. The pang hurt less than before. I must not give a crap.

"Thanks, man." I patted Leo on the shoulder as I exited his little Subaru.

I ran upstairs to my place. Nate was passed out on the couch. I opened my computer at the table and started my research.

I first went to Facebook to find the link. The Likes number was overwhelming, it had been shared a massive amount of times. I clicked on it and the link took me to YouTube. As much as I searched around there, I couldn't find anything about her. I clicked on the YouTube channel to see what other things had been posted by this person. After a few lame videos I went back and tried to find where it came from. The pent-up frustration ate at my insides. Everything I tried led me to a dead end.

I went back to Facebook and investigated, typing in the person who originally posted it. Some online click-bate had picked it up and I couldn't find the source. I couldn't find any pictures of Adri.

Adri.

Adri what?

Did she tell me her last name before? I knew she had. When? I tried to think back to the hundreds of conversations we had had. What if I simply asked her? What if she appeared in my dream tonight?

I closed my computer. Sleeping was my best idea yet. Just go to sleep.

When was our last dream together? It had been a while. A few months, maybe. Stars and an empty spaceship flashed into my memory. Had she told me then? Dreaming together was never something planned, it just happened. It always happened when I needed her, when we needed each other.

Was it her break up? No. It was after. I thought the guy she dated got married. A strange burning fire lit my heart at the memory. It was true too, her break-up with the guy I couldn't stand. She wasn't attached. She wasn't dating, as far as I knew. Once she knew I was real . . .

Sleep. I needed some sleep.

I went to my room, didn't bother changing, and lay on my bed. I closed my eyes waiting for sleep to take me.

And it didn't.

I lay there. I adjusted the pillow behind my head and sighed. Eventually I opened my eyes. I stared at the ceiling. "Adri, where are you?"

I thought about all our conversations and placing them as real events, something I had never considered. So many experiences we shared but didn't. Did she even know how many times she came with me on every date I ever had? She was always with me. She had been with me since the day we met.

A rush of memories overwhelmed me, thinking they were dreams. My heart completely swelled. I had to find her.

And I waited.

I waited for the sleep that would eventually come. I kept my mind on the meadow. I had its image. I could feel my body relaxing, the sleep coming.

"Please, Adri, I need you." I spoke heart to heart and hoped she was listening. "Come find me. I need you."

Since my nap I felt very awake. I hadn't watched this version of Jane Eyre in a long time and it held my attention, along with my popcorn and a hazelnut cocoa. I used my closed laptop as a table, keeping away the temptation to open it and talk myself into rejoining the social media scene. I switched my phone off completely and set it on the charger. It was nice and calm as I lay comfortably watching Jane and Rochester, nothing but the light tussle of tree leaves in wind. I had a peaceful four-in-the-morning moment, the kind you never truly get at four in the morning, but I needed it and it was here for me.

Jane Eyre took close to five hours to finish, but I enjoyed this BBC production the most. Before I knew it, the sky brightened. I had stayed awake all night.

As the credits rolled, I sunk in the pillow and thought of sleep. I flipped over my phone and saw the quiet black. I pressed power and let it awake. As it did, a few messages came over, all from my mother. How in the world did she find out?

I scrolled through them. Yes. She knew. Someone had told her, but she didn't mention who. It was early, but she would be up. I swiped her name and the phone rang.

"Adrianna." My mother's calm voice said every syllable with deliberate resignation. "How are you? I 'ave been zo worried."

"Hey, mom. Everything's fine. No worrying about me."

"Jonie Lilyvite came and zaw me last night. . ."

I sighed. Of course it was Mrs. Lilywhite. I wasn't allowed to call her Jonie. I forgot it was her first name. She was my old piano teacher growing up in Michigan. Mrs. Lilywhite knew everything about everyone. How she found out of my public humiliation was beyond me.

". . . She suggested I check on you. She zaid there was a terrible wideo being passed around about you in your underthingz."

"Geez, mom. It's super fine. I fell over a railing. I didn't strip or anything like that." I tried smoothing it out as best I could. "If it helps any, I tore a hole in the green chiffon dress you made last year."

My mother made a disapproving hum in the phone. "Oh, now, how iz that supposed to make me feel bet-ter? I don't think I could fix a hole in the dress. Chiffon does not fix."

Typical behavior from my mother, worried more about things and her reputation in the community than my feelings. I was losing patience. I shouldn't have called her. "I'm good. I'm great. I am super excellent, mom."

"It iz not too far of a drive, you know." I could tell she meant it. I hadn't been home for a while. I used to go all the time, but I've been too busy and too . . . too . . . not wanting to go see my parents. "At least were you wearing descent under things?"

"Mom. What? Yes. They were clean if you're asking. I'm not ten years old."

"Many girls now-a-days wear those thong pieces that go right up their—"

"It's early," I interrupted by faking a yawn. "I need to sleep. Seriously. I'm good. Give hugs to Dad." She made a few protests, but I said goodbye and tossed the phone to the other end of the couch.

I buried my face in a pillow and sighed. The only noise came from the gentle awakening of my quiet neighborhood. I lifted my head a little. Delicate light framed the outside window. Sleep was coming. I finally felt the tired heaviness spread through my entire body. I let it relax and appreciated the calm. I closed my eyes.

"Adri."

The voice rang clear in my mind.

My eyes popped open. The room was empty. My ears held his voice. He spoke my name as if we were standing alone in our field with only the wind to carry it.

"Simon?" I sheepishly said his name. I don't know why. I knew he wasn't here. I knew he wouldn't be in the room with me. I sat up waiting for the haunting to go away. He felt so near. I needed sleep. I needed to dream. Of all the people, he was who I needed to talk to, he was the one who would understand.

"Ha." I laughed to my own thoughts. Actually, Simon would be the one who would give me the worst time, but he would be understanding. I suddenly felt very lonely. I grabbed the blanket and placed it tight over my shoulders.

"Simon." It came out like a sigh. I placed my head back on the arm of the couch. I didn't expect the tears. A strange despair hit me like a crushing wave, pounding me with all the resignation of my single, lonely life. "Simon, I wish you were real."

Miah did little things, little mannerisms I liked because it reminded me of a boy who was not even real. I felt so pathetic, so small.

Would I ever find anyone who met the expectations I set by my imaginary dream guy?

I already knew the answer.

I shuffled in the coverings trying again to get comfortable. Memories of the meadow, our tree, and the face I missed kept me awake. I could never think of the meadow and get there; it was usually when I had problems and unconsciously needed to see Simon. Right now, I was consciously seeking him and couldn't connect. I couldn't relax enough to get my brain in a place where it wanted to talk it out.

My phone buzzed with a call. I looked at the clock—8:30 AM. I stretched over the couch to grab my device. It was my sister.

"Hey, Viv," I half-yawned.

"What's up with you. I tried to video chat and I couldn't find your name."

"Yeah, I removed it for a while."

Viv let out an exhausted sigh, the sigh that meant the conversation somehow was about her. "Because of this thing? Mom told me—"

"Nope." I stopped her right there. What my mother told and what my sister heard were probably two very different things. I calmly explained what happened, leaving out a few major details, but the gist was there.

"Miah was never right for you."

I sighed. "Let's not talk about him."

"It's true though," Viv said. A soft crunch muffled between the words. She must be eating something. "He never celebrated your quirkiness. You know? You're adorable."

"Eh, Viv. Adorable? You always called it dorky."

"He tried to change you. Why? You need your glasses, your hair color, your artsy-shabby smart look."

"You're making me sound un-dateable."

"Ugh, you know that's not true."

I slumped down on my pillow. Pauline's door opened. She gave a sad smile and headed for the bathroom. "Well, after this video fiasco, I'm definitely hitting the bottom of the dating world. I'm down in the ocean with all the other bizarre ocean dwellers. I'll have to grow some weird third eye to become appealing to anyone."

"You should come hang out with me. Roman has a cousin we could—"

"I'm not interested in your husband's cousin."

"But you could get away for a while. Come hang with me on the beach. Chicago is so cold. I don't know why you stay there."

It took a second to collect my response. I had fallen out of love with Chicago. When I moved here for school, Chicago was everything Michigan wasn't. I gravitated to its youthful, artsy side and the eclectic people it collected. That was before the town turned its back on me. Before I knew anything about the hard winters and muggy summers. My enchantment had disappeared after hard-trodden years of disappointment. With this strange new visibility, a change of scenery could be nice. California always felt like a vacation, never like home. Roman was handsome and tan with his exotic Persian background, and my nephews soaked up the sun in their skin. They fit into

California. But Vivian and I were polar opposites. Appearance was as important to her as functionality was to me. She needed the Greek God chiseled everything. I sought someone who could make me laugh. She was attracted to lifestyle. I was attracted to brains and cleverness, imagination and fun. I mean, I knew we came from the same DNA, but we couldn't be more different.

"Have you ever felt trapped?" I asked. It was a deep-seeded question, but I wanted an honest reaction.

"What do you mean, trapped?"

"I feel trapped here." I sighed as my thoughts spilled out of my mouth. "I have an existence in Chicago, but it's not a life. I don't want to go home to Michigan. Everyone I know is gone and moved, and I would rather die than drink tea with Mom's inner circle. I'm too poor to move away, and even if I did, where would I go? Not to California. I couldn't be myself there. I need to go somewhere quirky and interesting and artsy."

"What? Like Portland?"

"I don't know. Maybe." I heard the shower start and released the breath I was holding. "And I like Pauline, but she's not like me either. I don't think I can stay here another year. I just, I'm sick of being stuck. And I am really stuck."

The other side went silent. I don't think Vivian knew what to say. She had everything: marriage, kids, money, warmth, security. What could she possibly say to all my wallowing?

"Adri," she started. "I'm sorry."

Wow. To hear my sister apologize was something new. "It's not your fault. I'll figure things out."

"California is a great place to figure things out."

"I don't think I could leave the bookstore."

"Your minimum wage job? Why don't you use your degree?"

"There is nothing I'm qualified to do with an English degree besides teach. I'm a terrible teacher."

Her spoon clinked in her cereal bowl. "How about come here and write. Come finish your novel or one of your projects. Just finish something."

Could I do that? Up and leave everything to follow my childhood passion of becoming a writer? It sounded silly in my mind. Simon would love the idea.

"I'll think about it, Viv."

"Good." A few more excited words and she was off the phone. I stared at the silent thing for a moment, thinking about searching the video of my embarrassment, but thought better of it. I turned it to silent and flipped it face down. I sunk back on the pillow and fell asleep in seconds.

I didn't dream of anything.

Eight

Adri watches the passing clouds. "Have you been to California?"

Simon does not turn his head but looks at the different shapes. "Yes. Twice."

"Is it nice there? I've never been."

"Yeah, it's a cool place." Simon adjusts his head until it touches hers. "I think that one looks like an elephant."

Adri squints. "I see David Bowie with a microphone."

Simon laughs. "That's very specific."

Adri shrugs. "Well, that's what I see. Tell me about California."

Simon turns and looks at her. "Well, I don't remember much about the first trip. I was five when my parents took us to Disneyland. All I have are pictures. So I don't know anything about Disneyland, if you're asking." He stares back at the clouds, trying to see the David Bowie and not seeing it. "The
second trip though, I was eighteen and I went on a road trip with my buddies, Edgar and John." Simon laughs. "Whoa, yeah, that was a great trip."

Adri squints to see him better. "Sounds like you had too much fun."

"What's classified as too much fun?"

Adri raises an eyebrow.

"Okay, I get it." Simon repositions his head. "It was a great trip, though. Nothing that warrants too much fun."

Adri glances around. "Can you show me?"

"Huh. Let me try." Simon sits up and the checkered-worn blanket changes to vivid stripes of beach towels. A sun near the edge of the horizon changes the light to an orange-pink glow of sunset. The soft roll of waves crashes before them.

Adri quickly stands. "Are we there?"

Simon laughs. "Yeah, this is what I remember."

A blur of three young men running toward the ocean materialize down the beach, each one stripping off shoes and shirts before splashing into the waves.

Adri watches the memory, her hand shading her eyes from the sun. "Who's with you again?"

Simon points. "That's John splashing and Edgar's heading into the surf." He continues to laugh. "We acted like kids."

"When was this?"

"Right after graduation," Simon answers. "We left incredibly early in the morning the day after. We all hopped in the car and just drove west from Fort Collins. My mom encouraged me to go and have the best time. It took us a full day to get there." Simon casually puts his arm on her shoulder, growing more animated. "And the deal was, we drive as far west as we could before we could stop. We got to the beach near sunset. Isn't it beautiful?"

"Is the sand as soft as they say?"

"Who's they?" Simon asks. "It's sand, not magic."

"But California sand has to be different than Lake Michigan sand."

Simon crouches and takes some in his hand. "Try it."

Adri takes off her shoes and sets her toes in the sand. "This feels pretty soft, and warm. It's toasty."

"I hope it holds up to your imagination." Simon sits back down on the towel and tosses the sand in his hand. "But it's not about

the sand, it's about the—" he extends his arms toward the sunset,
"—everything. It's about looking west and knowing there's nothing
out there until you reach Hawaii, or Japan, or Australia, or
whatever is west of here. It's about living a life without limits."

Adri sits next to him. "And California is a life without limits?"

"Nah, but I think it lets a person dream bigger there, because
the dreams are all around you."

Adri rests her head on his shoulder watching the sky change
colors. "Seems like a dream place. I should have asked about
California before."

Simon sets his chin on her head. "But Adri, it's just a place,
like other places. They still buy their groceries and stuff." Simon
huffs out a breath, thinking. "What's in
California?"

Adri grabs his upper arm, mesmerized by the orange sky.
"My sister's moving there. Her husband is an entertainment
lawyer and got a high-paying job."

"It's good to have relatives here, I imagine. Nice to have
someone to stay with."

"I guess. I'm flying out in a few weeks to help with my baby
nephew while they unpack."

Simon looks back toward his memory. He and his friends
were now walking close to the surf talking. "You know, I was
mystified by the ocean. I liked picking up the seashells and skipping
them like river rocks. I kept one, though." He breaks away from
her and stands, walking closer to the memory.

Adri gets up and follows.

Simon pauses near his younger self and looks. "See? Look."
He points at what his memory pulls from the last crash.
"See that one?"

Adri marvels at the way the younger Simon checks out

the discovered treasure, the unique shape, the white and blue coloring. "It's really cool."

"It's broken but I like it. It looked like a piece of the moon." He points again. "See, it has a hole. Some bird originally pecked at it. It's the only thing I brought back for my mom. That's all she wanted. And she loved it. When she died, I took one of my mother's chains and slid it through the hole. I still have it." Simon watches as his younger self runs and catches up to his friends. He turns to Adri. "I hope to someday give the necklace to someone special."

Adri folds her arms against the ocean wind and smiles. "That's lovely. She's a lucky girl."

I didn't sleep much and I didn't dream. All I asked the cosmos for and I didn't get it.

The clock on my phone said 6:03 AM. It was only 7:03 in Denver and still too early to talk to Liane.

I sighed heavy, feeling the weight of her name. I swiped my phone open to the images I stole from the video. Real. And I couldn't be more positive about anything. I had to find her.

I went through all the "what if" scenarios in my head. What if it's not her? What if she just looks like her? What if she doesn't like who I am? Or how wild my hair gets? What if I'm completely crazy? But this morning, I didn't care. I didn't have room to care about failing. I was too occupied with doing this. There was no harm in trying to find her. I felt stupid for not trying before now.

"Adri," I exhaled, hoping somewhere in this world she would hear me.

I pulled off my covers and headed to my dresser. In the top drawer I had stuffed a bunch of odds and ends. I knew the notebook had to be in this pile of junk. I recognized the faded yellow near the bottom. I shoved the things covering it aside. As I pulled on it, the tiny brown box tumbled to the side. My attention wavered. I placed the notebook on the top of the dresser and grabbed the box setting it gently on the notebook.

It was my old watch box, too cool to throw away. The fake leather had rubbed raw on the side exposing the hard case underneath. I stashed a bunch of crazy things in it, like the giant steely marble I won in second grade from Javier Rubio and the ticket stub from my first Coldplay concert. I opened it. The random trinkets sat piled together as nothing important. A huge smile crossed my face when a delicate shell peeked through the monotony.

My fingers wrapped around the chain and lifted it up so I could examine it. The shell was as perfect as when I found it. A few small places were rubbed smooth where my mother would rub it during her chemo treatments. My hand clasped around it and didn't return it to the box. I lifted it around my neck and let it hang around me. I closed the box again and threw it back into the drawer.

I snatched the notebook and plopped back on my bed.

As I rifled through my old writing, stories, and song lyrics, I stumbled on what I was looking for. On the margins were scribbles of conversations I remembered having with Adri. My thumb rubbed the shell as I read.

"Lake Michigan." She lived near there, but I wasn't sure where. My brain raked over the details, but I honestly came up blank. Other words didn't connect immediately. "Freshwater." "DePaul." "Jeremiah."

"I have no idea what I'm looking for." It was now 6:07 AM. Time was not passing fast enough.

I headed to the bathroom before going to the kitchen for a bowl of Frosted Flakes.

Jessica was asleep on the couch. For the first time I didn't care. I crunched louder just to annoy her if I could.

My laptop stared at me on the table, daring me to open it. Within seconds I placed my nearly empty cereal bowl on the table and pushed the power button. It opened back to my social media page, searching for any link to her. I typed her name and a ton of names popped up and I scrolled down. No face I recognized. My privacy settings kept me from scrolling too far. I couldn't believe I was in the settings changing my account to public.

I promised myself to change it back as soon as possible.

A small ding came on my computer. A friend request. I read the name. It was an ex from a few years ago. Ah crap, not good.

I typed in Adrianna again in the search bar. Little changed. The same faces popped up again. I scrolled and I still couldn't see her. My computer dinged again. Another request. A high school friend.

I added the last name DePaul to the search. A bunch of new faces appeared—not many, none her. I erased it. It didn't sound right. A college page popped up. Was that a school she attended? Maybe I could look up schools.

Another ding—a chat window. What was happening?

I wasn't getting anywhere, and in fact, things were getting worse. I went back to Maria's page and pulled up the video again to read through the comments. There were so many now. What did the YouTube comments say?

Another ding.

"How are these people finding me?"

I went back to settings and changed my account back to private.

"Who you stalking?"

I jumped. Jessica was near my ear wrapped up in a blanket. She was laughing.

"Do you mind?"

Jessica strolled to the refrigerator. "Since when have you ever been on Facebook? You must be stalking someone."

I didn't respond and shut my computer. "I'm not stalking anyone."

"Ooh," she mocked, grabbing my orange juice and pouring herself a glass. "You totally are. Why would you shut your computer if you didn't want me to see?"

"It's not like that."

She took a sip. "Ha, then you're trying to find someone."

"Yes," I cleared my throat. "But I'm not stalking. I found her."

Jessica looked unimpressed. "You found someone?"

"Yes. A girl I met a long time ago."

"Does she have red hair?"

"Stop it, Jessica." I grew flustered. "She is the original red head."

Jessica stopped smiling and blinked. "Oh freak, you're serious."

"Of course I am."

"Well then." Jessica sat down across from me. "Tell me about her. Do I know her?"

"No. She's not from here. I don't know where she is right now."

"How did you guys meet?"

"When we were kids. She found me carving on a tree."

Jessica set down her drink. "You don't carve on trees."

"I was young."

"Are you in love with her?"

I stared at the girl who I tried as a replacement for Adri. My head again became dizzy with thoughts of her. "Probably. Yes. Yeah, I think I am. I've always been."

Jessica smirked. "I knew it. I knew there was something you were holding back." Her grin grew until it lit up her face. "This is great."

"How is this great? I don't know where she is."

"Then how did you find her?"

The truth came rushing out of my mouth. "She is on this YouTube video being passed around the internet."

"And that's why you were on Facebook."

"I know it sounds crazy. I have to find her."

Jessica tapped her fingernail on the glass "Now?"

"Yes. Now." I ran my hands through my hair. My frustration mounted. "I lost her. I mean, I haven't had any idea where to find her. I still don't."

"Well, what's her name?"

"Adri."

"Adri what?"

I looked at her hopeless and shrugged.

She laughed again. "She's a ghost of a person. Here. Let me see."

I felt helpless and opened my computer. I ran the video from the beginning. "That's her," I pointed.

Jessica watched and didn't laugh like the others. She made a few "ouch" and "eweh" noises before she said, "Back up."

I was startled and tried to grab the bar.

"Stop there." I paused it and she pointed. "See that?"

I scanned under her finger. "What am I supposed to be seeing?"

"It's an address."

"A what?"

"An address. Isn't that a mailbox?"

I backed it up and looked again. "But I can't read what it says."

"Well, study it." She drained her juice and went back to the sink to rinse out the glass. "If you want to find this girl so badly, an address is a good place to start."

For the next hour Jessica helped me decode a little of what I was seeing.

"What if it's a last name?" I halfheartedly mentioned, after looking at the words near the porch.

"Always a possibility," she mentioned, scribbling something down. I glanced at her paper. It had little word combinations, since the name of the street wasn't as clear as we originally believed.

I watched the back of her neck as I used to when we were dating. She had a slender tattoo behind her ear. I thought it was peculiar that anyone would tattoo behind the ear, a place you would never see. But yet, I had always liked it in a rebellious kind of way. "Why are you helping me?" I finally asked.

"You deserve to be happy." She tucked her hair behind the same ear I was looking at. "I won't ever make you happy, even if we tried. This girl," she pointed to the monitor, "she will. And it makes sense to me now."

"Jess, I . . ."

But she just shook her head. "Don't." She started scribbling again. "Friends." She eyed me. "You know that."

The apology stopped dead in my mouth.

She handed me the paper. "I think these are the best words I can decipher."

I glanced over the list. There were three words. "But these aren't words, are they?" I read them aloud, "Cataba. Catalpa. Catalba."

"Yes." She pulls over the laptop. "Right here. I think that's a *p*, but it could easily be a *b*."

"You don't know the word, this is a guess. I don't think anyone would live on a street called 'Cataba.'"

"Why not?" She opened up Google Earth and typed out 'Cataba.' "Look. There is a Cataba Road in California."

"California?" Adri had mentioned California before.

She continued trying another word. "Catalba isn't anything. Catalpa brought up some things."

"Too many things. Look at this." New York. New Jersey. Illinois. How was I to know which one it was? "I'm overwhelmed," I admitted. "I feel lost. What should I do now?"

"Street view." Jessica smiled. "I can help you."

It still felt hopeless. I stood up and made coffee.

I woke from my quiet nap on the couch to a knocking at the door. In my delirium, I wasn't sure why I slept here and not my bed. The knocking came again. I peeked through the blind and recognized the bright yellow crooked hat. I sprang up and unlocked the door.

"Oh, Addy, Addy, Addy." Julsie rushed at me and squeezed me tight. "That movie you made on Friday is just the absolutely funniest thing happening on the planet!" She squeezed me again. I let her.

"Oh, thanks. I tried," I said through her quaff of hair.

She pulled back and examined me. "Girl, you go on and get dressed."

"I don't feel like it."

"Oh, come on. You go get dressed. I'm gonna take you out."

I loved Julsie. Our friendship was a strange yet brilliant one. Julsie was eccentric and lively, and a true free spirit. She had several good years on me, but it didn't matter. We spoke the language of art. I met Julsie at a writer's conference where she was my mentor, being an accomplished writer of several best sellers. I was a nobody who hadn't finished a manuscript. She immediately liked me, complementing my shabby librarian style and eccentric hat choice—a 20s fascinator I found at a thrift store the day before. I renamed it my Julsie hat. We had been close ever since. Out of everyone in Chicago, she was the one person who might succeed in getting me out of my media doldrum.

"Did Pauline text you?"

Julsie's face lit up. "Of course, sugar. But it's not like I didn't recognize that skinny little behind on my feed."

"Ah, geez. It was totally my fault."

"Go get dressed and we'll talk over brunch."

We walked past the park to a corner café and talked about writing. I ordered a Spanish omelet and hibiscus tea, while Julsie ordered the waffle special.

The waitress eyed me as she took the order. "Sorry. You look really familiar."

My cheeks flushed. "Must be one of those faces."

The waitress was satisfied with my answer and left.

"Maybe if I showed her my butt, she would know me."

Julsie's hearty laugh made me glow inside. "You delight me, you know. How is that butt anyway?"

"Sore. I'm sore all over." I turned my head toward her. "And, you know, you're the first person to ask if I'm okay. Glad the bruise under my eye is easy to cover with make-up."

Julsie laughed. "Don't be putting any make-up on your butt. Got it?"

We both laughed.

"How's that manuscript coming?" she asked sipping at her drink.

I sighed and looked up at the exposed pipe ceiling. I didn't want to tell her I hadn't finished it.

"You know," Julsie said, breaking from a sip of her coffee with a giggle stuck in her throat. "I've known you for three years now, and I think this is the same story you've been writing."

"Well, it is, and it isn't. I rewrote it, remember?"

Julsie hummed in her coffee. "And revised it. And restored it. And all the things you need to do to improve it. Everything but tell the story."

"I'm getting there."

Julsie put down her mug. "I don't think this is the story inside you."

"What do you mean?"

"You have so much talent. I've read your short stories, even your poetry, but you come back to the same romance drivel, thinking that's where your voice is."

I wasn't sure if I should be offended. My writing is very personal, but I trusted Julsie more than any other writer. She believed in me. "Romance is what sells, so I'm trying my best. I mean, I think that is all I have ever written."

"You may have a romantic elegance to your writing, but that doesn't make you a romance writer. Do you see what I mean?"

I considered what she said, but honestly had no reply.

"Do you like to read romance?"

I thought about my favorite books and my to-be-read list, and not many were romances. "Well, not really. I figured romance was the only way to make it as a writer."

"And look at my books," Julsie laughed. "Are any of those romances?"

"Well, they have a hint of romance to them. But I can't write like you. Mysteries are too smart for me."

Julsie laughed on and slapped the table. "Do you know how many books it took to get me that smart? I write what I want to read, sweetie. You should be your first fan."

I sat back. Julsie had exposed my demons, but in a gentle, friendly way. I had never been a fan of myself. I hid under goofy clothes and other peoples' words. She was absolutely right that I wouldn't ever read the books that I was writing. I actually abhor the genre, so why was I trying to write books I couldn't be proud of?

But it wasn't just the things she said but the way they were placed together that stunned my nerves. I had heard this speech before. "Someone else told me the same advice."

Julsie leaned forward. "Oh yeah?"

"Yes." A little smile crept up my face. "A friend told me the exact thing a few years ago."

"Well, your friend is right."

The waitress brought us our food. The cheese smelled heavenly. I didn't realize how hungry I had become. We talked about nothing particular while we slowly picked away at our meal. The conversation eventually moved back to writing.

"What did you do with that short story you wrote, the time traveling one?" Julsie asked, setting down her fork.

"Oh," I said with a mouthful of toast. "Well," I tried to swallow, "nothing much." The time traveling story came out of me at a writer's retreat she hosted at her home in Lake Forest. It was the first time I really got to know her, writing with other wannabes while Julsie mentored us and fed us delicious food. She took us to Fort Sheridan for inspiration. My eyes brightened at the idea of Fort Sheridan and the lush meadows, where I found the beautiful tree that reminded me of dreaming, where I first came up with the time traveler story. The quick piece involved two people meeting from different eras, two people who were never meant to meet. I sketched out my plot under the tree that reminded me of Simon.

"I liked that story," Julsie added, breaking into my memory. "It had the romantic tones you like to write about. And the two characters were smooth and clever. It was a beautiful story."

"Thank you." I felt my cheeks warm. I didn't know what to do with compliments, especially coming from someone I admired. "I published it on ZagMag last August."

"I remember. It's a good step." Julsie picked up her coffee and took a sip. "My advice—turn that story into a novel. Or even a screenplay."

My mind was filled with these two characters clearly stolen from my own life. "I don't know how it ends."

"We all know the ending we want." Julsie grinned as she lifted the last of her coffee to her lips. "Did you ever see Somewhere in Time?"

I shook my head.

Julsie set down the mug. "Christopher Reeve. Jane Seymour. Beautiful film. Will make you cry. It's much like your story: two people never meant to meet, but somehow are tethered together through time, and it's a simple magic that brings them together. Make it your homework tonight."

I appreciated the idea, but was wary of it. The story was created from a longing and sadness I didn't like feeling. "I was in a different place then, I mean creatively."

"Not much different. The writing was pure, energized. Do you think you've lost that? As I remember, you were in a relationship that wasn't very special when you wrote it."

"My imagination is very complicated."

Julsie motioned to the waitress for her check. "Your imagination should be somewhere you go to escape. Don't let it be complicated. Let it envelope you wholly."

Julsie believed in me. I didn't want to disappoint her. "I'll look at it."

"It's a wonderful story. Would make a great screenplay, ya know."

"But I don't know how to write screenplays."

Julsie placed her hand on my arm. "Oh, honey, if there wasn't this wonderful thing called the Internet. I bet you could find out."

I grinned. "Well, I might be taking some time away from the interwebs. No one needs to see me that much."

The waitress brought her the check and we stood. "Thank you, doll," she replied to me as she took it. "Do what you need to. Take time for you. Get away if you can. You are always welcome to my place if you want to duck out and just write. I have plenty of spare rooms. Trevor left back to Stanford, so the house just has Gerald and me again. I keep beggin' Lucy for a visit, but she's stuck in D.C. I miss my girl."

"I was thinking maybe of going to California. See my sis. Go hang out on the beach."

Julsie cocked her head back. "Well, that sounds downright lovely, though I'm a heck of a lot closer." She laughed and squeezed my side. "Shake off this moment. They happen to all of us."

"Not to you."

"Well, I must be blessed." She nudged me. "Even to me. I just react differently than most. I go with it when I can. Laugh along. Sometimes it hurts. None of us are immune. You know," she stopped mid-thought. "You should come stay with me. You know Gerald loves you. Always wants you to come over. We have a meeting of the minds tomorrow night. You should come."

Julsie was kind to think of me. "Thank you," I squeezed. "Maybe next time I publicly humiliate myself."

Nine

Simon studies the pages but remains silent.

Adri fidgets in her seat. She studies his face as he reads. She looks around at the emptying library then back to Simon, drumming her fingers on the oak table.

Simon eyes her fingers. "You know, other library patrons may get upset by all your noise," he whispers and turns back to the papers.

Adri stops and lays her arms crossed, waiting. Her heart pounds. He hasn't finished reading. Her head starts questioning what he must hate about it.

Simon lifts over the page.

Adri makes a low grunt.

"Excuse me. Some of us are trying to read."

Adri sits up. "You know you can't really read in dreams, it's just what your brain thinks of the words."

"Says who?"

"Dream theorists."

"Well, what do they say about us meeting in dreams?" He continues staring at the pages and doesn't look at her.

Adri furrows her brow. "Good point. It's just taking you forever."

Simon looks up from the page. "I'm digesting it."

"Well, I'm not used to people reading my words. I'm never around when they do. But I can't escape this time." Adri drops her head on the table. "It was stupid of me to have you read it." Her voice muffles in her arms.

Simon looks at her puzzled. "Why are you freaking out?"

Adri lifts her head and leans on one hand. "It's taking you a long time. And I can't bear watching you read my words. I probably did something wrong."

Simon's lip curls up. "Why do you think that? Because I'm not shouting"—he cups his hands and whispers—"'it's wonderful' through the library?"

Adri shrugs. "I don't know. Maybe? I thought you'd have some kind of reaction by now." She sits straight and crosses her legs on the chair. "You're the writer. You're the clever one."

Simon grimaces. "What? You devour books. And, I should also say, you arrange words very well."

Adri's chin lowers, bashful.

Simon sets the page down. "You know what you've written here?"

Adri raises her eyebrows. "A time-travel story?"

Simon sighs. "In a mask of a time-travel story, sure. But you know what I'm talking about." He leans forward and captures her eyes.

Adri doesn't dare look away. "Do I?"

Simon whispers, like the library might overhear. "This is about us."

Adri doesn't know how to respond.

Simon rummages and finds the first page. "I'm reading this slowly because this is the first time I'm understanding what you're thinking."

"It's fiction."

"It's inspired fiction. And you know why I know?" Simon sets down the page and places his hand on hers.

Electricity fills the touch, spreading a tangible energy between both of them.

"How are you doing that?" Adri looks at her hand.

"How are we doing any of this?"

Adri watches his finger brush her thumb.

Simon lifts her hand and examines it carefully. "Your story is beautiful and tragic."

"Because there's time between them," Adri whispers.

Simon cups her hand in both of his, not letting it go. "Because it doesn't have a happy ending."

Adri adjusts her breathing. "It's a short story. Should it?"

Simon studies her fingers before looking back to her eyes.

Adri feels her cheeks warm.

Simon half-smiles, thinking. "Man, I hope so. Can I continue reading now?"

Adri nods.

"What's goin' on?" Nate wandered out of his room around ten in the morning to see Jessica and me with three different computers and the TV all linked to Google street view.

Liane was on video chat with me looking through Illinois, Jessica focused on New York, and I had Florida pulled up.

"Morning." Jessica hopped up and went and gave Nate a big morning squeeze and noticeable butt grab. I didn't feel jealous, exactly, but more a longing for that to happen to me. I went back to the video chat with Liane.

"How's Illinois?"

"Dull," she returned. Her concentration was slightly diverted by the toddler sitting on her lap. She kept bouncing her knee and talking quietly. "Lily. Don't touch the keyboard."

I laughed watching the silly little girl do exactly what her mom told her not to. The little fingers reached forward and banged as hard as she could. Liane said sweet no's to the girl, but I could see the frustration grow on Liane's face. I loved my sister, but there was something so satisfying about seeing her have a child who was exactly like her growing up.

"Hey Lily." I waved and the girl grew excited and banged harder on the keyboard, giving a wicked laugh. I chuckled.

"Oh, hold on." Liane grabbed her daughter and tickled her wildly which made her giggle and walk out of the room.

"What's goin' on?" Nate wandered out of his room around ten in the morning to see Jessica and me with three different computers and the TV all linked to Google street view.

Liane was on video chat with me looking through Illinois, Jessica focused on New York, and I had Florida pulled up.

"Morning." Jessica hopped up and went and gave Nate a big morning squeeze and noticeable butt grab. I didn't feel jealous, exactly, but more a longing for that to happen to me. I went back to the video chat with Liane.

"How's Illinois?"

"Dull," she returned. Her concentration was slightly diverted by the toddler sitting on her lap. She kept bouncing her knee and talking quietly. "Lily. Don't touch the keyboard."

I laughed watching the silly little girl do exactly what her mom told her not to. The little fingers reached forward and banged as hard as she could. Liane said sweet no's to the girl, but I could see the frustration grow on Liane's face. I loved my sister, but there was something so satisfying about seeing her have a child who was exactly like her growing up.

"Hey Lily." I waved and the girl grew excited and banged harder on the keyboard, giving a wicked laugh. I chuckled.

"Oh, hold on." Liane grabbed her daughter and tickled her wildly which made her giggle and walk out of the room.

The camera on her computer went quiet and I turned back to my own screen.

California was not the right place to look. I felt it in my gut. All the homes were homes, with yards and fences. I studied the screenshot of the tall brick residence I took from the video. The style was wrong. The age and period looked completely out of place. It didn't fit in California from the street views I had, not even in San Francisco. This home was old and used and the greenery wasn't the same.

"It's not California," I said to Jessica.

"Got it." Jessica took the pencil from her makeshift bun and scribbled out the state on her list of possibilities. New Jersey and Ohio were also crossed out.

"Should I check Florida again?" I kicked back my feet on the coffee table.

"Florida has the same problem as California." Jessica said, pushing the pencil back into her hair. "It's too green. I mean, look at that!" She pointed at my phone with the picture on it. "It's obvious this place has seasons. Look at the way people are dressed, the tree in the front yard. I still think it's near the east coast."

I felt my frustration rise up my throat. It was illogical to look for a place where a theoretical girl from my past may or may not live. The hope that was once taking over all my actions now waned.

Jessica could see it on my face. She shook my knee with her hand. "We haven't checked Oregon yet. Maybe she's here."

The idea didn't give me much comfort. Never had Adri mentioned Oregon. I shuffled my feet off the coffee table and sat up again, wiping away the address in Florida and typing

under the faucet. The
me down.

"Simon." Jessica

"I don't need t
dripping in the sink. '

I turned to see J
silence filled all the
crunching his cereal–
make the sounds.

"Dude, you can
"Sy!" Liane's voi
can't believe we foun

Jessica pointed a

My stomach chu
she went to school in
stupid. I knew it. I
Chicago."

I still remained ir
His milk must be so
yelling for her husban
over me, I didn't feel
hauling me over to th

On the screen sa
the wrong season, wit
pumpkins on the stair

"I can't believe
toppled over." I wen
the harder it was to s
the funny mailbox on
Catalpa.

Catalpa and Oregon. It only gave three results, which was nice. I started with the first one.

"I'm back," I hear in my headphones. Liane had returned to her computer. "The little monkey is with her daddy."

"I can't wait to see her again." I commented. "I gave up on California."

"Told ya," Liane said in singsong.

"California has some green, shady places."

"Like Northern California, which none of those addresses were in."

"But, if you want me to go with my gut, California has a place. Her sister lives there. This I know. Not sure where, but I do remember that."

I could see Liane looking at her screen and not at me. "But you tried. That's important."

I sighed. I moved the little man down on the street and began scanning up and down. It was tedious. Everything for the next few minutes remained quiet while we all looked. Jessica's hand worked frantically scribbling off more streets. Nate leaned on the kitchen counter eating his cereal and watching the madness.

"No way!" The exclamation came in my ears.

"What? You find something?" I asked, more attentive but still focusing on my own street.

Liane popped up and down on her seat, moving in and out of view. "Sy! SY! I think I found it."

"What?" I bolted up right. "Where?"

Jessica unplugged my headset from the computer so she could hear Liane.

"Holy crap, I think this is it."

"Where? Wher
my head and I coul
"Where am I?
Chicago. I look
through conversatio
"Chicago!" I ra
in Chicago."
"Wait. Wait."
her paper. "What's
Liane rattled s
down. She went to
The process wa
headache suddenly
crawling over my fc
my gut. The emotio
Adri, the girl who ne
chasing a dream gir
had happened to m
toes went numb, m
out? What if the a
swept so fast it for
hopes up. I had to c
could not be real.
Jessica took th
screen.
As the resoluti
the kitchen.
"Simon?"
I covered my n
stubble and scratch
turned on the sink a

And every nerve ignited at once, like a spasm, and yet I felt paralyzed unable to move. "I can't believe this. What do I do?"

Jessica shoved my back playfully, getting me out of my trance. "You go there, idiot."

"But I can't go there. I work."

"You don't do anything at work that Adam couldn't handle." Nate said after he slurped his milk.

"Not after the crazy day we had on Friday." I ran my hands through my hair. "I can't just fly to Chicago and knock on someone's door."

"Why not?" Jessica demanded. "How long have you been searching for her?"

I slumped to the ground. "Too long, not counting the last five hours." My emotions bubbled and I tried to hold them back. The pain in my chest increased, a longing pressed hard on my heart, my lungs struggled for air. "I . . . I can't believe she's real. I mean, just so long. It's been too long not knowing . . . I just . . ." I knew I was mumbling. I searched for the right words. "I ache for her." The words got stuck in my throat. I had to stop talking before I lost my cool completely.

The room went silent. I found Jessica's face. She was crying.

"What did I do?" was my immediate reaction. I've made her cry before.

Jessica wiped her nose gently with the overlength of sleeve from Nate's flannel. Nate was not emotionally prepared for anything happening and remained as still as possible watching his girlfriend quietly sob.

"This is the Simon I never knew, you know. The guy I always wished you were."

"What?"

"I guess I should have known there was someone else. I would never be enough for you."

Nate rubbed his neck looking uncomfortable at this talk and slowly tried to back out of the room.

"I don't know what to do," I admitted. I could see the screen of my sister yelling something. Jessica had muted the screen. My eyes turned to Jess, who sat cross-legged across from me. Her eyes were indeed red, more from holding back tears than from actual crying. She reached out and rubbed my knee.

"You have to go find her."

"I can't." I gasped. Both my hands were through my hair and down to my face. "I can't. There isn't anything I can do."

"You should fly to Chicago and find her."

"No. I can't." I was adamant. I brushed off her hand as I tried to think. "I have a job. I can barely pay rent. It's irresponsible."

"Again, Adam could handle it." The voice speaking was Nate. He was now in the kitchen leaning against the door jam. Nate and I had met at ADA Specialty before they downsized. He knew how Adam could basically run everything himself. "Call him. No harm in asking."

"This is insane." I stared at both of them. "Flying to Chicago in search of a house this girl once visited, just to find out where she is . . ." I breathed rather fast at the actual thought of it. "I can't. Honest. It's too much money. I can't fly somewhere without a plan. I don't have extra money to plop down on a theoretical idea. This is creepy stalker stuff. I can't."

I buried my head down on my knees hiding the aching swell of longing. I was overwhelmed and exhausted and so clueless.

Jessica shook me. Her expression was rather soft. There was a look in her eyes I didn't know, part mischief, part surprise.

"What?" I spat, harder than I wished. "I found her. She exists. Holy freaking shit. And I feel powerless."

Jessica grinned. "I can get you there." She hopped up and ran out of the room. She returned quickly with her phone in her hand, dialing a number.

"Who are you calling?" I sat up right before someone on the other end answered.

"Mom. Hey."

She had called her mom?

". . . nah, I'm good. Great actually. I have a favor. Do you have any sky miles left?"

Jessica's mother worked for an airline, though I didn't remember which one. My heart hammered with this explosive idea. What the hell was I about to do? Could I up and leave? Could I really go to Chicago? Could I find Adri? I didn't know she was real until last night and here I was planning a trip halfway across the country.

I watched Liane freaking out on the screen wanting to know what was happening. I moved to the couch and unmuted the screen.

"—of all the rude things to do. Whoa." She stopped, realizing I could hear her now. "What did you mute me for?"

"I didn't, but Jessica is trying to get me tickets to Chicago."

"What? I'm coming."

"You can't come."

"Well, you can't go without me. Stop in Denver and pick me up."

"What about Lily?"

"She has a dad, you know. It's called parenting. And I have family here who will help."

She rubbed in the family part.

"I can't believe this is happening."

Liane giggled and danced on the screen. "It is, baby. Whahoo!"

Chicago, IL

I messaged my sister as I walked back to my apartment. When I got home, I dabbled with looking at airfare and my bank account. I received a message back from my sister:

'*Seriously?*'

I didn't think about texting her back.

Pauline walked in as I frantically typed on my computer. "What's happening?"

"I'm moving."

"What?" Pauline slammed my laptop down.

I didn't appreciate it, but my mood gave into her temper. "I need to."

"No, you don't. Who told you that?"

"Well, nobody. I've decided there's nothing here in Chicago for me anymore."

"What?" Pauline sat next to me. "How can you say that? I'm here."

"I know, and you're great, but there is seriously nothing else. I'm too close to my parents and not close enough to my sister. I don't even have a very good job."

Pauline sat back. "But you love your job." She was right. "And you have six more months with me in this lease. Don't forget."

And I had forgotten. "Okay, maybe you have a point."

Pauline shoved me in the shoulder. "Snap out of it. Meeting with Julsie was supposed to cheer you up not make you move away."

"She got me thinking."

"That you don't belong in Chicago? That's crazy."

I shuffled myself on the couch. "No, but I should do something more than what I'm doing. I was so driven to be a writer. I went to school to be a writer, and here I am working in a bookstore. I'm not doing any writing."

"That's not what I see. You spend all your available time with your computer."

"And I hate everything I write."

Pauline crinkled her nose in confusion. "Then why are you writing it?"

My mouth smirked in contemplation. "A professor once told me that to be successful as a writer you have to write either sweet romance or erotica. I tried to do both, thinking it's what people would read. I'm struggling with what I think others want and what I desire to write."

Pauline slapped my arm playfully. *"Why on earth would you write something you didn't believe in?"*

I watched Pauline speak, but it wasn't her words echoing in my mind. It was *his*.

"I want to be able to make money as a writer."

"But you're not. You're a bookshop girl." The words stung, though I know Pauline didn't mean it to hurt. I still felt dazed by how similar this conversation was to one I had earlier.

"If . . ." I started. "If I asked you to read something, something I believe in, would you?"

"Yeah. Of course." The sincerity showed in her face. "I've read your stuff before."

I stood and went to my room and grabbed the little folder tucked between my mattress. I still had the story on my computer, but I liked the beat up, marked up copy. I brought it out and handed it over to Pauline.

Pauline took it thoughtfully, examining the unicorn on the cover. "How old is this?"

"Not as old as the folder," I promised. "It's my favorite folder. I kept it from when I first started writing. I put all my favorite things in there. Now it only has my story in it. Julsie knows about it. Actually, I got it published in a dinky online magazine. I think I told you. Julsie wants me to continue writing this story."

Pauline opened it up with delicate fingers and looked it over. "You want me to look over this now?"

"Oh, sorry. I just threw this on you."

Pauline ruffled her shoulders. "Let me grab a drink or something."

"Right." I sat back down as she went to the kitchen and came back with ice water. "Kay. Let me look at this thing." She took off her shoes and settled back into the couch, manuscript in hand.

I curled up on the end watching her read my words, speculating what each facial expression meant. "When did you meet Miah?" she asked, her head still in the words.

"Miah?" The pain of my nightmarish drinking moment came back to me. The cut on my face felt deeper, to the bone.

Pauline looked up from the pile of papers. "That's what this is about, right? This is a love story."

"I knew Miah when I wrote it"

I sighed deeper than I intended. "It's not about Miah. I wrote this story about someone else. Miah came along when I was trying to fill a hole."

Pauline stared at me like she hadn't seen me before. "You kidding me? There's someone else? I've only ever known about Miah."

"Well . . ." I squirmed. "This other guy has a different history and it's not easy to explain. I don't like talking about him."

"Girl, stop. You gotta dish."

I fidgeted nervously with my hands. "That's not what I meant. I gave you the manuscript. Finish it and then we can talk."

Pauline rolled her eyes but went back to reading.

"Sorry, do you have time? I mean, it's not long."

Pauline suddenly sat up, still bugged. "And this will help me understand your wanting to move? And your crazy-ass behavior?"

"Well, no, but it might help you understand me better."

Pauline nodded and sat back eyeing the first page.

I left her alone in the living room, reading. I took the time to finish my laundry. We were lucky to have a laundry unit in our apartment. I cleaned up the kitchen while switching the loads. I peeked in on her a few times, and eagerly watched her eyes roving over the pages. It was hard to not think about what she was reading.

I knew the story well enough. I went and fixed it a bunch of times, but I hadn't touched it in a while. I liked how raw it was from the freshness of when I wrote it. So much had happened between Simon and I after I shared it with him. Our relationship changed in a way. The dreams suddenly flooded me and I felt the pull inside once again, an electric energy that started in my chest and pushed fast throughout my body until I remembered it wasn't real.

I snapped back and the sadness was overwhelming. I couldn't dwell on something not real, non-existent. I blinked a few times, realizing tears had formed in the corners of my eyes and I couldn't think about it. I checked around me, the piles of laundry now folded on the kitchen island. "This is real," I said to no one. "This is my life. Laundry. Get over him already."

I picked up my clothes and headed toward my bedroom to put them away. The sniffling startled me and I stopped. I knew what part she was at.

"You okay—"

Pauline held up a finger telling me "not now."

I backed into my room and put my clothes on the bed. I did a crazy, happy dance knowing I had her. She liked it. I knew it.

I placed my clothes in my drawers and straightened up my closet. In the hamper was my green dress, the one with the shred. I didn't bother washing it—it was ruined, and not to mention dry clean only. I picked it up and placed it against me. Was it really that bad? I checked it out in the mirror and as I did, the scrape on my face highlighted the bruise around my eye. People couldn't see it much with the glasses, but I could.

I knew it was there. I threw the dress in the trash and went to put some make-up under my eye to see if it helped.

A knock came at the door. Pauline stood there, her eyes puffy and red.

I stared at her, unsure of what to say. She had come to me. "Okay?" squeaked out of my mouth.

Pauline came in and sat on my bed, the manuscript still in her hand. "Kay . . ."

I kept staring at her. "Did you like it?"

"Yes. And no, but mostly yes. But still a bit no."

"It was the ending, wasn't it." I was matter of fact. It was tragic.

Pauline glared. "I've read your mush love stuff before, you know, whoever your other characters are in your book, but this . . ." She held it up. "This has heart and passion and longing. It made me sad. I don't know why, honestly. I've dated a bunch, and I don't have this kind of passion with Danny. I don't think he is capable of anything like this. There's no distance, no reason for distance, but it makes me want to miss something or long for something. I don't even know what to say."

I slunk to the floor and leaned against my dresser. "So, you did like it."

"But what happens?" she pressed.

"You've read it. That's the story."

Pauline pushed my shoulder. "But I know you've written an ending in your head."

"Short stories don't need endings."

"Bullshit." She slammed the manuscript on my bed.

I straightened. Was she really upset about this?

"It's a story, Pauline."

Pauline pressed her palms together. "So, tell me. You said you wanted me to read this, and now I know what it is. So tell me what it's about. This is not about Miah, but this someone else."

I nodded.

"Is this someone you knew in your teenage life? Those are the hardest to get over, I think. The first loves."

I nodded. "He was before teenage years even. He was . . . always."

"Oh seriously, Adri. Where is this guy?"

I didn't want to answer the question. I slumped down on the carpet by the bed. "His name is Simon. I guess you can say we grew up together. We, um, haven't kept track of each other. Our relationship is long distant, you could say."

Pauline learned forward. "And you don't where know he is, right?"

I sighed waiting for the words. "I've been searching for someone like Simon my whole life. He's the perfect scale of nerd for me. He inspired me to write, to pursue writing. He always believed in me, and I pushed him away. He also wanted a happy ending to this story."

"So, he's read it?"

"I shared it with him."

"Like through email or something?" Pauline glared. "But he hasn't written you back? Did you try and find him after you and Miah broke up?" She stopped and covered her mouth. "Oh, shut up. Is he dead?"

I chuckled. "Not dead. But, not around. Not available."

"Is he in prison?"

I had to be up front with her. I knew she would think I was crazy. "Pauline, this person I wrote about, does he feel real?"

"More real than your other characters."

"But what I mean is," I didn't know how to clarify it. "Simon is as real as anyone. But, I made him up too. He is an imaginary friend I had when I was little and I grew up with him."

Pauline's shoulders hunched down. "Are you kidding me? You made him up?"

"I started dreaming about Simon when I was eight. And I continued to dream about him until, well, now."

"And Simon also aged, like you, 'cause that would be so creepy if I just read a story about an eleven-year-old."

"Yes. He did. And he felt real, and I shared things, special experiences with him." I reflected on what Simon was to me. "Simon was . . . is . . . was my best friend. I couldn't wait to go to sleep so I could dream about him. He taught me things. He was my first kiss, in a way. He prepared me for my first kiss, I should say. Simon is my dream guy. He is everything. I know his heart and I know his mind. I want him to be real." My emotions came up. I rested my arms on my knees and wiped my eyes. "He feels so real."

Pauline was quiet. I don't think she knew what to think.

"I know this sounds crazy," I said. "I dreamed him up." I crawled over to a drawer and pulled out a sketch pad. "Look. I drew him." I flipped to a page with a juvenile drawing of me and him holding hands.

Pauline took the notebook and flipped through the pages to other drawings. My artistic styling got better as I aged, but

I kept drawing when I could. "Is this accurate?" She held up the last one I did. Simon's eyes were centered and sparkling.

I nodded. "It's the best I could do."

"Not bad. Definitely got that nerdy vibe down."

"I guess I have a great imagination." I glanced at the different pictures as she turned the pages. They were memories. "Funny though, for a while, I could have sworn he was a real person I could share my life with. When I learned about the brain in my psychology class, I made the separation that this wasn't real. My own wanting created a perfect image of what I needed. Maybe my own need for a brother or for approval from my parents or whatever adolescent need people create for themselves. It's what Simon became to me. A perfect illusion."

"What was this one about?" Pauline held up a sketch with Simon over a grave.

"When his mother died."

"You created a guy in your head, and his mom died when he was a teen?" Pauline's mouth opened wide in shock.

"I know, right?"

"What about this one?"

It was a sketch I had started and scribbled over.

"That's when I broke his heart." I took it and examined it closer. "We both understood this was only dreaming. We had imagined it both. My imagination even wanted to test if it was real. He asked me to call him or something. We argued. I woke shortly after that, so I didn't get to set it right. Next time I saw him, we didn't mention it. He was different, colder to me. Like he knew too it wasn't real."

"The way you talk about it doesn't make it sound like it's imaginary."

"Tell that to my therapist."

"I just . . . can't believe this."

"That your roommate is crazy?"

"You dreaming of the same guy for years is pretty insane, you know."

"Sure, I get that. But it's also painful. It's something I can't get away from."

Pauline handed the sketchbook back to me. "Do you still dream of him?"

"I have." I rested on my elbows lost for a moment remembering the last time he appeared. "Not like I used to. He never tried to contact me, I mean, in the waking world, not the dream world. I think my brain finally accepted he wasn't real."

"It's your subconscious." Pauline rolled her eyes. "Maybe he has an email address."

I laughed as I shoved my sketchbook back in my drawer. "Yeah, next time I see him I'll ask for an email."

We both laughed for a second until Pauline glanced at me. "When you wrote this story, it was how you imagined your relationship with this Simon. He is in one time and you are in another. And that's why you didn't end it, because you left hope at the end."

I brushed my hand through the carpet. "I wanted it to be real. I still want it to be real. I don't know if I can write an ending because no relationship has made me feel as complete. I need to find something like this."

"Maybe you should go up to Julsie's and talk to her about this instead of taking off to California."

I considered it. "Maybe."

"I think it needs a happy ending."

"I don't know if I can write one." I grabbed the unicorn folder. "I'll see what I can do."

Pauline's phone buzzed. "Oh, yeah. Wanna go out with Danny and me? We're heading to poetry slash comedy night at the Whinery."

"Not really."

"But will you?" She shook my shoulders. "Come on. The Whinery is dark, no one will recognize you or see that black eye. No one will know you."

My shoulders sunk. "Why do you think I need to get out? I'm okay with staying here. I have books."

Pauline glared. "Best thing for you to do is shrug it off and keep moving."

She was hard for me to turn down. I hated her superpower. "Fine. I'll ask Brody if he wants to go. He loves poetry."

"Perfect." She stood up and slugged my arm. "Thanks for not moving away."

I smirked. "Can I at least take a shower?"

Ten

"Did you see that one?" Simon asks.

Adri rests on Simon's chest as she stares up at the night sky watching the meteor shower. "Yes."

"Did you make a wish?"

Adri sighs. "Always." She feels Simon's chest rise and fall. "Your breathing feels real."

"Well, that's a silly statement." Simon brushes his fingers through Adri's hair. "I breathe just like you do—in and out every day."

Adri rolls over on her elbows, watching his breathing. "I guess it's silly. It feels so real. You know, I often think I'll run into you on the bus or train. I find you everywhere."

Simon props himself up. "Funny. Me too."

"I don't know how it's possible. You being here with me, in an incredibly romantic moment. It's like you were created to fulfill my dream fantasies in my subconscious. My brain doesn't even need to work hard."

Simon laughs. "Well, honestly, it's partly true, I guess. I mean, you definitely fulfill mine."

Adri's mouth gapes. "Daydreaming of me?"

"Always." Simon sits up straight. "I keep searching for you. I know you're real. You have to be real. I couldn't dream you up. As creative as I pretend to be, I couldn't in a million years make anyone that checked every box."

"Every box?" Adri gasps. "I don't check all the boxes. You only know dream me, not the real me."

Simon sputters. "I have only ever been me here," he argues. "I'm more me in these shared dreams than I am anywhere else."

Adri's face reddens. "You're the one who isn't real. I'm as living and breathing as what your chest was doing."

Simon grabs Adri's hand and squeezes. "Tell me. Do you feel that?"

Adri does not flinch. "Of course."

"See." Simon exhales. "It's real. Believe me. I'm real."

Adri pulls her hand away. "But it's a game, Simon. And my heart suffers every time you pull me closer. Every time. And I don't know what to think or do. I'm lost."

Simon looks around at the beautiful night. "This is us. This is what we have. I asked you to come here, and you came. I needed to see you. I wanted to share this space with you. And look," he points to the shooting stars, "the Perseids. Now you can see them like I did. Look it up. It's a real thing."

"I know it's a real thing, but what if it's just my subconscious wishing or filling in the gaps?"

Simon shakes his head. "We're both here, right now. I'll take every moment I get with you."

Adri feels a strange tug in her chest unravelling the truth in her. "I . . . I can't do this, Simon." She starts hitting her head with her palm.

Simon pulls at her arms. "What are you doing?"

Adri's breath hitches. "Trying . . . to wake up."

Simon panics. "No. Why? Stay with me."

Adri bangs with her palms with every syllable. "You aren't real."

Simon tries to pull her in. "Yes, I am."

Adri resists, tears welling in her eyes. "I spend my waking hours waiting to go to sleep so I can see you. I daydream of you. I draw your face over and over. I search for your face everywhere."

Simon finally pulls her arms down. "I can't help it if I want to spend every moment I can with the woman I'm in love with."

Adri pushes back. "You can't love. You aren't real."

"Stop saying that. I am."

Adri's hands came up to her face. "Why do I torture myself?"

"Meet me," Simon states flatly. "Let's meet. I'll call you. Tell me where you are."

Adri still hits her head. "Not real. Not real." Tears wet her eyes.

"Adri, please, trust me. I love you. Stop doing this. Stay with me."

Adri stops hitting herself and stares at him. "You what?

"Lo-o-ove you." Simon sang the word. "I'm so in love with you it drives me crazy."

Adri's tears fall down her face. "This isn't love, Simon, it's something else."

Simon stares back. "I'm crazy in love with you. I want to see you in the daylight. I want you to meet my family. I want to date you like a normal person."

Adri's breath staggers. "But it's not possible. I made you up."

"No." He grabs her hand and presses it to his chest. "Feel this. It's a heartbeat, my heartbeat. It beats faster when you touch me or talk to me or even when I think of you in daylight, which happens much more often than I should admit." He caresses her fingers. "Meet me," he whispers.

"No."

"Yes."

A dark roll of thunder sounds somewhere in the distance. A strange wind sweeps through the trees.

Adri pulls away and stands. "Morning is coming, I know it."

Simon feels the wind. "I'm real, Adrianna. My name is Simon Moon, I live in Fort Collins, Colo—"

"Morning. No. It's coming." Adri yells over the wind. She suddenly feels scared. "Don't leave. No. I don't want to be alone."

Simon rushes to her. The clouds quickly cover overhead, the thunder grows louder. He takes her face in both of his hands and kisses her deeply, pushing away the doubt.

Adri tries to pull away, but melts into him, feeling the weight of it, the overwhelming urge of wanting.

Lips brush and part.

Adri wraps her arms around his neck and drinks him in. "Be real. Be real."

Simon pulls her close, his gentle fingers skimming her cheeks.

Their hearts syncopate as they press against each other. Each wild with the excitement of the moment.

Thunder rolls overhead.

Simon reaches for her with more passion, but his fingers pass through air. He opens his eyes.

He stands in the darkness alone.

Chicago, IL

The Whinery was mostly a comedy or poetry club, with a few random stage plays performed here and there. I hadn't been here since Miah and I broke up, but as a couple, we came to this place quite a lot, knowing my lame love of dinky poetry. I flashed my ID, paid my entrance fee, and passed through a black curtain revealing a flight of stages. The room was cozy, filled with different eclectic seating. Brody said he would meet us here. I couldn't see him in the dim light—of course, I entered wearing dark glasses, like I was a celebrity. I was incognito. Danny and Pauline went to grab a drink. I asked for a water and sat at a table on the left side near the back. Gentle conversations happened around me. It was nothing much to hear, but I liked feeling like I was in the conversations even when I wasn't.

"Here you go." Danny handed me the water in a crisp, glass bottle.

"Ooh, so fancy," I said, rather capriciously. "Match my mega-star sunglasses and kerchief."

He laughed. I don't think Danny knew how to react to me, so he laughed uncomfortably most of the time.

"Are you gonna wear the glasses all night?" Pauline asked as she slid in next to me.

"Nah, I'll ditch them in a minute, once it gets a little fuller in here."

Brody stood near the stairs. I waved him over.

"Well, hello movie star." We faked kissing each cheek. I loved when he played things up with me. He shrugged off his jacket and placed it on the back of the chair. "I'm heading to the bar. Do you think they have food here?"

"Oh, if they do, I want some fries."

"On it, your highness," he teased and was gone.

"I think I'll head to the restroom before it starts." I got up. "I better leave these here or I may kill myself getting there." I handed Pauline the sunglasses and kerchief before I headed to the back of the room.

The bathroom was rundown and graffitied, but in a charming kind of way. I liked the little doodles and inappropriate words. I picked the last stall and locked myself in. I pulled my phone out of my pocket so it wouldn't fall into the toilet.

The door of the bathroom opened to the crowd noise and instant chatter as women came in continuing their conversation. I felt like I was accidentally eavesdropping.

". . . he didn't admit it. But I know he did it."

"Did he text you?"

"I muted it. I have no idea."

Okay, this wasn't the juiciest of conversations, listening to an alleged unfaithful boyfriend trying to reach his girlfriend. I quietly tried to finish up, zipping my pants as soundlessly as possible while still pretending to be invisible. The conversation grew personal rather quickly and I heard a few muffled sniffles through the stall door.

The two girls didn't know I was there, obviously. I felt awkward. I've been in here too long, I couldn't just leave. I took a seat, leaned over, and grabbed my phone. Maybe if I texted someone to come in, these two would leave and I wouldn't feel so stupid. I felt trapped. I had been in here for five minutes. Someone might start to worry or think I'm totally constipated. I didn't want that. I sent a quick message to Pauline telling her I was trapped in the stall. There was no response.

Didn't anyone need to use the restroom?

"She's such a bitch. I have always hated her. Thank God my face doesn't show up on that movie."

"Don't worry. She's getting it now. The vid is everywhere."

I froze, like completely froze in every place. I wasn't even breathing. Were they talking about me? I began to sweat everywhere, even my palms itched. I should have figured Miah and Lydia would come to this place. I hadn't considered the matter when Pauline invited me. I wanted to curl up very, very small and flush myself down the toilet.

"Where is he tonight?"

"Don't even care. I stayed at Steph's. I don't think he's over her. He says he is, but whatever. Who would do that? We've been married three whole months. Plus, she's ugly. She hardly wears any make up."

Well, that wasn't very nice. As if makeup was what makes a person beautiful. I leaned my head on the side of the painted cement wall. There was a silly drawing in sharpie of some anime and it stole my attention for a moment.

My phone buzzed. I fumbled.

The chatter stopped.

"Is someone in here?"

I went to silence it and quickly tucked my feet up creeping up on the toilet. It buzzed again.

"What freak would listen in on our conversation?"

I sighed deeply trying to think of a way out of this. "No Engles," I tried to say in my smallest voice.

The door opened. "Adri?" It was Pauline.

The women stopped. "Oh my gawd . . ." Lydia drawled the words out of her mouth.

"Holy, holy, holy crap," I said to myself.

"Lydia, right?" I heard Pauline ask. "Miah's wife?"

"What are you doing here?" Lydia shot her nastiness toward Pauline. "So, Adri is in this bathroom right now?"

"I thought she came in here," Pauline returned. "I must be mistaken." I could hear Pauline making up her words to try and help the situation, maybe even get the two girls out altogether.

"The husband-stealing bitch is here? Tonight?"

"We are here to watch Lincoln's stand-up."

A scoff. "Of course, I should have figured you guys would come."

"Whoa. Watch it. No need to be hostile." Pauline was the most upfront and rational person I knew. Patience was not something she carried. If she gets pushed, she will push back harder. "Adri did something wrong, but she apologized, and believe me, she is sorry."

"That's right she is."

There was a pause. I knew Pauline was ready to explode. "You're lucky your ass isn't as prominent in the video, because you'd be getting the same treatment right now."

"She deserves it."

"Now, you stop." I could hear Pauline's lioness come out. "I think you should leave before another fighting video comes out. Is Miah here?"

"I came without him."

I felt a little better knowing Miah wasn't here, but that didn't mean I wanted to see or talk to Lydia. I lost my footing on the toilet and slipped. My foot went in the toilet with a terrible splash, and my phone tumbled out of my hands and into the bowl.

"Shoot!" I forgot about everything happening around me and dug into the scummy bar toilet to grab the only thread I had to the outside world. I pinched it with two fingers and opened the stall door.

Lydia and a tall, dark-haired girl stood behind her, both with disgusted looks on their faces. Pauline stood by the door and immediately came over.

"You listened to everything we said, you eavesdropping whore."

"Like I had a choice." I put the phone on the counter and immediately grabbed paper towels to dry it. "Trust me, this is the last thing I wanted to happen."

It's not in my nature to be rude to people. I expected her to be upset. I didn't want to fight her Friday night. I had only been in one other fight in my entire life and it was with my sister. So, even in this instance, I gave Lydia the right to hate me, to be angry. It was a drunk kiss, but still a kiss, with rational thought behind it. I had wanted to do it, and that was the worst feeling, knowing I wanted to.

I glanced over at Lydia's face. She also had a bruise under her eye. There was some satisfaction knowing I gave it to her. I looked at myself quickly in the mirror. I didn't look too bad, but the ring scrape burned deeper seeing the girl who gave it to me.

"This is entirely too soon to see you," I muttered from the corner of my mouth.

"Stay away from my husband."

"Done," I said, grabbing more tissue and dabbing at the screen.

"Do you think they have rice here?" Pauline asked, ignoring the other girls.

"Doubt it."

"There is a Chinese market down the street," Lydia's friend offered. Lydia glared at her. "What?"

Lydia came close. "Miah left you a long time ago. You had no right going after him. He is my husband." She flashed her left hand.

The gesture stung and I started losing my thoughts. "I know, I know." I twisted toward her, all the words boiling up. "Sure. I did it. You attacked me Friday night without even asking me anything."

"What were you going to say? 'I'm sorry?'"

"Well, yeah," I squeaked out. "But there is more than that."

"Oh, please. Enlighten me." Lydia crossed her arms waiting.

I went to say something but stumbled in my thoughts. My thoughts had always been slow to process the right things to say in the moment. It would mull over it for an hour or so and then spit out something brilliant that I should have said. I brew out a breath, still thinking.

Lydia threw her hands up. "Thought so."

"I'm going to ask if they have rice." Pauline placed her hand on my shoulder.

"No, don't leave me," I whispered.

"Come with me then." Pauline shuffled me out the door, my wet phone cupped in her hand. She turned back, anger rumbling in her low tones. "And you better not ever think about touching my friend again. So help me. I will mess that pretty little face so hard, you won't be seeing straight for a week."

Once we were out, I covered my mouth with my hand and gasped. "I can't believe . . ." I mumbled through my fingers, hyperventilating.

Pauline marched me back to the table.

"They didn't have any fries—what happened?" Brody knew something was wrong.

"She dropped her phone in the toilet."

"Uck." Brody recoiled.

"I didn't wash my hands," I said to Pauline, nearly crying.

"Here." She rummaged in her bag, pulled out some hand sanitizer, and dropped a small amount on my hands. I was still in shock and barely rubbed my hands. The alcohol stung the scrapes I received from the bush I fell into.

"What happened?" Danny could see things were not right. Lydia appeared in my peripheral. "Do we need to leave?"

"Maybe." Pauline said, tossing the sanitizer back in her bag. "We're running to get some rice."

"Uh, okay," Danny said. "I can take you home."

"No," I said, grabbing my sunglasses. "I don't want to ruin your night. We'll be back."

Pauline swung her arm around me and shooed me away.

The Asian market was a block south and they had a perfect, plain old bag of rice, which I purchased for two bucks, and quickly slipped my phone inside. The cute lady who helped us laughed at what I was doing.

"I can't believe it, Pauline," I said on the way back.

Pauline kept a fast pace. "I should have thought about them coming after Lincoln invited us."

My mind went to the Lincoln guy I met at the party. I didn't remember much, but I remembered a little before I drank. He seemed nice enough. "So, is he a poet?"

"No. He's a comedian."

"Oh." My opinion changed slightly after knowing he was a comedian. I had unfairly associated his name with politics. "How do you guys know him?"

"He's Danny's friend. I think they know each other from Loyola."

I wrapped my sweater around me, holding the bag of rice in my hand as I walked. I kept thinking about this guy Lincoln. "Was he the one who shot the video?"

Pauline stopped. Her hand shot out in front of me. "What if he did?"

My stomach turned over. "Do I talk to him about it?"

"You could ask him."

"Should I though?" I suddenly got light-headed.

"Does it matter?" Pauline threw up her hands. "If he did or if he didn't, what would you do about it anyway?"

I was shocked by the irritation in her voice. "Are you mad?"

Pauline slowly shook her head. "No, well, not at you. I really don't like Lydia. The old me wants to kick her ass. She deserves it. But girl, when are you gonna stand up for yourself? You don't need to keep apologizing. Stop beating yourself up." Pauline exhaled, exasperated. She tugged me forward. "Come on. You'll be fine."

I begrudgingly stumbled with her pull. I could feel her frustration.

When we entered, some comedian was on stage, but I didn't know who it was. We quickly made it back to our seats. I inspected the crowd for Lydia and her friend. I didn't see anyone I recognized.

Brody still had a few chips, but I still felt the need to sterilize my hands. The comic wasn't funny, though maybe I wasn't in the mood to laugh.

I viewed my sorry, stupid phone. Maybe I should take out the battery. I hadn't yet, but I didn't have a key to open up the back. I completely lost track of what was happening on stage.

A few claps and laughs later, someone called Lincoln's name and I looked up.

It was the dark-haired man I talked with the other day. He started his comedy routine and he was slightly amusing, talking about his mundane, corporate job.

"So, Friday night I had an experience. Have you seen the video of the girl falling over the railing?"

Several people started laughing and talking, like this was something the world had in common. My stomach roiled with an anxious unknown about to be spewed from the mouth of this comedian.

"Right? I was there. It was better live."

"Nope," I said to Brody. "I'm not staying." I grabbed my bag of rice and started crossing the floor. Pauline grabbed my arm but I yanked it away trying to get out as fast as I could.

"Is that her?" someone said in the crowd.

Ah crap, my sunglasses. I had left them on the table.

"The fight happened in Chicago?"

"I haven't seen it."

"I think that is her."

I quickly scanned. Was Lydia still here too? Would she publicly beat me up again? I hunched over, not caring if anyone was coming behind me, and left as fast as I could.

The fresh air felt wonderful. The tears streamed and I ran to the train with the bag of rice clasped tight in my hands.

Denver, CO

I left Portland at six in the morning. I couldn't sleep. I couldn't eat. My stomach knotted itself tight. Nate dropped me off and, strangely, gave me a hug—well, a guy hug, like he would never see me again. My co-worker Adam wasn't as cool with me leaving as I thought he would be, but I promised to do as much work as I could when I got back. I wouldn't be gone forever, only a few days. He still needed help cleaning up the technical debt, so I did what I could while waiting at the airport.

I got to see the sun rise from my seat window. It was a new, different sun. It still did its job and warmed up the world, but it felt different. This gutsy impulse to chase a dream invigorated each cell in my body. There was a tangible freshness. I wanted to study this sun and feel it on my skin. I rubbed the shell still hanging around my neck to ground me from freaking out. I got an idea and pulled out my dream notebook from my backpack under the seat. I took my pen and drew a sun with heat rising and different clouds around the cover. My artistic skills were rather weak, but I knew what it was supposed to be. It was a beginning, and if anything, the effort of trying.

I landed in Denver around nine and headed toward my connection. I knew the Denver airport well enough it felt like coming home. I rode the train to the middle terminal, and when I got out, I saw my sister waiting at the gate.

Liane had the smart, black curls and quizzical Asian eyes my mother had, but she got the disapproving scowl and strong will from my dad. The rest didn't come from anyone, it was all her. I watched her talking to her phone, making cute faces obviously to her daughter, or at least I hoped it was her daughter. She hadn't seen me yet, and I wasn't sure I wanted her to. I liked watching her from a far—the quiet before the storm.

A coffee cart wasn't far, so I went and bought us each one, her mocha extra sweet and my boring regular with two creams. When I returned, she was off the phone and had her head pressed against the back of a black airport bench. I still couldn't believe she was here, coming with me on this ridiculous mission.

"Hey," I snuck up.

Immediately my sister wrapped her arms around me, squeezing so hard it shook the perishable coffee still in my hands.

"Hi there." I tried to hug back but the coffees prevented it.

Liane finally let go. "Hey!" She squealed. "Did you get me coffee?"

"It was a rough morning for me."

She laughed. "I bet."

I handed it over and she sipped it carefully. "Oh, this is so good," she said, making a yummy sound in the back of her throat. "Coffee tastes better when you didn't buy it."

We sat back down on the bench. Liane sat sideways on her seat like a little girl. "So? Are you out-of-your-mind excited?" She shook my knee.

"I guess not as excited as you."

Liane brightened. "I mean, come on, when was the last time we road tripped together?"

"Driving me to Portland, I think." I took a deep gulp of the earthy, warm liquid.

"That was before Lily was born. Before she was even thought of." She giggled. "Well, maybe thought of, but not really planned."

Those brief moments with her in the car driving with me through Oregon flashed in my mind. We talked non-stop. A reminiscent feeling passed over me, how I had missed the joy of experiencing something together. I perked up. "This is different though. We only have today and tomorrow. It's not much time. And I'll need to remote in to work while traveling around."

Disgust crossed Liane's face. "Forget it. No. I'm sure your work will be fine. You're with me, and I doubt I'm going to let you work." Liane was relentless.

A tremor hit me from head to toe. The fear of everything. "I can't believe I'm doing this."

"I know, right?" She shook my knee again in excitement before sipping her drink. "You did a really good job. This is way chocolatey. I love it."

"Well, I know you."

She raised her eyebrows together like a cartoon character. I busted laughing. "I knew you missed me."

I resisted the desire to place her in a headlock and rub her head like I used to when we were little. "Yeah, you're right."

The plane announced our departure. Both Liane and I didn't have assigned seats, with the late purchase of our tickets, and I hoped we would still be able to sit together. Luckily, we made it to the back of the plane where a back row was available. Liane filled me in with everything happening in her household, Lily's antics, Ian's never-ending school projects, and her preschool job. Not until we were in the air did Liane ask about Adri.

"So, what are we doing here? We're flying to Chicago—and then what?"

"Find my dream girl."

"Which I can't wrap my head around." Her head rested back in a cute way, looking at me with strange admiration. "Tell me about her."

I wasn't prepared for the question. "Well . . ." I started to think, and daydream, and I grew dizzy at the idea of her. "Too many things."

"What's her name?"

"Adri. Adrianna, but likes the nickname."

"Adri what?"

I rested my head back. "I don't know. I don't remember."

"But what do you know about her? In all the conversations you've had over the years you—"

I shushed her and reached deep into my backpack. I pulled out the banged up old notebook and handed it to her. "These are all the notes I have."

Liane's eyebrow raised. "I remember this notebook. I stole it once and colored in it, and you were so mad a me."

"I still am," I mocked. "I kept the page. Look." I flipped toward the back were Liane's little hands drew a house and a swing set, snowcapped mountains in the background.

"Aw, you kept it?"

"Well, when I got there in the writing, I was old enough to appreciate it." I smiled. "I'm sure Lily will do the same to your special things."

She laughed. "No kidding." Liane thumbed through the pages thoughtfully, reading my immature handwriting and hurried dream script. "Is this day one?" she asked.

"No. There is no day one. I didn't start writing it down until it kept happening." I pulled her fingers back to the first day I began the journal. "Here you go, but you don't need to read the whole thing. It gets *really* personal toward the end." I emphasized the word really while I stretched my arms forward. "If fact, don't read the back entries. Stop around your drawing."

Her shoulders shrugged. It was a tease. I knew her well enough she would respect my wishes. I rolled up my jacket and placed it under my head, thinking I could get some sleep.

I slightly drifted, not enough for deep sleep, not enough to see the meadow or talk with Adri. The plane dropped with turbulence and I opened my eyes. Liane kept reading like nothing had happened. I skimmed the page she was on. And then I heard a small sniffle.

"Lee?" I asked, but I knew why she was crying.

"She knows about Mom."

I forgot about the hard stuff I had written in there. "Yes, she does."

"How much?"

"Well, everything. She was there for all of it. I would subconsciously ask to see her when I needed her. And she would come, not every time, but a lot."

"And that changed?"

"Yeah. Kind of." I straightened to face her better. "When Mom died, I slept a lot. I sloshed through life. I needed Adri much during that time. I know I went through a big depression. Me disappearing all the time was me sleeping it off. I moved out shortly after 'cause I thought that might help. I went and stayed with Grandma, remember?"

Liane dabbed her eyes without smudging her mascara. "I was fifteen, you know. You could have stayed for me."

"I probably should have." I rested back my head. "Adri and I's dependency on each other had grown strong, it was hard to want to do anything but dream. Dreaming became better than reality. Then the doubt came."

"The doubt?"

"Before the doubt, everything was possible. I mean, we both couldn't believe each other existed. I suggested we meet. I confessed I was in love with her. She freaked out, of course, and then I knew," I paused gathering myself, "I knew I had made it up and I shouldn't try and meet her again. Things changed."

"How?"

"They just did. We moved on and I never talked to her the same. Our first kiss was in that dream."

Liane's mouth dropped. "You kissed her in the dreamworld?"

I smirked. "Yeah, of course. That's what you do in dreams."

"Ha. I guess I never thought of this. Nothing further?" She started rifling through the pages with feverish intent. "Is that why you don't want me to read the last pages?"

"Ugh, stop." I pulled at my notebook. "It wasn't like that. It was all fantasy, and promise; the want was there, but it never went *there*. If that makes sense."

Liane started laughing at how embarrassed I became.

"Will you get serious? Here." I found a specific page and handed it over. "Here is the dream I was talking about."

She eyed it. "But it hardly says anything."

I read my writing. "I know she's real. Why won't she believe I'm real too?"

Liane ran her finger along the edge and read, "the storm is coming." What does that mean?"

"She said those words before she disappeared."

"She woke up?"

"And she disappeared out of my arms." I felt the crush in my chest as if it had just happened.

Liane slapped my knee. "Yeah, but the sun is coming out. See?" She pointed, and in the fair distance I could see a tall city near an enormous lake.

My heart flipped. A surreal, understatedly beautiful moment crept on me as I looked on Chicago for the first time. The plane understood my need for peace as it quieted for one, still second in time. "I can't believe we are here."

Liane snuggled my arm. "Me either, big brother."

Eleven

"There you are." Simon yells over the crowd.

Adri stands behind a counter in a dark, crowded room. She continues wiping the bar. "And there you are."

"Where have you been?" Simon strides forward and takes a seat across from her.

"Working. Can't you tell?" Adri leans toward him. "I've been waitressing and bartending. It keeps me up at night. Looks like I'm dreaming of it too."

"Yeah." Simon looks around. "Hey, I'm sorry. Classes get me up early."

"Makes it hard to see each other, doesn't it?" Adri smooths out the cloth. "I'm glad you found me. I applied for a new job, day hours. I think I might like it. Less money, but I can't take the nights."

"Cool."

"Yeah."

"So . . ." Simon smiles.

"So . . ." Adri stares confused.
"Do I get a free drink?"
"Psh." Adri laughs. "Not you. Uh uh."

Adri starts to walk away but Simon grabs her hand. "I've missed you."

Adri squeezes it back. "I know. Sorry I've been away. Sleep is unpredictable. I'm currently knocked out with a cold. On some Nyquil or something. Trying to sleep it off."

Simon gets up and hurries around the bar to her. "Sorry to hear you're sick." He looks at her. "You don't look sick."

"Trust me. I look like death."

"Nope, I don't see it." Simon brushes a strand away from her
face and places it behind her ear.

"Simon," she starts. "Simon, there's someone—"

"Oh." Simon stops mid-gesture and crosses his arms. "Oh,
okay."

"I think you'd like him. He reminds me of you."

"Oh?"

"Yeah, he's charming and funny. His name's Miah."

"Miah? For a guy?"

"Well, it's short for Jeremiah, but he goes by Miah."

"I guess." Simon shuffles his feet. "And you met him—"

"In class, I mean, he's in my major."

Simon stumbles back past the bar. "That's great. I mean,
yeah. So, so great."

Adri eyes him. "What's wrong?"

"Nothing's wrong."

Adri comes forward. "Stop it. You know I can tell when you
lie."

Simon huffs a laugh. "You know I wouldn't lie to you."

"Stop telling me it's great when clearly it's not."

Simon's shrugs. "Yeah, well, it's not great, it actually sucks
quite a bit." He stops to gather his thoughts. "I've been
waiting to find you, to see you again, and I finally get to dream
about you, and here you are with someone else."

Adri puts down the rag and comes to stand right before him.
"I'm trying to be responsible and be a stupid adult." She gestures
to the dream around her. "I'm working this lame job that is killing
me and infiltrating my sleep." Adri places her hand on his chest.

"All I want to do is take Nyquil and dream of you all day. But I can't see you during the daylight and I hate it. So, I'm trying my best to find someone as close to you as possible. Miah is the closest I've found so far."

"I should, I should do that too." Simon fumbles toward the door and away from her touch. "Though, I don't think I ever will."

Adri rushes in a hug.

Simon takes it but then pushes away, walking away from her. "I . . . I can't," he says and disappears.

Monday morning, I opened the shop, relieved to get back to normal life and normal work. Annette greeted me as she walked into the back of the store. Her wild, white hair stood up in spikes which complimented her tiger-striped scarf and huge hoop earrings. Annette always dressed for an after-dinner party, even at nine in the morning.

"I hear you had a hard weekend." It was a playful comment, but it still irritated me. "Wanna talk about it?"

"Nah. Everything's fine." I waved it off as I grabbed the till and went back up front, placing it in the old register before logging on to the store computer.

Annette sauntered back to where I was, her coffee in her hand as the soft clips of her boots made a sophisticated clack around the empty store. She stopped about ten feet from the counter and stared at me. "Brody said you might move to California."

I blinked. "Where did he hear that?"

Her fabulous hand flipped in the air. "Oh, darling, I don't know. But is it true?"

I sighed. "Nothing has been decided. Annette, I promise, I'll do the right thing if I need to leave this place. I would give you notice."

"Good." She sipped her coffee. "I don't want to lose a peach like you. But if you need to take time away, let me know."

I stood up straight and contemplated what she meant. "You serious about that?"

"Of course." Annette came closer and placed her coffee on the counter. "You have been here a few years and I never expected you to stay. You are one of my best employees. We've grown like family."

"I like this place. It suits me. I don't know if I have what it takes to be a writer."

Annette scoffed. "You've been too focused on this store and helping me out. When I had my surgery, you took over because I couldn't trust anyone else." She looked at me with her heavily mascaraed eyes. "You are very special. Don't ever doubt."

Annette glanced at the pile of books yet to be put away.

"I like running a bookstore, you know. I feel it's my failed attempt at being a writer. But I chose this instead." She tapped her nails on a copy of Fahrenheit 451. "What do you want to do?"

"I . . ." Did I know this answer? I felt like my world was collapsing. "I honestly don't know."

"You are still young."

"Yes, but I'm old enough to have a career and should be starting my life. My college friends are now having kids. I should be in that stage of life."

Annette threw up her hands. "Oh heavens. You want to have kids?"

"Well, that's not what I'm talking about. I'm nowhere near ready for that, it's just at least they have a grip on life."

She shook her head at me and returned to her point. "Listen. If you need to take some time and figure it out, you can. I'd miss you, but you can."

"Really?"

"Yes. I owe it to you."

"Okay." I nodded, though I was still deciding. "Maybe a few weeks in California might do me good."

Annette lifted her coffee. "That's the spirit."

"I can't believe you want me to go."

Annette placed her hand on my shoulder. "I don't want you to go, but I want what's best for you. Take some time and figure it out. I did. After Douglas died, I toured the world trying to figure out what I wanted and needed, and this is where I ended my journey. It's okay to take time and figure it out."

"Thank you."

Annette turned the Closed sign over to Open and unlocked the door.

The first few hours were nothing special. A mother and her two daughters recognized me and one of the girls asked to take a photo.

"Okay?" I agreed, but it came out as a question. She was ready to shoot a selfie but I stopped and checked my surroundings. "Okay. I don't want the store name in the picture."

The girl smiled and we grouped together, and I did a cute peace sign hoping this picture wouldn't go viral as well.

The new girl, Samantha, came in. She was a sweet, bookish kind of girl I liked very much. Seeing her meant I could go to lunch.

"Do you want anything?" I asked her and Annette before I left.

"Where are you heading?" Samantha asked. "There is this new cupcake place—"

I pointed at her. "Ooh. I know which one you're talking about. Bake My Day, right?"

Samantha clasped her hands in excitement. "Yeah. They have a lemon custard cupcake I am dying for. I've been craving it all weekend."

I laughed at her simple charm. "Yeah, I can do that. You want one too, Netty?"

Annette shook her head and waved me away.

I grabbed the paperback copy of Jane Eyre that I'd been reading off and on during downtime before I left. My phone was still drying in a bag of rice, and I had no connect with the digital world. It felt nice to be unplugged. I casually walked with my nose in a book, like I had before the smartphone. The day was overcast but not windy, which I liked. Chicago wind was a character all its own, and me being rather slight meant I had been swept up in its grasp more than once. The little shopping area where I worked was in Andersonville and not right off the lake; the wind traveled here but wouldn't blow me over, usually.

Sweet Julip Café sat on a quiet corner, and I grabbed a warm bowl and found a peaceful table to myself. I liked people watching and I tended to sit where I had a nice view of the street as well as the door. A few people came and went as I sipped my tomato basil. I skipped ahead in the book to the juicier parts when Jane first meets Rochester.

"Funny, I just read that."

I looked up. A woman near my age, sporting adorable puffy pigtails on each side of her head pointed to the book. She wasn't really talking to me, more to herself, but I smiled back.

"It's a classic, always good to reread"

"Exactly," the girl walked over. "I read it in high school but hated it because we were forced to read it. But I just reread it and loved it. Maybe I'm in a better stage in life to appreciate it."

"Yes, exactly." I agreed.

The woman inched forward. "Hey, do you live around here?"

I set the book down next to me. "Well, this isn't my neighborhood, but I know it pretty well. I work down the street at Moonstone Books."

"I'm trying to find Catalpa."

"It's not far," I said, remembering oh too well where my panty-flash-to-the-world happened. "It's about five blocks north and all the way east there."

"Cool. Thanks. My brother and I ditched the Uber and thought we'd get some lunch."

I looked at my watch. "Yeah, speaking of that, I better head back." I spooned up the last of the soup. "Hope you find what you're looking for."

"Thanks. Me too." She waved briefly and walked back to the counter.

The little bell rang as I exited thinking about lemony frosting. I didn't realize I was skipping to the cupcake shop.

We touched ground.

"Let's get some lunch." Liane was practically dragging me down the terminal. It was getting close to lunch time, but I didn't have any idea where we were.

"You mean at the airport?"

"You get grumpy when you haven't eaten. I want you to think straight."

"Yeah, but I don't want to eat here. I can't eat yet."

"Fine," Liane pouted. "But I'm buying a Snickers." She left and returned a few minutes later with a healthy chunk missing from the unwrapped candy bar. "Here. Have a bite."

I bit into the goodness and it tasted delicious. "Should we take a train or Uber?"

Liane check the time. "What if we Uber there and then took the train? I booked us a night in an Air BNB somewhere near the address?" She turned it into a question, looking on her phone to check the reservation.

I walked slowly to a large window revealing the vastness of Illinois, a state I had never been to. It felt way too big. Chicago was a mythical place I only knew in movies, and here I stood as if I were in one. Somewhere here was a girl, one simple girl, someone I ached for. My feet felt like lead, weighed down by the impossible task of finding this someone. We only had two days, actually a day and a half, and everything slipped from being probable to impossible.

"How are we going to do this?" I said to myself, but Liane put her hand on my shoulder.

"By trying. Come on."

I was immeasurably glad my sister was here. I couldn't do any of this if she hadn't jumped at the chance to go. Even when Jessica found me the SkyMiles, I still wouldn't have done anything so crazy if Liane hadn't insisted on coming.

Liane went to an app on her phone and hailed an Uber. "Seven minutes," she stated, indicating the wait time.

"What address did you put in?"

"The house we found."

My stomach lurched. "You mean, we are going right there?"

"Of course. That's why we're here. If we find this Adri early enough, we might get a chance to see the city too."

"Holy shit." Reality slapped me back.

"You're going to be fine. Let's go sit outside."

We walked through the sliding doors and into the crisp Chicago air. The clouds rolled along without a break. I couldn't tell which direction we were facing. Growing up in Colorado, I had always known my directions. We had mountains and they were always on the west. Even when I went to college and eventually moved to Portland, I still had to orient myself to direction. Looking out at Illinois and seeing nothing but clouds and trees, I felt completely lost.

"What direction are we facing?" I asked Liane.

Liane casually scrolled through her map. "Says east. Look." Her finger pointed and I could see the grid pattern. "Lake Michigan is this way. It's always on the east side."

"Helps me a little."

Liane continued to scroll. "Where we are heading is away from the lake."

I huffed. "Well then, that doesn't help me at all."

"Here is where we are trying to get to."

She was right, it was nowhere near the lake, but I could see the streets lined one by one. It was only yesterday when we found the street, and here I was minutes away from seeing the house with my own eyes. "Chicago is big."

"Oh look, it's here." Liane stood forward and a black sedan with all tinted windows drove up to meet us.

Liane started idle chatter with the driver, and I put my backpack in the trunk and got in the back.

"I'm Willard," the driver introduced himself as he set off driving through the airport lanes. He was older, but distinguished with lighter tuffs of gray peeking out from his paperboy-style cap. "So, you're off to the old Rosehill Cemetery?"

"Is that where the address is?" I asked, shuffling on my seat.

"Nah, I'm teasing. Very nearly close, though. Is this your first time here?"

"Yes." Liane answered for me. She loved to talk. Looked like the driver, Willard, would fill her in on everything.

"Well, welcome to Chicago, my hometown. What brings you here?"

"Oh, you know. We are tracking down a mythical girl we saw on the internet."

Willard laughed. "You're what? Now, that sounds crazy."

"I know, right? My brother here knows her from his childhood, so it's not too bizarre."

"Sounds like a true adventure."

"It is." Liane told him about the viral video and the girl who starred in it. I didn't add much—I was listening to how insane everything sounded. I kept my focus on the big town I was beholding for the first time, the skyscrapers in the backdrop, the endless sky of clouds above.

"I know that video." Willard laughed harder. "It made number one on the Best in Chicago yesterday. Million or so likes on some app or whatever. Something ridiculous. My daughter, she's fourteen, yeah, she sent it to me."

Liane leaned toward the conversation. "My brother's in love with the girl."

I shoved her, surprised she was letting out so much information to a stranger. "Liane."

"Which one? The panty girl?" Willard asked.

"That's the one," I pointed to myself.

Willard laughed deep and hearty. "And now you're off to find her? Man, that's sweet. And darn right creepy, but in a sweet way."

I was softening to the conversation. I mean, maybe it didn't sound too crazy. "I flew across the country to find her."

"Wow, that's beautiful. Not every story starts like that. I hope it works out for you."

"Thanks," I returned.

Liane shook my knee again. "It better." She smiled, still optimistic.

Willard took us off the freeway and we headed through different intersections. I had never seen so many monasteries and cemeteries on one street. My stomach became increasingly uneasy as we crept closer and closer. I needed to be stronger than this.

"What if she's not here?" I asked, mostly to myself. "What if it's a girl that looks like her?"

"Then you get to hang out with me in Chicago. I'm sure they have some tasteful bars you can get drunk in."

"Yes, ma'am," Willard returned, still listening. "There are some nice Blues clubs you can lose your miseries in. Music is amazing. And add a side of chicken wings to the misery. Mmm." He laughed a hearty laugh.

Something roiled in my stomach, like the bit of snickers was trying to get out. "I don't feel good. I think I made a mistake."

"No. Simon. You'll be all right." Liane started rubbing my back, but it didn't help. A few more turns and I felt the Snicker bits folding over and over in my stomach.

"I think . . ." I stopped and sat up. "We may need to stop."

"Sir, you need me to pull over?"

"Could you?" Liane finished for me. The car pulled over between two cars and stopped. The driver Willard put on his blinkers.

I unlocked the car door and unfolded to the ground, crawling on the asphalt until I reached the curb where I could sit. The cool, fresh air felt so much better. I don't know why the car felt so stifling.

"Would you like me to stay?" I overheard Willard ask Liane.

"How far are we?"

"Oh, not far. Up the road a few."

"I think we'll walk. Thank you so much."

Willard smiled a big, toothy grin. "My pleasure. You take care of him. I hope you find the girl." He popped the trunk and Liane retrieved both of our bags.

I waved very slightly as the car pulled away.

Liane came and sat by me on the curb. We sat there in silence for a moment before she busted up laughing. "You are too funny."

"What?"

"You're so worried." She rubbed my back very motherly, like she did to calm her baby.

I breathed in. "I can't get over this. I can't process it."

"Do you need to eat? You know, something other than a Snickers?"

"I don't think I can."

"But do you need to."

"Probably."

"There's some cute places around here." Liane slugged my arm. "You want a cupcake?"

My stomach dropped at the thought of all the sugar. "Nothing sweet. Maybe just soup."

"Come on. We'll try this café."

I stood, hoping to shake off the light-headedness, but couldn't, keeping my head down as we walked. I didn't catch the name of the café as we walked in grabbing a seat at the little soda bar. I ordered tomato basil and a water, while Liane ordered herself a grilled cheese.

"Reception is lousy in this place," Liane commented, trying to map where we were.

I glanced down at her phone. "Well, your battery is nearly dead."

"Yeah, I know. Candy Crush wipes it out."

"Why do you play it?"

"It's fun to watch all the candy fall when you clear the board."

I sipped my soup quietly as she showed me the different screens. She knew I wasn't interested but she showed me anyway. It was an irritating quirk I found charming.

The food made me feel better, the water especially. "Stop playing your game, if you want to save your battery."

"I'll just turn it off." Liane went to power down her phone but got distracted by Pinterest.

I laughed. "You're such a dweeb."

Liane shoved me. "A dweeb? No one uses that word. Only dweebs would use the word 'dweeb.'"

"Fine. I'm a dweeb." I slunk off the bar stool—"I'll be right back"—and headed for the toilet.

The single occupant bathroom gave me the quiet space I needed. I relieved myself and washed up, splashing my face from the tap. I took my wet hands and ran them through my hair, refreshing my thoughts. In the mirror I looked hollow, a shell of myself. My eyes had the bruisy look from lack of sleep. My face had the scruff of days without shaving—not that I was big on shaving, but I wished I hadn't been in such a hurry and had cleaned it up. Even wet, my hair bounced back into its normal shape, sticking up in places where I wished it wouldn't. I had learned from years of trying that my hair didn't care what I wanted and did its own thing.

"Snap out of it," I said to myself. "You don't want to meet her being a dweeb." In the mirror, I evaluated everything—my raggy Voltron tee shirt, my aged but comfortable jeans—everything. I was in no shape to meet Adri looking like this.

A voice came in my head, Adri's voice. *I don't care what you wear. Why would I care?*

"I'm about to meet you in the real world," I answered. "There's a lot of pressure."

Her calm voice came to me again. *I'm not attracted to your clothes.*

I closed my eyes and could almost see her again. When I opened them, I stared at a new me, the renewed me.

"I got this." I gave my mirror self a fist bump and walked out of the bathroom.

"Wow, geez. There you are." Liane leaned on the counter waiting for me. "I talked with a local. She said the street is not far from here. Are you ready for a walk?"

In my best Big Trouble in Little China Jack Burton voice, "I was born ready."

Twelve

"You said this was a phone interview." Adri sits uncomfortably on a beat-up couch covered in a homemade denim blanket. "Does it matter what you wear?"

"A video interview," a voice shouts from a side room. "There's a difference. They'll see what I look like."

Adri plays with the tied yarn in between the quilt squares. "So you wouldn't really need to wear pants."

Simon pokes his head out of his bedroom and glowers. "Are you insinuating something?"

Adri giggles. "What? No. But you wouldn't, would you?"

Simon returns to his room. "I would still wear pants, because I would know I wasn't wearing pants and it would make me awkward."

Adri laughs and falls on her side, resting her head on a crocheted pillow.

Simon laughs too. "Great. I'll be thinking of this conversation during the interview."

Adri chuckles. "Oh, I hope so." She straightens along the couch and takes in the strange, old apartment. "How long have you been staying with your grandmother?"

"Not long, and it's just until I get a job. Saving money."

"It's charming." Adri turns her head up to the sparkles on the popcorn ceiling. "Why don't they fly you to Portland?"

Shuffling sounds come from the room. "This is a little company. They can't afford to fly me out."

"But they can afford to move you out."

"If they like me enough, yes. I'm ready for a change. I need to get away."

"You only just graduated college. I'd take my time and travel."

"The student loans don't agree with your idea."

Adri grows impatient, giving up on the particulars of the conversation. "When did your dreams get so boring? They used to be fun. Now I'm helping you pick out a tie for an interview. Where is the adventure?"

Simon's head pokes out of the room again. "I was trying to find this pink shirt I got for a wed—"

"Pink?" Adri waves her hand.

"But it's a nice—"

"Not for an interview. You want to be taken seriously."

"Okay, good point. I couldn't find it anyway, so I have this one."

Simon walks out of his bedroom wearing a slate gray shirt with a casual blue and black tie and appropriate black dress pants. "Too much?"

Adri stops playing with the yarn and sits up, taken aback by his dapper appearance. "Simon. You look great."

"You think so?" Simon smooths out his shirt. "I haven't worn this since my mom's funeral."

Adri contemplates this. "Oh. Right."

Simon waves her off. "It's all right. It's a nice shirt."

"How long ago did she pass?" Adri asks, reevaluating the blanket. "I don't remember. Years are blurring together."

"Right after I started college. Four-ish years."

Adri stares back at him. "Has it really been that long?"

Simon sighs. "Yeah. And you know what? I'm still sad about it. I mean, it's okay, but I miss her."

"Tell me about her."

"You would have really liked her. I mean, she had a way
to make everyone her favorite, but I think she and you would have
been great friends." Simon loosens his tie and walks nearer. "It
wasn't done fair."

"Fair. What do you mean?"

"She was sick for years. I felt a little cheated out of having a
mother."

Adri scrunches her face. "I don't know how I would be if my
mother passed. My mother is a stern, difficult person. I don't think
she likes me very much. I feel like such a disappointment to her.
We've never gotten along."

Simon sits down by her. "You've never mentioned anything
about her."

"Honestly, there isn't a need to. My mother has a hard
history and she keeps it private. She's German and met my dad
when she shouldn't have, married young, left her country. I don't
think she had a very good example of a mother. Does
that help?"

Simon snickers. "Yes, that does help."

Adri brushes her hand down his silk tie. "Don't think about it.
It's a nice shirt."

Simon rewires his thinking back to the clothes. "The nicest
thing I own."

"You should wear it." Adri's mouth turns up. "I think wearing a
special shirt like this will help your confidence."

Simon smiles. "You think?"

"Of course." Adri looks in his eyes. "I don't care what you
wear. Why would I care? What you wear is not the person I know
in here, in our dreams together. It's not someone I see.

It's you," she pointed right at his heart, "the person I know right here that I care about."

Simon makes to grab her hand.

Adri pulls it back.

Simon clenches his empty fist. "It's just me."

"And that's the problem. Remember?" Adri looks around the room. "This little home is incredibly charming." She stands before she speaks again. "You know I'd choose you if you were tangible. I don't have a choice right now. I'm trying to

expand my relationships to those who don't exist only in my head."

Simon lifts his eyebrow. "And how's it going?"

Adri swirls her hands in the air. "Not sure yet." She eyes him seriously. "Nothing's easy."

Simon stands and looks down at her. Neither speak. He reaches toward her face. "You have a . . . just stay still."

"Okay?" Adri freezes as Simon gently places a finger near the corner of her eye. Every nerve pulses at the gentle touch.

"Eyelash." Simon pulls back his finger and shows her the tiny lash.

"Does that mean I get a wish?" Adri smirks.

Simon shrugs. "I guess so." He holds it out to her. "Make a wish."

Adri closes her eyes. "You too."

Simon half closes his eyes, still watching her. "I always do."

My sister and I stepped out of the café. I looked north, the direction of the street. My nerves were wrecked, but my newfound bathroom confidence pushed my feet forward.

Liane bounced next to me. "This is too exciting." She couldn't contain her energy. It was adorable and irritating. I side-hugged her and we started walking.

"Miss," a voice called from behind us. We both turned around to see a young woman dressed in a black smock approach us. She must have been one of the servers from the café. "Hey, did you leave your book here?"

"No, not us." Liane stared at the book, a worn copy of Jane Eyre.

"Oh no," she said. "She left it."

"Who left it?" I asked.

"It's not mine, but I think I know who it belongs to." Liane held out her hand and the lady handed over the book. "Thanks."

The server nodded and walked back to the café.

Liane studied the book. "The girl I asked directions from, this is hers."

"Looks pretty beat up. She could probably use a new copy."

Liane batted me with the book.

"What?"

"The condition of the book is exactly why we should get it back to her. Look at this!" She flipped through it. "The bent pages, the worn rubbing from years of fingerprints. This is a treasured book. Someone's read this over and over."

She stopped on a page bookmarked with something.

"See, look." Liane held up a business card. "Moonstone Books. This is where she works. Let's stop there on the way back."

"Sure, I guess." I tugged her forward. "Come on. I need to do this before I lose my courage."

We started forward again, walking the dilapidated concrete sidewalk lined with trees. I felt a gentle buzz in my pocket. It was a text from Adam, my co-worker. The server was down again. That wasn't good. I quickly texted "I'll log on soon" and shoved it back in my pocket.

"Did you ever read Jane Eyre?" Liane asked. "Didn't you have to read it for school?"

I eyed the back at the book she was carrying. "I've read it. Not for school or anything. Someone asked me to read it." *Adri,* I thought but didn't say.

Liane laughed. "Didn't think you would like something like this."

"I didn't say I liked it, just that I've read it." I walked around a broke piece of curb as we crossed a street. "I want to be a writer, eventually. I don't want to be ignorant of the classics."

"Yeah, there aren't enough dragons in here for you."

"Jane Eyre with dragons," I said to myself. "I might be able to tie the two together."

"Ugh. Please don't ruin Jane Eyre." Liane hopped gingerly onto the sidewalk. "You ruined James and the Giant Peach for me."

"I improved it." I laughed at the silly memory.

"Leech and Moth did not chase after James and try to eat him."

"That was my favorite part."

"I think Mom stopped having you read to me after that."

I laughed harder. "Mom *asked* me to read it to you. I read it to her first. She believed in my talent."

I watched Liane's smile increase. She was much like our mother—contagious energy and a strong determination. She would have liked what we were doing now.

I felt a tiny drop on my head. It was beginning to rain. "Did you pack an umbrella?"

Liane glared at me. "No. I didn't think of it." She stopped and unzipped her pack, grabbed her jacket, and slipped the book inside. "Where we live, we wear hoodies. It doesn't rain enough to justify an umbrella."

"Portland has two seasons—'raining' and 'threatening to rain.'"

Liane snort-laughed, which made me die in laughter.

"Geez, Lee. It wasn't that funny."

"I miss your humor." Liane struggled getting her arms in her jacket sleeves, pulling the hood up, and we continued to walk.

Liane was silly, almost like a kid, noticing the oddest things.

She halted. "Do you see how this sidewalk winds around the tree?"

I looked down to see how carefully the cement molded away from the old root. "Well, the tree was here first."

Liane laughed. "That's right." She stuck her finger in the air, marking the point. Liane continued on, observing little details of things, on the houses or mailboxes. "Do you see this?" She ran around a large trunk of a tree. "Do you know what this is?"

I followed her and noticed the white box, like an old medicine cabinet with frosted glass for windows, mounted to the tree. Liane opened the little doors. "Books?" I questioned.

"It's a neighborhood library."

"People do that?"

Liane's eyebrows crinkled. "Yes, you hermit. You can swap books or read books and replace them. I wish we had this. When Ian and I get out of our dumpy apartment and into a house, I want to put one in our neighborhood."

"You could put that Jane Eyre copy in here."

"No," Liane said, admiring the mechanics of the mounting. "I'll take it back. I'd like to go to a bookstore anyway. It's a charming way to spend your time."

"When not stalking a mythological viral video superstar."

I reached in the little library and took out the first book in the stack. Something struck me when I held the book, mesmerized by something unexplained. I flipped the book over and flipped inside.

Liane spotted my confusion. "Little Women? You into the female protagonists?"

"Maybe? But it's not about reading it, it's . . ." I trailed off, thumbing through it again. "I don't know. It feels familiar."

"Is it the had-a-paperback-when-you-were-little kinda feeling?"

"No, well, maybe?" I didn't know how to describe it beyond it feeling familiar. "You know Grandpa's old bookcase with all those old paperback westerns? It's like that. I know I wouldn't read it, but knowing it was his is like sharing his memory or experience of it. Holding this book is similar."

Liane shook her head. "Maybe you're a book psychic."

"Shut up." I hit her with the copy before putting it back. "Forget I opened up to you."

Liane kept laughing as we walked, the rain becoming steadier.

The sidewalk ended and I stood at the corner of the street, the sign reading the words "Catalpa Avenue." I said it out loud and my stomach sank.

"We're here." Liane hopped up and down. "Come on." She dragged me forward again as she searched over the house numbers. 153. 147. "132!"

And there it was. 132.

My knees wobbled and started to buckle.

"Whoa, what's happening here?" She grabbed my arm from the elbow.

My breath left me. I sat on the curb and tried to even my breathing. I stared blankly at the house across the street. It was like looking at the movie. I pulled out my phone and opened the screenshot. The white blossoms covering the bushes were still blooming.

"The video must have just happened," I exhaled. "I can't believe this." My hands couldn't stay out of my hair—my nervous habit. Liane stood patiently. She knew enough to give me some time to process this.

An overwhelming reality settled around my heart. If this girl was real, I was minutes away from discovering the truth. Questions filled me, simple questions like, does she live here? Is she familiar with this neighborhood? Are we walking the same streets?

I couldn't concentrate on one thing, but it was time to find some answers.

I stood, brushed off the dust from my pants, and quickly crossed the street, Liane following.

I stopped mid-crossing. Liane bumped into me. "What do I say?"

"Don't think," she shoved me onward. "The words will come."

She pushed me out of the road. I stumbled onto the sidewalk and Liane was already bounding up the walkway.

"Come on," she urged. She radiated excitement.

I swallowed. I couldn't get over this moment, the hugeness of it. It was too overwhelming to think about, and my slow, overthinking brain told me not to. Don't think about the enormity of what is playing out, it's a house, with a walkway, and a buzzer, like other houses. Don't notice the broken bushes where someone might have fallen and, ouch, probably scraped herself good. Don't notice the sitting area on the porch where the cushion was still indented from someone's elbow. Or the glass screen door that has a tinny squeak on its hinge where someone opened it in the middle of a girl fight.

The same tinny squeak woke me back to my senses. I was standing at the door. I had made it up here. Liane had already buzzed the house, and the door had opened. A man stood behind the glass— a huge mess of black hair, overgrown and wild, matched his wooly beard and black-rimmed glasses.

"Oh, man, whatever you two are selling, I'm not interested." He went to close the door.

"Wait," Liane grabbed the screen. "You don't know why we're here."

"Not interested."

"Was this where the girl biffed it over the rail?" The words rushed out of my mouth before I could filter anything.

The man stopped. "Are you guys from the Sun, because the Tribune was here about an hour ago." He made a huffed laugh and went to go inside.

"We aren't from either," Liane rushed.

"Yeah, but you're here because you found my famous house on YouTube or whatever and just had to come see."

I felt panic. "You mean, other people have been here?"

The man stopped. "Yeah, I don't have time for this."

Liane stuck her foot in the door. "What? You have a pressing Overwatch meet-up?"

The man looked around him. "Possibly. Who are you guys?"

"Can we come in?"

"Nope." The man stepped out to the porch. "Things are not tidy, you know." He made his way to the sitting area on the porch. "And I don't trust you two, you look too put together to be at my place."

Liane made it over to a wicker chair. I preferred to stand, watching them. The man gestured to a chair. I shook my head and kept standing.

"Whatever, man." He waved his hand. "So, you are here to see the famous house."

Liane eyed me. "Well, sort of. Simon?"

I knew I needed to say something, but I didn't know where to start. "Adri," popped out of my mouth.

"Adri?" the man said, a scoff. "Adri who?"

"I don't know. I mean, I don't know her last name."

The guy cocked his head. "You know, the guy from the Tribune wanted to know all sorts of details about the girls. Let me tell you what I told him. I am not about to sell out my friend and his girl so pervs can stalk her just for some money."

His girl. The words stabbed me. His girl? She was somebody's girl? The last time Adri and I had spoken together in the field she was nobody's girl. I was positive.

"We aren't from any news anything," Liane said. "We are trying to find out where she lives."

"Why, so you can stalk her like all the other people who have asked? I told you, I'm not interested."

The man made to stand up, but I impulsively walked over there. Nothing was going the way I envisioned, and without his help we would never find her. He was our only key.

"Hi," I extended my hand out. "I'm Simon Moon, this is my sister Lee."

Liane did a small wave from her seat.

"What's your name?"

The man took my hand and shook it. "I'm Greg."

"Greg. It's awesome to meet you. You have a great house." I didn't know where my conversation was leading. "Greg. Do you believe in fate?"

"Ah, geez. I don't believe this."

"Please, hear me out." I sat next to him and pulled out my phone. "I flew from Portland this morning. Portland. To find this house."

"Whoa, Portland." He looked genuinely surprised. "Things travel, don't they."

"I watched the video, and in it is a girl I knew from childhood. This girl."

Greg glanced at the screen. "Man. Seriously?"

"I've been searching for her for years." I briefly summed up a roundabout story of our meeting and knowing each other without sounding completely crazy.

Greg scratched his beard. "Yeah. Very stalker. But as I said, I don't know Adri."

"But you said *his girl*. You must know her. She was here at your house, your party—"

"Yeah, there were a lot of people here that night I didn't know." Greg rubbed his hands. "The girl on your screen shot," he points to my phone, "is not anyone I know. See this girl?" He points to her opponent. "She's married to my workmate, Jeremiah. That's who I meant by *his* girl."

"Oh." I sat my shoulders back and closed my phone. "Has anyone been asking about Adri?"

"I don't know anything."

I felt the weight of a dead end coming again.

Liane shuffled. "Are you saying this to protect against creeps like my brother?"

Greg smirked. "I'm messing with you, but I, no fooling, don't know much about her. Honest."

Liane picked up on something. "But why would these two girls fight?"

"It was fun, I'll say that. The other girl, this Adri you named her, had no idea what was coming. I don't think she has fought a day in her life. Lydia wouldn't have fought unless it meant something."

"Lydia?" I asked.

"Yeah, Miah's girl. She has pure Chicago guts. It was awesome." He put emphasis on the last word, like referring to a wrestling match.

My ears burned. "Miah? He goes by Miah?"

"Yeah, he works with me at JD publishing. He's a content editor."

"But how long have you known him?"

"About six months. They got married about three months ago."

"What's his last name?"

"Ashfield. Why?"

"Is he on Facebook? Maybe I can find her that way." I fumbled again with my phone trying to find the Miah. A conversation came back to me. *No one would be lame enough to go by Miah.*

"I guess so." Greg smiled. "Okay, I get this now. This Adri girl knows Miah, has a history with Miah. Right on." He backhanded my arm, like we were friends. I laughed uncomfortably. "All this time I thought it had something to do with my friend Danny."

"Who's Danny?" Liane asked.

"Danny and I are close mates. Great guy. We game a lot. Dating this dynamite girl. Pauline is her name. Yeah, and I know this girl left with Danny and Pauline. As far as that, I don't know."

Liane stood. "Can I get Danny's number?"

"Nah, still don't trust you guys. I gotta protect my friends, you understand? A lot of people have been asking and you are the first I've actually told anything to." Greg stood. "But how about you give me your number, and I will ask to see if Danny knows anything and send you info that way."

"Okay." Liane pulled out her phone. "Crap. It's dead. I forgot."

I sighed and opened my messaging. I rattled off the number and Greg sent me a quick text. "Nice. It worked."

Greg shook my hand again. "I really hope you're not a creep."

I wasn't sure how to respond. "Thanks?" I shook it back.

He went back into the house and I stared at Liane.

"It was kinda helpful, right?" she returned my absent gaze. "Come on, let's go over to that bookstore."

"All right," I silenced my phone and shoved it into my pocket.

I stopped at Bake My Day Bakery and grabbed the cupcake for Samantha. I couldn't help it and grabbed a second lemon curd. I had eaten half of it when I entered Moonstone Bookstore.

"Lemon was a great choice." I smacked my lips as I walked in the door. I stepped into the back office to put my purse down.

"Oh, hey," Annette said from behind her computer. She was working on the store accounts, like she usually did around this time. "Someone was looking for you a few minutes ago."

I started to blush. "Ah, geez. Is it a reporter or a YouTube stalker?"

Annette lifted her eyebrow. "I don't remember who it was, but he's a friend, I know that. He seemed like he knew you very well. Called you Adri and everything."

"Oh." I poked my head out of the office to gaze around. The store had few customers, but no one I recognized specifically.

"And where's my book?" Annette lowered her chin. "You said you were borrowing it."

"Oh, bother." I examined my empty arms. "I think I left it at the café."

"Try to track it down."

"It's just a Jane Eyre."

"But it's a Bloomsbury 1960 printing with the green jacket. It's not common."

"Ope." I swallowed in shame. "I'm sorry. I'll try."

"Thank you." Annette went back to her paperwork, but I knew she was kidding, well partially. Annette knew obscure details I could only dream of.

I walked back to the floor and straightened some of the displays. I covered the register without incident so Samantha could go eat her cupcake. I kept craning my neck to see if there was the mystery person who knew me but couldn't see much beyond the customers.

After I finished ringing up the young college reader, an older woman came up to me.

"I can't find your cookbooks."

"Let me show you." I walked around and led her to the back corner. "We don't have many, and some of the ones we have aren't the newest."

"Doesn't matter." She waved her hands in front of her. "Cookbook's just another challenge. I went through that Julia Child book. Tell ya, I skimmed some, but still, I feel I can do anything."

I laughed and pointed toward them—and stopped dead.

Someone stood near the end of the aisle, and at first, I wasn't sure I was seeing right. Was my crazy mind making things up?

"Miah?" I didn't mean it as a question, but a statement. He smiled and it was stupid charming.

The lady I was helping quickly noticed the awkward tension. "I think I can find it from here, dear." She turned down the wrong way.

I thought of correcting her, but Miah strode forward.

"Are you the person looking for me?"

"Probably," he said. "I couldn't reach you."

"Well, I deleted all my social media accounts."

"And I texted."

I brushed my hair behind my ear. "Well, my phone hit the bottom of a toilet. I thought your wife would have told you all about it."

Miah's smile vanished. "I haven't seen Lydia." He moved a few more steps toward me, like a lion stalking prey. "You've seen her?"

"Yes. She's why my phone is sitting in a bag of rice at home."

"I haven't talked with her."

He was a shoe-length away from me now, and I didn't know exactly how to act. I crossed my legs like a ballerina trying to act casual, though I was anything but. "You're married. You should talk to her."

Miah didn't blink. "She doesn't want to talk with me."

"Why?" I breathed. "I think I know why. Don't answer."

Miah squared his shoulders. It was obvious he had prepared something to say. But it didn't matter what he had to say. In this moment, I had to pretend to be brave. Even though I had never been brave in my life.

"Adri—"

"Look," I cut him off. "Before you say anything, Lydia is great and you deserve her and . . . and . . . and I am a terrible person. I can't believe what I did. I learned my lesson, promise, because I think my panties have a million likes by now."

My feet did a pirouette in the other direction.

"Wait." Miah grabbed my shoulder. The touch held my bravery still. "No, that's not it. You are not a terrible person."

I turned back to face him. "No, really. I can be. You can say it."

Miah still held my shoulder. "Adri. You know me, better than Lydia."

"How can you say that? You didn't ask me to marry you, you asked her. Clearly, she has something I didn't."

I began backing out of the aisle.

Miah grabbed my hand and pulled me into the fantasy section. "Just listen, please."

He sat me down on one of the soft puffs in the corner. I stared, silent, as he pulled up a crate, meant to be a side table, and sat down.

"You kissed me. You shouldn't have. It was wrong of you." Miah softened his look. "It was tremendously wrong of you, making me think and relive feelings in that moment."

I didn't like the direction of this. A lot of blame was coming at me. My brain ran through any blame I could send his way, just to get back at him for saying things like it, but I bit my lip and stayed quiet.

"I also did something wrong," he started. And I was surprised. "After you left, Lydia and I got into a very big fight, our biggest yet." Miah placed his hands on his knees and leaned forward. "Lydia fights with me a lot. It's like she wants to change who I am. She doesn't like any of my sweaters. She doesn't care for my nutmeg brew."

I nearly gasped, but held it in. His seasonal coffee was quite good.

"That night I think she understood that I will never be the guy she wants."

And now I understood what he was saying, and my mind started skipping ahead. "But you are married. The big 'M.' You're not available."

Miah sighed. "I don't think I was meant to be married."

"Don't say that." And why was I saying this for? My brain scrambled. This was my chance to get Miah back. But did I really want Miah back? YES! My brain quickly answered, but then the heart tugged and I wasn't sure what I was saying. No. Shut up, brain. "You chose her, not me. You had your chances to marry me."

Miah sat up. "But I was still trying to find you, Adri." He grabbed my hand and started stroking the back knuckle. My stomach caved in. He knew I liked that. "Sometimes I had you all to myself, but then, there were times when you were searching for something else. I asked you once if you wanted to spend your life with me."

"I don't remember you asking me that." I pulled my hand back trying to think. "Honestly, you did?"

"Yes. You said you would sleep on it, and we never talked about it again."

"Oh," I remembered something else. "Maybe I was." I quietly answered. "Maybe I was looking for something else."

"Did you find it?"

I started, then sighed. "No." The sound I made was hardly no, but more an echo of my thoughts.

Miah rested his hand on my knee. It tickled but I didn't laugh. I kept any emotion bottled. "Lydia isn't right for me." He gazed so deeply, I worried he would see the truth, but if he did, he didn't let on. "I think I made a mistake with you. Your kiss woke me."

"And not the brawl?" I reflexively itched my cheek where Lydia's ring had cut me. I stood. I didn't know what to say, but I knew I couldn't be in that corner with him anymore and I began heading away through the aisle.

"Adri. Wait." Miah pulled on my shoulder holding me back. "I still need to say something."

"I don't want to be that person," I whispered. "The one who ruins your marriage."

Miah could see my swelling tears. There was an emotion-driven silence between us. Unspoken memories flooded the space holding us both in place. I didn't know what to think or what to say. The sadness of my own loneliness filled in any empty space the memories couldn't find. I wanted Miah more than almost anything. Everything pulled me toward him. And I wished so hard that I wasn't broken, that I could be in love with him and everything would be fine, that a life together wouldn't be a constant reminder that I made a huge mistake and ruined his marriage.

"I . . ." he started to say. I didn't want him to say it. Please don't say it. "I . . . was the one who uploaded the video."

Without a word, I slapped him so hard the red immediately bloomed on his cheek. He was shocked and couldn't speak.

I left him standing in the aisle between Sanderson and Tolkien and walked out of the store.

Thirteen

Adri stands in the wind alone, watching the gentle breeze tumble the colored, fallen leaves. She stares at the tree curiously.

"I was wondering when I might see you." Simon says from behind her.

Adri turns and sees Simon walking toward the tree. "I'm not a fan of your time zone."

Simon takes in the landscape. "Where are we? This isn't our meadow. Is it?"

"But it's close. Right?" Adri bounces around excited. "I went to this writer's retreat in Lake Forest and swear I saw our tree, and I went searching and found this exact spot. I've come back a few times, you know, when I need some peace. Fort Sheridan is lovely, especially in the autumn. I wanted to show you the colors changing."

"Lake Forest? It sounds like a made up, dreamy place. I guess that's fitting."

Adri brushes her fingers against the trunk. "It's where I first came up with my time travel story I read to you."

Simon notices her clothes. "You're wearing a dress. I've never seen you in a dress."

Adri bites her lip. "I haven't seen you in a while. I thought I'd try and look nice."

Simon's breath catches. "You always look nice."

"You big, fat liar."

Simon points his finger on his chest. "Hey, you were the one who told me it was the person in here that you liked."

"Do you remember everything I say?"

"Usually."

"How?"

Simon grabs the back of his head. "I . . . uh, I write them down. The dreams. I write down the things I remember."

Adri cocks her head. "How sweet. And creepy, you weirdo." She brushes her hand on her skirt and smirks. "Kidding. I draw, sometimes. I've tried to draw you several times."

"Like a cartoon artist? I've only ever seen your cute stick figures."

Adri laughs. "When we played Pictionary." She shoves him playfully. "Stick figures are what you do. No, I do draw. I'm not the best, but I like it. I haven't shown anyone." Her eyes study his. "I have one I'm really proud of."

Simon moves a step closer. "I wish I could see it."

"Maybe someday I could redraw something like it for you."
Simon resists fixing a random strand of her hair and blinks his thoughts clean. "So, where have you been?"

Adri playfully moves her dress side-to-side. "Remember what else I said in that dream?"

Simon runs his hand through his hair. "What do you mean?"

"You keep things in your journal. What else did I say? Do you remember?"

Simon remembers. "You would choose me."

Adri feels a lump form in her throat. "I would." She chokes on the words.

Simon grasps the emotional pull she has on his heart and gently runs his hand down her cheek. "And you would dream all the time."

Adri closes her eyes, melting in his touch. "Yeah, about that."
She opens her eyes, tears settling in the corners. "I think I would
rather be here though, feel this, than be alone."

Simon can no longer resist and pulls her in, wrapping his arms
tight around her slender frame.

Adri doesn't pull away, but drinks in the embrace. "Let me be
with you."

"I've missed you." Simon whispers near her ear.

"Me too." Adri speaks in his shirt.

"What happened?" Simon asks, wishing he hadn't.

Adri's head lowers further into his chest. "My life is a lie. I
can't love Miah. I can't be honest. And I will never be honest with
him because he's not the person I'm in love with. I want you.
Always." Adri pulls back and looks at him. "Always."

Simon kisses her deeply, without any hesitation. The warmth
feels so real, yet so distant.

Adri lets him have his way, for once.

Adri's Apartment

I hopped on the Brown Line and tried to evaporate. Different people came and went in blurs of motion as I rested my head on the back of the train car. I didn't think about anything specific—I was numb and embarrassed and hurt. I wanted to disappear completely. My brain dreamed about seeing Simon, hearing his voice. My brain even tricked me into seeing him step off the platform as I passed. Soul sickness took over. The tears stung rubbing the last of my make-up into my eyes, as I rested in the corner and passed time on the train.

Hours later, I walked off the train platform and trudged home.

It wasn't dark, but the light was falling. My stomach made an angry twist. The gentle soup from lunch was not enough to sustain me and it was time to eat. I didn't want to eat though. I was rebelling.

It was too early in the season for the lightning bugs and cicadas, but there was a gentle buzz of nightlife coming out as I opened the gate to my apartment. The porchlight was off. Pauline must not have come home yet from work. Good, I thought. Made leaving easier.

I entered and when to my bedroom. I grabbed my laptop from my bed, wrapped the cord around it, and shoved it into my backpack. I grabbed some jammies, fuzzy socks, my favorite college hoodie, and random items close at hand I might need.

My eyes glanced at the notebook with sketches, the page left open. I ran my finger gently along the picture, wishing Simon were actually here with me. He would tell me what to do. He would help. He always tried to help.

I had room in my bag for a few snacks. I would probably need them. And sometimes, especially on a bad night, you just need Doritos.

I rummaged the pantry, found a few things, and snatched them. I shoved a few pretzels in my mouth as well. Then a few more. My emptiness growled inside more, not just the hunger but the anger. I was much more impulsively angry on an empty stomach and the few pretzels told me so. I needed to eat in order to think clearly and I had no idea when I would have the chance to eat again. I placed my bags down and looked in the fridge. It looked rather bare, but a scrambled egg sandwich sounded really good. I grabbed the carton and a skillet. The pan warmed and I threw on the eggs, dashing salt and pepper as they grew all lumpy. When I pressed down the bread in the toaster, the door opened.

"Hey girl!" I yelled from the kitchen. "I think I'll take your advice and disappear for a while."

I didn't hear her respond. The eggs looked about done, so I took the pan off the stove and turned . . . to see Miah standing there, a bundle of roses in his hand.

I screamed and dropped the eggs. The hot pan hit the ground, sending bits of egg everywhere.

Miah set down the flowers and started scooping up the eggs in his hands.

"What are you doing here?"

"Cleaning up eggs." Miah evaluated the mess and we both knew the eggs weren't salvageable. I pulled out the garbage from under the sink.

"How did you get in here?"

"You left the door open."

"I did?" I jumped as the toast popped up. I pretended it was nothing and set to buttering the toast while they were still warm. "That doesn't mean you can walk in."

"I wasn't going to stand at the door. I know your house and your place." Miah dusted the lumpy egg off his hands. "And I don't think you would have let me in if I knocked."

"Look." I bit into the bread, knowing I needed food for this conversation. "I can't be-weeeve whaah you did."

"Uploading the video?" Miah wiped the last bit of egg off the ground. "I showed it to a few friends. I didn't know what would happen."

"But I'm a meme now. Holy lord, a meme! There is a gif of me falling over the rail and back again. It's the most clever thing I've ever seen. Up and down and there she goes up and back down and, whoa, back up again."

Miah snickered. "I think you're overreacting."

"When your butt gets its own Twitter account, we can talk about overreacting."

I took a bigger bite of the toast. It was rather dry, so I grabbed a water bottle from the fridge and took a swig.

Miah stepped closer. "Look, I'm sorry. I had no idea this would happen."

"Why did you film it in the first place?"

Miah half-grinned and studied my face, especially the ring-shaped scrape on my cheek. "I had two girls fighting over me."

I felt sick. "I was defending myself, not fighting for you."

"Look, I didn't intend for this to upset you. I came to apologize." He reached over and grabbed the roses, all white—a peace offering, I guess. They were the tiniest bit of pink on the ends. Gorgeous, absolutely. I loved them. And the sight of them made my heart soften. What a stupid power roses had—a magic revealed in subtle bloom.

Miah pulled one rose from the bundle and held it out to me. My hard shell was beginning to crack. "Please, don't."

"What you did made me realize how much I missed you. How Lydia and I don't make sense, and how we do."

I apologized to the flowers, wishing so much that I could keep them.

"Miah. I'm in love with someone else."

Miah crossed his arms. "Since when. You came to the party with Pauline, not anyone else. You haven't been dating anyone. I know." He raised his voice with each sentence. "Tell me, Adri. Because that kiss didn't tell me you were dating. It told me the opposite."

I went very quiet looking at him. His eyes were those deep blue people always mistook to mean something beyond what they saw, the same eyes I thought held all the answers but were just masking the fact that he didn't. I had kissed those lips only days before, but I couldn't remember what they felt like. The scruff from his unkempt beard rubbing against my chin was never comfortable. Taking in all of him, how could he be mad at me for loving someone else? What did he see in me that was anything remarkable?

"I learned a lot when I was with you." I set down my toast and stared at the counter. "I will never be a whole person if we were together."

"What are you talking about?"

"Simon happened a long time ago, long before you."

"Simon?" He scoffed. "Simon. This is the first time I'm hearing his name."

"Because I never talked about him." I threw my toast in the sink. "I never wanted you to know."

"Simon, huh? Was Simon happening while we were dating?"

I bit my lip and answered truthfully. "I'm not sure how to answer."

Miah stood very straight and looked right through me. He knew I was telling the truth. He didn't need to know anything more.

"You cheated on me?"

"No. It's not like that." I felt the anger rush through me. "And you can't tell me Lydia didn't happen before you dumped me. I know she did."

"Where's Simon now?"

I breathed. "I don't know."

Miah shook his head, disbelieving. He appeared seriously hurt by this. Good. Serves him right for posting a video of me in my panties and humiliating me.

Miah heaved a few times, his temper flaring. "I can't believe you. I thought you were in love with me. You were so pathetic, you couldn't get over me. Why else kiss me like that? But there was always someone else. Always. I can't believe you, you little bit—"

I sprayed the rest of my water bottle in his face to stop him from finishing that sentence. The water dripped down his eyebrows into his eyes. I grabbed the roses and smacked them on top of his head, the petals exploding, each puff of magic left in the flowers gracefully plummeting like snowfall in winter.

"Get out!" I shoved him hard out of the kitchen. He sputtered and wiped the water from his eyes. I couldn't understand what he was saying until he was close to the door.

". . . it's angora and shouldn't get wet."

"That's what you care about? Your sweater?" I got him on the porch. "Go find your wife. You two belong together." I shut and locked the door.

I heard pounding and shouting. "Adri! Open up. There is no Simon. You made him up! I know it. I know you better than anyone alive. Open up. Let's talk."

It continued on. I snatched my packed bag and snuck out the back kitchen window.

I received a few more texts from Adam. He was desperate. "I gotta help him. Is there someplace we can get internet?"

"Sure." Liane took another bite of cupcake. "I booked us a place above some restaurant. Let's head there. It shouldn't be far, I don't think. The bookstore can wait."

I checked the CTA, and the trains system seemed pretty understandable, so we headed toward a platform.

A few stops later, Liane and I hopped off and walked the two blocks toward a restaurant called "Bluey's" on the corner of Irving and Southport. A little bluebird sitting on top of a big letter B told me we had arrived. Liane talked with the man inside and came out with a key.

"Come on," she said marching through another door on the left. Inside sat a very old staircase, completely shining with wear. We went up two flights to an old door. Two turns of a key and we were in.

The old apartment smelled of rotting wood and a remembrance of too many cats.

"Nice." I said rather sarcastically.

Liane immediately looked in the rooms. "If we are staying in Chicago, I want to have a real Chicago experience."

"Be careful about that, I hear there are not-so-nice neighborhoods."

"Oh, look at this," Liane shouted from the kitchen. "There is an old balcony that has these scary stairs by it."

"Fantastic." Another sarcasm. I immediately went to work setting up my computer and Wi-Fi connection.

"Seriously, this place is charming."

"Uh-huh," I returned. My screen came on and I logged in. Opening my work email, I could see what Adam was talking about and I started replying to some of the emails. I messaged Adam and told him I was online.

"How long do you have to work?"

"I have no idea," I replied honestly. "Just give me an hour or so."

"Okay. I think I'll go shopping. This looks like a quaint area, and there was a cute shop we passed just across the street."

"Do you want to charge your phone?" I suggested, getting out my headset.

"Good idea."

Liane pulled out her plug from her bag and set it up to charge. I already had my headset on and IM connected when she left.

I worked as fast and as furiously as I could, trying to answer what Adam was trying to fix. I wasn't as much help here as I hoped. I knew the problem, but Adam was on it. I was his wingman for the moment, cleaning up the technical debt. There was a two-hour difference for me in Chicago. I didn't notice when it said 5:00 on my computer, it was actually 7:00 PM in the Central time zone. It felt like a very long day.

Liane returned with a few bags and some food. She fixed a quick meal of sandwiches, powered on her phone, and called her husband.

"Don't worry," she said to her husband, Ian. "We have a solid lead, and I'm going to start looking for her once I hang up with you." A few more gooey words and she hung up.

"So," I started, shutting down my computer. "Tell me about this dynamite lead."

"Solid lead," she clarified.

"We can't do anything unless this guy Danny calls."

"But we are going back to the bookstore, remember?"

"That's just wasting time."

"Is it?" Liane cocked her head.

"Yes." I stood and put on my jacket. "Is this a vacation to you? You've gone shopping and eaten at your fun little café you've always dreamed about. Are you taking this trip seriously?"

"Says the man working for the past two hours." Liane knew this tone, and how to defuse it. "I am helping, promise." She stuffed her phone into her purse. "But we got to get this book back. The store will close soon. And as you said, we have to wait until this guy calls. We've done everything we can do right now."

"I'm not going to find her." I had been feeling this despair ever since I realized she didn't live at the house, and the guy wouldn't technically help us. "I flew out for what?"

"For a chance." Liane shook my shoulders. "Don't lose hope. We have tonight and a lot of tomorrow."

"It's not enough time."

I know Liane was trying to give me a boost of confidence, but her disappointment showed on her face. "I will do everything I can to help find her."

We left the quaint apartment and started back toward Moonstone Books. I watched Liane's spring in her step as she admired the city, chatting about this and that. Being around my sister made me feel young again, made me feel like I could do anything. I missed that, a lot.

Moonstone Books was everything I hoped. It was small but lively, with eclectic furniture strewn about to form reading nooks. A vibrant older lady sat at the front of the service desk.

"Hello there. Your first time in?"

"Yes," Liane stated. "It's such a cute place."

"Thank you. I try to make finding a book an experience."

"As it says on your door," I remarked, fanning my hand out over the logo.

She raised an eyebrow at my comment, but I could tell she was amused. "Are you looking for something?"

"Sort of." Liane placed the book on the counter. "Someone left this at the café up the street."

The lady laughed. "My Jane Eyre circa 1960." She laughed harder. "It's returned home."

"I found this inside. I thought I would bring it back." She lifted the business card place marker.

"How tremendously honest of you. Thank you."

"I had a brief chat with the girl reading it. She said she worked here."

"Yes. Thank you. She's left for the day, unfortunately." The lady flitted her eyes like she was averting a question. "Please look around. If you have any questions, please ask."

I shuffled around and browsed the shelves. Liane went to the kid's section, probably looking at something her daughter Lily would like. I went over to the Fantasy. A lot of the books were old paperbacks—the small standards first production in mass marketing unlike the newer, bigger books. I picked up a few of my favorites like Jim Butcher and Terry Brooks, checking out the old covers and quality before wandering to the Horror section and flipping through some of the Stephen King I hadn't read.

There was something about the smell of books, like trapped memories trying to escape. Old books carry treasures, fingerprints of those who once owned them and loved them. I thumped through the old paperbacks admiring the art skillfully hidden in certain chapters. They didn't have sketches in books anymore. I missed that.

The edge of the aisle had a shelf for employee picks. It didn't look like there were many employees. Some of the books I didn't recognize, but I did see an Ender's Game sticking near the bottom and it made me smile. I picked up the book. It was the original cover version, the one I remember reading, with the bold lettering and grave game ship. It only had small turned up corners and held its condition very well, but I could see the worn spine. Someone read it and liked it, from what I could see.

"Nice pick," I said to the invisible employee. I glanced down at the employee's name. "Adrian—na," I breathed the last syllable. "Adrianna."

A vision of a field crossed my mind. A playful conversation about books. I see her face, her smile clear in my mind. But her favorite book was Jane Eyre. I read it for her. She asked me to. And here I was staring at the book I recommended.

"It can't . . ." I said aloud. "Adri isn't here. This isn't her store. This can't be." I shook my head, but it was possible. Did I know she worked in a bookstore? Yes. I knew that. But it was too coincidental. It was wishful thinking, but of course it was wishful thinking, this whole experience had been wishful thinking. My heart panged and all good sense left my body.

I snapped my fingers, like an idiot, trying to get the store owner's attention. "Hey, hey."

I looked over my shoulder. There wasn't anyone around me. I went back to the counter, still with the book in my hand. The polite woman came over and smiled.

"This book," I showed her. "It's one of your employee's favorites?"

"Yes."

"Is she here?"

"Sorry, no." The lady sighed. "She went home for the day."

"She worked earlier?"

"Well, yes." Her eyes crinkled at the edges. "You returned her book." The woman took me in, like she was looking at me for the first time, not saying anything for a few long seconds. "Do you know Adri?"

"Adri." Her name out of my mouth sounded strange, but out of her mouth it sounded perfect. "Adri. Yes. I mean, I think so. Where is she?" I feathered my hand through my hair. No way was this real. "I can't believe it."

And in those words, the world stopped. My knees went weak. I completely froze and forgot to breathe. My Adri worked in a bookstore. She knows my favorite book is Ender's Game. She read it. Did she tell me she read it? No. She never told me.

"Can't believe what?" Liane saw me wobble. "Whoa there, soldier. What happened? Simon?"

"How do you know Adri?" the lady asked again.

Liane's face brightened. "Is Adri here?"

The sharp dressed lady came around the corner and waved me to a wall near the entrance. "Do you know this Adrianna?"

My eyes went to where she pointed to see a group photo with the employees who worked in the store. There, on the right, in a black floral dress, her leg propped at a modelish angle, a wide smile on her face, like she was mid-laugh—stood my Adri.

I put my hands to my face and wept.

Fourteen

Simon gazes out at the nighttime lights of Portland, his warm coffee cooling in his hands.

A figure he immediately recognizes runs toward him changing his focus.

"What's wrong?" Simon lifts his arms as he sees Adri crossing the Tilikum Bridge.

Adri runs and embraces him, knocking his coffee cup to the ground.

Simon strokes her hair, shocked to see her. "I've missed you. Where have you been? It's been months."

"Doesn't matter." Adri's words muffle in his shirt.

"Are you hurt?"

"Only on the inside."

"You don't need to tell me." Simon presses his cheek next to her head. "I've got you."

They stand together as the river winds sweep around them.

"He's getting married." Adri whispers into Simon's shirt.

"The Miah guy who broke your heart?"

"Yes," she exhales.

"Well, that's soon."

Adri nods her head. "I didn't ask details. I learned from a friend. He didn't have the guts to tell me himself."

Simon pulls back to look at her and sweeps the hair from her face. "He was a jerk to you, remember? We talked about this."

"But, it's different when you hear it."

"Lots of girls I dated are married now."

"But, did you ever give over your heart?"

Simon hesitates. "No."

"Why?"

Simon heaves a breath. "You know why."

Adri shakes her head. "If you are real and you do live somewhere, then you have to forget about this dream."

"No." Simon looks in her eyes. "I don't work like that." He lifts his arms up. "This is where I live. This is Portland. It's real—you can find it on maps. I'm real. I'm so real. Dammit, Adri. Why won't you believe it?"

"It's not possible."

"Why not?"

Adri feels the tears again. "You couldn't be real."

Simon cuddles around her. "Believe in the impossible. Just believe. We dream together. That's not possible either."

"If you were real, you'd know way too much about me." She curls back into him.

"And I don't forget anything." Simon laughs. "Miah is missing the best thing ever created. I'd gladly punch him for you."

Adri giggles slightly in the tears. "I'd like that. I'm afraid, Simon."

Simon rests his chin on the top of her head and breathes. "Believe in me."

Simon stands alone near the tree, his name still mars the trunk, now grown over the years. He brushes his thumb above where Adri's name was awkwardly scratched.

He looks at the valley. Adri was just here, he thought. Wasn't she? Where did she go?

"Adri?" he calls. "Adri! Where are you?"

"Are you okay?" the nice lady asked me. She grabbed on to Liane's arm, who was admiring the picture and jumping up and down. "Is he okay?"

"More than okay," Liane answered for me and spontaneously hugged the owner. "Where is this girl?"

The woman—Annette, according to her nametag—went back to her counter. "Now, before I give you any information, I need to know more about what's going on."

"Sure." Liane started to answer when I stopped her.

"Wait." I shoved out a hand from my face, still wet with tears. "It's my story."

"See, he's been searching—" Liane started again, but I shot her a glance which shut her up pretty quickly. It was the 'I'm telling Dad' look every sibling knows.

"I'm Simon Moon. I've known Adri for years, but I didn't know where to find her. I've been searching for her. I've flown in from Portland today to find her, and I only have today. I have to fly back tomorrow."

Liane jumped in. "It was the viral video she was in that made her—"

"Lee. My story." I cut her off again.

"I'm just so excited Sy. You found her."

Annette lowered her eyes below her reading glasses. "You flew here from Portland? How did you know where to look?"

"It was not easy." I quickly threw in some details about the Google map quest and the skyping.

Annette put her hand to her chest. "I don't know whether to be excited about your discovery or very nervous. This whole situation with the video has been such an incredible stress on her. She canceled her media and broke her phone."

"And that's why you couldn't find her." Liane pointed a finger at me. "She made it harder to find her."

"But you can see why," Annette interrupted. "Who is there she can trust? Many have found her a celebrity and want her picture. It's been scary for her. And to be so humiliated."

"But that's how I got here," I returned. "It was the video that gave me a clue to where she might be. I have to find her."

Annette considered me. "You do look like a good kid. Give me a minute." She walked away to the back office.

"I can't believe this, Sy. It was the girl I talked to at the café. It's the same girl." Liane went back to the picture. I followed.

"She wears glasses. Did you know that?"

"Vaguely," I muttered. "Though, she never wears glasses in the dreams. Doesn't matter. She's adorable."

Liane laughed. "Adorable? I think that's the first time I've ever heard you use that word."

"Lee. I'm losing my mind. Look at her." My finger traced the picture. "She thinks I'm a figment of her imagination. How do I do this?"

"We'll find her house and surprise her," Liane smiled. "You know, like any normal person would."

"She looks smart in glasses." I ran over her name in the description. "Adrianna Freshwater." I laughed. "Freshwater?"

"What?" Liane inspected the writing. "That's her last name?"

"She did tell me. Do you still have the journal?"

Liane rummaged in her backpack. "It's right here," and handed it to me.

I grabbed it and flipped through until I caught the name Freshwater scribbled on the side. "She did tell me, but I didn't know."

"Well, but how would you ever guess that was her last name."

"Good point. I've never met a Freshwater."

Liane giggled. "Well, I think it's beautiful."

Annette walked back over with a tall, blonde man wearing half-rimmed glasses. "Brody can help you."

"Hey." Brody extended his hand out for a shake, which both Liane and I took.

"Brody works here. He knows where Adri lives."

Brody had a huge grin on his face, shaking his head. "And I have a car."

"Great!" I shook his hand harder. "Holy mother, this is happening."

Brody turned to Annette. "You got this?"

"Oh sure." Annette winked. "You came right before closing time. Brody usually helps close."

"There's a poetry slam at nine that I'd love to attend. This helps me out." He made a small chuckle and I joined him. "Should we go?"

I suddenly forgot how to walk.

"Come on." Liane grabbed my shoulder and pushed me to the exit.

Brody drove a small Volkswagen beetle parked on the street a few shops down.

"Slug bug Yellow." Liane punched me in the arm like a ten-year-old.

I was numb to the pain of her weakling slug.

Liane climbed in the back, while I slid into the front seat. Once Brody started the car, he said, "You two are old friends of Adri? That's what Annette told me."

"Not me," Liane jumped in. "He is. Simon came all the way from Portland to see her, once we found her in Chicago."

He pieced it together. "You mean, from the video? I'm impressed. That's gutsy to come all the way to Chicago to find a girl."

"She's not just a girl," I mumbled as Brody swerved around a parking car. I didn't finish my thought.

"I was working with her when the vid went viral," Brody added slowing for a red light. The bug rattled to a stop. "I've been worried about her. I've never seen her upset to the point of being physically ill. She nearly lost her dinner in my passenger seat."

"She sat in this seat?" I sounded like a little boy, marveling the worn leather

"Yes." Brody moved the car back into first gear and it shot out again in traffic. "We get along well."

"Where does she live?"

He waves his left hand. "Over on Alder, not far."

I grew familiar with Chicago from the rain streaked window. A lot of lights, and churches, and trees, and brick. And there were a lot of pizza places. The gray sky had settled into dark lamp-lit streets. We turned left again. The maze of grid life was different from the quaint suburban living near me, but the free spirit expression felt the same. I could see the monolithic skyscrapers in the background, but I hadn't reached them yet. They were like the mountains in Colorado, standing and protecting much like a castle guarding its kingdom.

A question came to my mind . . . *what next?*

The question was never what would happen next, it was always about find her now. Here I was, traveling to her house, to her actual living space. What next is not the question I should think about. I quickly smelled around me. I hadn't showered. I didn't smell great. Did I even think about that? I checked my breath. Not bad, but it needs to be better. I looked in the small side mirror. My hair was sticking up again, doing its own thing.

Liane patting my shoulder. She must have seen me checking myself. "You look fine. I don't think she would care."

"Doesn't matter." I ran my hands through my hair trying to fix the problem and gave up. Yeah, I guess it didn't matter.

Brody made another left down a tiny street. Cars lined every inch of space. "Oh, there's one." He went forward, heaved sharp on the wheel before swerving back in a very tight parallel. He was good. "The hornet can fit anywhere," he said predicting my response.

I got out and flipped my seat forward so Liane could get out from the back seat. The rain was really starting to come down now. I was kind of glad now that my hair wouldn't be an issue, just a mop of wet hair and a perfect excuse.

"This way," Brody beckoned, and we followed him up the street to an iron-gated house. We moved through the gate to a small door below the stairs.

As we grew closer to the walkway, my heartbeat thumped harder and harder. I was so close to her. So close. My vision blurred at the thought of everything I was about to see. My palms sweat. My muscles twitched with nervous energy. Every step weighed heavier and heavier. I was here. Adri was here and I would see her and . . . and . . . my mind blanked. And everything!

"What are you doing here?" Brody asked as he approached the door.

"I was talking with Adri."

Adri. Everything was just becoming too real. My head started swimming again. "She's here?"

The man scanned me, quickly casting judgment, and turned back to Brody. "We were just talking."

Brody checked the door. It was locked. He knocked not as gently as I would have liked. "Adri?"

This was real, my heart said to me again.

A few painful seconds passed. No one came to the door.

Brody reached around a shrub and produced a key.

"She told you where a key was hidden?" the man threw this statement out like an accusation.

Brody continued without responding and unlocked the door. "Adri?" He pushed through and we followed. "Adri, you here?"

I walked into a small living room, furnished in the college ramshackle style. Knick knacks of two different lives were nicely placed on surfaces, dressing up the space with two distinct personalities. I smiled. A charm smothered every sense I had. It was much like my place—a place to leave your stuff, but not a home.

What was I doing here? I examined the apartment. This was where she lived. I considered the gently crumpled pillow on the couch. Is that where she slept? Where she dreamt? The connection I tried so hard to have with her just the other night, did I reach her here?

Brody continued inspecting the place. I was so distracted I didn't notice the argument between the two men. I stood near the couch listening to my heart thump, expecting her to appear out of one of the doors, seeing me with her eyes for the first time.

I felt a tug on my arm, taking me out of my cloud back to earth. I looked over at Liane.

"I don't think she's here," she whispered. "That must be an ex or something."

My head shot back up. "Of course." My head returned to their conversation. "Miah."

Liane didn't say anything, though her eyes opened wide, taking in every truth I had written in what she had thought was a fictional journal of dreams. I knew she was impressed with how names and places were clicking together just as much as I was.

"We were just talking," the man explained with big, unnecessary arm movements.

"But she threw you out." Brody was in the small kitchen now. "She's not here. And you can't be here."

"You are trespassing just as much as I am."

"I have permission, you don't."

The man sank down on the couch. "Look. She was just here. I don't know where she went. I'm waiting for her to return."

"Where did she go?" I heard myself say without thinking. Both men stopped and stared at me.

"I don't know," the man said. "She was mad, but she doesn't stay mad for long."

Brody came back from the kitchen. "Listen, Miah, you can't be in here."

I heaved. I was right. Miah. The Jeremiah I made fun of in all those dreams. This was the man I had all the fear about. He looked like I thought he might, with the scruffy face and wild hair, but now I had a face for the name, and I wasn't as afraid of him as I had been. Names have a bigger presence as names, nearly forgetting that they are people too. They eat, and drink, and use the bathroom just like the rest of us.

"Miah?" It was a voice from behind us that made me turn.

A woman with dark waves and stern eyes came in.

"Why are you all in my house?" She walked in and threw her coat on the couch. "Get out. I didn't invite you in here."

"I'm here for Adri, Pauline. *We* were just talking." Miah stated.

The woman named Pauline quickly scanned Miah up and down. "I doubt Adri asked you to stay."

"Hey." Miah stood up again. "This doesn't concern you."

"The hell it doesn't. You're trespassing." She shoved him. "You can take your friends out of here." She grabbed Brody's arm. "But you can stay."

"Oh, I'm not his friend." I motioned to Miah standing there. "I actually hate the guy. I promised to punch him if I got the chance."

Miah studied me. "I don't even know you."

My heart thumped in my ear. Something was about to snap in me, and I needed to keep it reigned in, to keep control, like the Incredible Hulk. I'm not one to lose it, but I knew the heartache this man caused the girl I loved. "I know you better than you think."

Pauline scanned me and didn't say anything, just stared. She took in my sister, who stood by the window trying to stay out of the way.

Miah walked forward toward me, his chin propped up. "And who are you to care about Adri?"

I didn't say anything at first. I mean, who was I to be so important? I didn't date her for months like he did. I didn't break her heart. I'm this stranger that hopped on an airplane to find her. "I'm Simon," was all I could say.

"What did you say?" Pauline grabbed my arm. "Wait, what?"

I felt fear from my head to my toes. "I'm . . . Simon?"

"Stop." She shoved me now.

"Simon." Miah flashed with rage. I guess he did know my name.

And now the whole room turned to me and stared, even my sister.

Pauline put her hands to her face. "Oh my gawd. Oh my gawd. Oh my gawd," she kept repeating.

Miah still stood way too close to me, sizing me up. "You were the guy Adri was seeing while we were dating."

"Wait. Really?" I didn't know that side of the story.

Without expecting it, a fist came at me and I felt the pounding force drive into my left cheek. I toppled backward, hitting against the side table. Liane was there quickly.

"Are you okay?" Liane checked my face.

"Miah. What the hell—" Pauline came over to me. "Are you okay? Do you need some ice?"

I rubbed my jaw. "Maybe?"

"I'll get it." Liane popped up. Pauline motioned to the kitchen.

"I got a text." Pauline rummaged through her bag and whipped out her phone. The case had more sparkles than should be allowed. Her thumb did some scrolling. "There's a guy named Simon looking for your friend," she read aloud. "I got this from Danny about twenty minutes ago. His friend Greg contacted—"

"Greg!" Liane shouted from the other room. "The guy. In the house, that guy."

I understood what she was saying, and it clicked. She came rushing back in with a few ice cubes in a wet paper towel. "Yeah, sorry. This is my kid sister, Lee." I don't know why I felt I needed to introduce her.

Pauline's concern poured over me. The whole room had frozen and I didn't know what to do. I didn't like everyone staring at me. I shrugged in a nervous motion.

"Let me help you up." Pauline lifted a hand to me. Liane was there too, both lifting me back to the sofa. I placed the wet ice on my cheek and glared at Miah.

"Simon." Pauline evaluated my face. She gently pinched my cheeks and my lips went together like a fish. I let this happen, even though it hurt my bruising jaw. "Simon."

"Yish?" My yes came out as a weak question in my fishy face. She let go and walked away into the next room.

Miah came closer. "Who are you, Simon?" He spat my name out of his mouth.

I started massaging my cheeks. "I know who you are, Jeremiah." I wasn't about to call him 'Miah' like a chump. "I know exactly who you are."

"How?" He made another step toward me. "What did she tell you?"

"Enough."

"Enough, huh." Miah's face reddened with anger.

Truth though, Adri didn't talk much about Miah, her real boyfriend, while she and I didn't exist. She casually mentioned things here and there that made the blood in my veins icy with jealousy. I remember very clearly the day he broke her heart.

And here I felt very out of body, as I stared at a living, breathing person. He was nothing I expected, nothing like me. His cool indie vibe was way cooler than my introverted geekiness. And yet, if there was a competition, I knew I had won. He had lost. He had given her up, went a different direction, and I was pretty sure he was now married.

I owned up my position. "I'm not Adri's boyfriend."

Miah relaxed a little but didn't step back. "She has more class than dating you."

"Wow, you don't even know me."

"You're after my Adri."

My hands expressively shot out. "She is not yours. She was yours and you chose someone else. And yes, I'm glad about that."

It was like Miah's eyes started on fire.

"I think you have somewhere else to be." The voice was Brody's. I had forgot he was in the room. "You don't need to be here. Go home to your wife."

Miah faced him not saying anything.

"Simon." I looked back and Pauline was in the doorway. "Simon, come in here, please. And you," she shot Miah a glance. "Get out of my house."

I watched Pauline grow taller in front of me. Miah's face paled.

"Go home, Miah. Adri is better off without you. I know you sold the video, you piece of shit. So you can leave and forget where we live. Go live off of someone else's humiliation. Hope you feel great knowing you destroyed something precious with someone amazing. Go!"

This was all news to me, but I felt a strange heat burn in my face, like this private information made the situation worse.

Miah remained silent but let the door swing closed behind him.

I walked and walked. The rain was already pounding and I didn't have my umbrella.

I eventually went into a corner Starbucks and ordered an ordinary coffee. As I dumped two packets of sugar in there, I formed a plan.

California needed more planning. I knew Viv would take me if I asked. I could go to my parent's house if I were super desperate. My canopy bed was still set up in my old room, as if I had never left.

But Michigan would take planning as well. I couldn't afford the Uber.

The sugar crystals swirled until they disappeared and fell to the bottom. I watched them fall. I wanted to disappear, but not completely, like sugar in coffee. Chicago had become my home. Could I stay here? I didn't want to go to California, even with its glorious sun and gorgeous tans. That wasn't what I wanted. But I needed time to heal, somewhere away from here.

And I knew where to go.

I reached for my phone—but it was still in a bag of rice on my counter. I felt like I was missing my right arm. I wished I had it. I didn't want to surprise Julsie, but I didn't have much of a choice.

I could find her online, but I deleted all my social media.

I pulled out my computer and logged on to the generous network Starbucks supplied. I opened my email and sent Julsie a quick message, hoping she might open it while I journeyed there. I thought of sending Pauline an email too but shut my laptop instead. I could email her later.

I took my cooling coffee, stuffed my computer in my bag full of random things and headed toward the Ravenswood stop in the rain. The rain didn't bother me so much. It was still the cold rain of a warming spring, but not freezing like the stinging rain of winter. I actually welcomed it during my walk. The sips of coffee warmed my throat as the caffeine quickly went to my head, helping clear my thoughts.

The fact was, I wasn't ready to give up my life in Chicago, but I couldn't face things as they were. I needed space. Julsie's place would give me everything I asked for. I'd stayed there a few times, during weekend writing retreats and once after Christmas, when the Chicago snow had kept me from Michigan to see my folks.

It wasn't too late in the evening, and my stomach missed the scrambled egg sandwich I didn't get to eat. I made a quick diversion into Dunkin, grabbed me a glazed, and continued on my way.

Within a few minutes, I walked into the station, glad to get out of the rain, and purchased fare to Lake Forest. I didn't have to wait long, and soon I found my seat and rested my head against the glass, watching the streaks of rain move across the glass windows of the train.

My heart ached in strange places, longing for something I didn't have and couldn't have. It was something I missed terribly, something not exactly real, but I ached for it—

something or someone that had no connection to this world that was such a mess right now.

"Oh, Simon," I said aloud to no one at all.

Fifteen

"Simon Moon."

Simon looks away from the fathoms of space. "Hmm?"

"How does one get the last name Moon?" Adri sits cross-legged before the glass window of the space station, staring toward the Earth. "Last names come from somewhere. Did you get it from the Moon?"

Simon crinkles his brow. "What? That's a weird question."

Adri laughs. "I don't know. It was silent, and I didn't want to waste time in silence."

Simon stretches until he is flat on the glass looking at the stars. "I don't know. Sometimes silence is welcomed."

"I don't like silence."

"Sometimes the world has too much noise." Simon rests his hands palms flat. "You shouldn't be afraid of a little silence."

"I'm not afraid," Adri retorts. "I didn't want to waste the time I have with you."

A small smirk creeps up Simon's face, but he tries to hide it. "Asking about my last name is a waste of talk. My dad was a Moon, his dad was a Moon. They're not astronauts. People think it's Korean, but my dad's heritage is Scottish. My mom happens to be Filipino, so people think it's an Asian last name, but it's not for me." Simon squints Adri's direction. "Is that why we're in space?"

"Maybe," Adri looks out. "But I think I fell asleep during Nova."

"Oh." Simon turns his back and faces her. "You may be avoiding your own question."

Adri straightens up. "What do you mean?"

"I don't think I've ever known your last name."

"Does it matter?"

"It might."

Adri lifts her eyebrow. "It's McGillicuddy."

Simon scowls. "No, it's not."

"Poindexter."

"I don't think you're saying the name right."

"Freshwater."

"Now you're just making up names."

Adri gives an incredulous look. "Well, I guess you wouldn't believe me even if I told you."

"It's probably Johnson, or Smith, which means I would never be able to find you."

Adri uncrosses her legs and rests on her elbows facing the glass front. "What if, let's say, you searched and searched for my name and found me in some city somewhere and met me in the daylight. What if I wasn't this?" She gestures to herself.

Simon blinks and turns toward her, propping his head on his hands. "What do you mean? Do you think I'd be disappointed?"

Adri doesn't reply and looks forward.

"I promise you I wouldn't be disappointed."

"How can you promise that?"

"So easy." He rests his head against the glass.

Adri sits up and moves next to him. Her head lays opposite to Simon and sees the large skylight revealing the moon. "I'm not a fan of myself right now."

"I wouldn't care what stage of mess you're in." He catches her eyes. "It's not about mess. I know you well enough I would care about you in all stages."

Adri stares back. The invisible bond between them pulls tight as they both stare beyond the color in the others' eyes.

"See?" Simon finally says.

"See what?"

"Silence is okay."

Adri's Apartment

Pauline threw up her hands as the door shut behind Miah. "I can't believe Miah showed up at my apartment." Her frazzled head shook. "Simon, seriously. Come over here."

I walked ceremoniously forward into what I could only fathom would be Adri's bedroom as Pauline closed the door.

I took a glance around. It was not super tidy, but not messy, just lived in—it was a room of a writer, a reader, an artist. Stacks of books near her bed held a cup of pens and pencils on top. Thrown clothes lay near the closet, with kicked-off shoes. And the pile of soft, plushy animals near her pillows on her bed made me smile.

A fragrance of some light citrus hit my senses, the scent of her. A fresh, clean scent I didn't know but wanted to desperately.

Pauline rounded on me. "Simon. Simon what?"

"Simon Moon." I breathed. "Why are we in here?"

"I had to find something to make sure you were who I think you are."

"What do you mean?"

"First, tell me your story."

So, I tried, a short glazed-over version. "Don't think I'm crazy. I've been searching for Adri for years. We . . . I thought Adri was a figment of my imagination. And then there she was on YouTube!" I felt emotion in my voice but held it down. My mind clouded. I didn't know what I was saying. "She was there. I saw her, and I had to find her, but she was impossible to find."

"But you found Greg," Pauline added.

"I found the house." My hands ran through my hair. Everything sounded crazy. "And she wasn't there. Did you know I flew from Portland?" I waved my hand in the air like a little boy sailing it through the wind. "And I only have today to find her. I have to fly back tomorrow. But she wasn't there. She wasn't."

I felt the emotion again, and this time I didn't hold it back. I sat on Adri's bed and put my hands to my face. "Where is she? I can't believe I'm here. I'm here. She's real and I'm here and she doesn't know."

Pauline held something in her hand, a notebook. "Here," she whispered, and handed me it.

I grabbed it, not having any idea what it could be. The old sketchbook had its pages worn smooth from obvious use. I squinted at the drawing and flinched.

"It's me," I exclaimed. "She drew me. She said she would. I . . ." I lost speech and put my head down. "You believe me," I choked out. "Don't you?"

Pauline wiped her running mascara. "She said something similar to me earlier."

"Where is she?"

"I . . ." Pauline sniffed. "I'm not sure. She's never gone long, probably went to Starbucks. I don't think she planned on seeing Miah."

"Miah." I half-laughed his name. "The thing is, if he hadn't've posted the video, I wouldn't have found her. It's his fault."

Pauline laughed. It was hearty and cute and made me laugh back.

"What do I do?" I asked her. "What do I even say?"

Pauline came and sat down by me. "I don't think you need to say anything. She knows you. This is the proof," she flicked the notebook, "she's just as crazy as you are."

"I need her," I blurted out. "She needs to be here. Should I go find her?"

"No." Pauline pulled out her phone from her back pocket. "I'll contact some people. Do you need to eat?"

"Probably." But I didn't want to.

"I'll go find you some food. What's your sister's name?"

"Lee . . . Liane." Pauline went to leave. "Can I just," I sheepishly said, feeling the emotion in my throat again. "Can I sit in here for another minute?"

Pauline grinned. "She'll be here soon. I'm sure of it." She walked out the door, letting it close behind her.

With the snick of the latch, an overwhelming emotion swept through me as I sat in Adri's private sanctuary. This was where she made her home, her life. The citrusy smell crept around me again, a clean smell that excited my senses. I let it fill me with memories that were not mine, but that I almost knew. I scanned her room, not wanting to see too much detail, but enough to know her better, something to connect us.

I saw a heap of green, the remainder of the stunning green dress she had worn in the video. I studied the dress casually thrown into the small trash can. The color was much better here than what the video had captured. A sudden pang of envy hit me in the chest. I wished I could have been there with her. We could have done so many things together. We could date. I could date her.

I casually picked up the dress and looked at it. A want washed over me so deeply I nearly lost my balance. I needed to find her. Some whispering urge made me touch the chain still hanging around my neck—my mother's shell I had given her. It was a touchstone of not only my mother, but my promise to show it to Adri someday. And I would.

I wiped the last tear from my eye and walked out the door to the living room.

"You okay?" Liane stood from the couch, where she had been talking with Brody. "Pauline ordered some Chinese."

"Nice," was all I could say. "I'm cool. Okay." I went to the blinds and peeked out. It was still raining and I couldn't see much around the bushes. I wanted to see her. The hunger was there. I needed her. I missed her.

"I messaged a few people," Pauline said from the kitchen. "Danny is coming over. He's my boyfriend."

"Cool."

"So," Brody broke my train of thought. "Can I hear the whole story?" he asked. "Liane has told me bits and pieces, but I'm not understanding it."

I flatlined. I had nothing but the truth to tell him. "I've known Adri for a long, long time, since we were kids. I've been searching for her ever since, and when I watched the video . . ."

"Oh," Brody stated. "That makes a lot more sense. Liane was saying something about dreaming."

"Yeah, don't worry about that." I laughed it off and changed the subject. "You work with her?"

Brody brightened. "Yes. We're pretty close, both writers and poets. She would hate it if she knew we were talking about her."

"Fair enough. Tell me about Miah."

Brody choked. "Him? Are you worried about him?"

"Well, kind of." I rubbed my still red jaw. "He's been with Adri for years."

"I never liked him." Brody waved his hand. "No, no. You don't have anything to worry about. Adri is fresh air and Miah wanted her to smell of coffee grinds. Am I making sense?"

"A bit," I added.

Brody's stare intensified. "Adri doesn't fit a mold. She is unique and charming. It was everything that makes her so bright that Miah didn't like. It's like he wanted her to be something she wasn't. Miah is high-maintenance and worldly, Adri is the simplest girl on the planet." Brody rolled his eyes, like he has been waiting to talk about Miah for years. "Oh, and Miah never believed in her. He hated her artistic inclinations. He never encouraged anything. The bookstore was never a place to be forever, just a stepping stone to a quote unquote 'real' job." I could tell that part bothered him greatly. Brody took a deep breath and exhaled slowly. "Miah was a poison I was very glad to see gone. Pauline too, right?" He gestured toward Pauline in the kitchen.

Pauline walked in still looking at her phone. "Oh yeah. Total ass hat," and went back to her messaging.

Brody nodded. "Adri tried to adapt to the change, and tried to be this person, but it made her miserable. She disappeared for a while."

I tried to think of the years of dreaming and what time this might have been, but details ran together.

Brody continued, "In the end, she couldn't. It smothered her vibrant spirit and she couldn't be that person. He dumped her. Probably started dating his wife while still with Adri. I don't know the details. But I'm glad to have my Adri back. She is sunlight. It's all those charming details that make her genesis, and how could anyone not love that? It is her story, her mythology. She needs writing and art to truly be Adri." Brody reached for a glass of water before him. "So, you can say I'm not a fan of Miah."

My heart swelled at Brody's confirmation of Adri's character. The exact person I knew and loved. I glanced back to the door. Where was she? I needed her here. I had to see this sunlight for myself. "I would never want to change her."

"Good to hear." Brody sipped from his glass.

I knew I was growing impatient. "Can you call her? Maybe I should. Should I call her?"

"Her phone's busted." Pauline motioned to a bag of rice unceremoniously tossed on the table.

"But there are other ways of getting a hold of her, right?"

Pauline came and sat on the arm of the couch, propping up her feet. "She deactivated all her social media after the video went viral."

"Email." Liane joined in. "She has to have email, right?"

Pauline brightened. "Yes." Still with her phone in her hand, she started clicking and swiping around. "I'll look. Brody? Do you guys have something at work you use?"

Brody set down his glass. "I mean, not really. Annette is rather archaic when it comes to bookkeeping."

"I don't know if I have an email. Oh, I have an old one. I'll try it."

There was a knock at the door, and my heart jumped into my throat. Pauline rushed to get it. It was delivery and she went about setting it on the coffee table before us.

"Where are your plates?" I asked trying to be as helpful as possible. Pauline started to wave her hand to refuse, but I stood and went to the kitchen to look anyway.

"Oh, we have paper plates in the pantry there," she indicated. Paper was a much better idea for this.

I opened the pantry door and searched around until I found something. I took in at a glance the different variety of food they had. There wasn't much, cans of this and that, but the cereal struck me.

"Frankenberry?" I questioned.

"That's Adri's," Pauline remarked behind me grabbing napkins and utensils. "She buys it every fall, like four boxes, and then works through it slowly."

"This girl," I uttered, completely charmed.

"Will you use chopsticks?"

I held out the plates. Pauline had pairs of nice chopsticks she obviously used and took care of. "Umm, sure. Though, I'm not very coordinated. People assume I am."

"Well, I do own forks, too." She laughed. "They are here if you need them."

We returned and sat around the little coffee table sharing the chicken lo mein. The door opened again, and I quickly stood up. A tall man with crazy curls leaping around his head walked in with a big, bright smile.

"Hey," he called. Pauline jumped up and kissed him.

"This is Danny."

"Hey," I saluted with my chopsticks. I felt foolish standing, so I sat on the couch again and began fiddling with how to hold sticks properly. I tried my best to eat, but I wasn't in the mood. I mean, where was she?

The slight conversations came around me of this and that, but it mumbled into absent white noise. I only picked up on things when it had to do with Adri. I was consumed. Where was she?

Soon Pauline picked up on the absence too and kept checking her phone.

I was fidgeting, Liane could tell. I leaned to her. "I can't stay here. I just can't."

"We are here, in her apartment. I don't think we can get much closer."

"Where is she? I feel like I should be out looking for her."

"She's not a little girl. She will come home."

"I didn't get an email back," Pauline said putting down her phone.

"Is there somewhere she would go? A library or something? Would she go back to the bookstore?"

Brody shook his head. "I doubt it. Is her computer gone?"

Pauline jumped up and ran to Adri's room. "I don't see it," she shouted from the other room. "Her computer bag is gone."

"What does that mean?" Liane asked.

"She probably went writing," Brody answered pushing around his noodles. "There are a few coffee houses around. It's getting late for those though. Things close."

"Maybe pizza places?" I asked, thinking only of cliché Chicago references.

"Sometimes she rides the train for a while, goes in town, walks around." Pauline shoved a big piece of orange pork into her mouth. "I mean, she cooould be annaywhay-o."

I stood without meaning to. "I have to go look. I can't stay here. Should I look around here?"

Liane stood too. "We aren't far actually. Just over on Irving."

I surveyed the three people frozen, eyeballing me. "What should I do? I have to find her."

Pauline finished chewing. "She doesn't disappear. She always shows up. I doubt she went far. I'm sure she didn't head to Michigan."

I panicked. "What's in Michigan?"

"Her folks."

"I can't eat. I can't sleep."

"But you should," Liane nudged me. "You should sleep." Each word was pushed out deliberately.

"But I don't know if she'll be around. It doesn't work like that."

Brody put down his plate. "I'll drive you around."

"And miss your poetry whatever it is?" I asked, remembering we were ruining his plans.

"I wasn't married to it," he returned.

Pauline straightened up. "And Danny and I will start with some of our friends."

"Thank you," I stated.

"Please eat something," Pauline gesture. "I promise, I'm doing what I think would help."

"I know," or did I? I didn't know anything. I sat back down and examined my plate of food. "When is our flight tomorrow?" I asked Liane.

"Five."

"So, that means you have until three," Brody answered. "Because you have to get back to the airport and through lovely security."

"But she will be here tonight," Pauline interjected. "I swear. She will be back." She quickly popped up and went to the kitchen returning with a fork. "Here."

It was hard to refuse the food now. Pauline knew how hard this was for me. The fork meant more than just eating, it meant friendship. "Thank you," and accepted the utensil.

She leaned over placing her hand on my knee, controlling the fidget. "You have landed, Simon. She's here. She hasn't run away. You now know where she is, where we are, always. Everything in your life from this moment forward has changed direction. Don't lose hope."

"Whoa," I exhaled. I twirled the long noodles with my clean fork and took a bite.

The Lake Forest stop came close and I got ready to exit.

"Sorry, can I get a picture with you?" a girl in her teens asked me. I had seen her on the train staring. She might have even taken a picture pretending to text on her phone. This was all new to me. I didn't know how to answer at first.

"Sure," I finally said. "Would you like me to bend over too?"

The girl went pale. "Oh, sorry. I guess I didn't think of that."

"It's cool." I leaned next to her and did a cute peace sign, that I figured was my thing now. Peace, love, and panties. The girl snapped the picture.

I casually walked away from the station and my brief moment of fame, down the beautifully lit streets and toward well-manicured front lawns. Lake Forest was not a neighborhood I worried about walking in the dark. It felt like a Hollywood movie set, probably because several movies were filmed here. It had the perfect atmosphere. I don't think I could ever live in any place so lavish. I was too simple for such extravagance.

My spring jacket was no match for the heavy, drenching rain. I stopped under a tree and rummaged through my bag, pulling out my college hoodie and slipping it on as well. I worried about my computer, so I stuffed everything else around it to protect it. All zipped up and covered, I made my way across the street.

Julsie lived a few good blocks from the station, but nothing not walkable. To live in Chicago, everything needed to be walkable. I was used to it. I enjoyed the walk, the crisp, rain smell refreshed my skin and helped clear my head. My temper had cooled. Miah had stung me but hadn't broken me. It was wrong to kiss him, even in my drunken state, but I realize even now that I know he posted the video. In that moment I wanted, just for a second, to remember him and us. But I no longer needed it. That happiness was artificial. And now, reflecting on the whole time with him, it wasn't a waste of time, but it taught me more about myself and what I needed and wanted from a relationship. I walked forward with confidence. We were even.

The familiar white-gabled home appeared as I rounded Green Bay. The modest dwelling sat quietly tucked across the street from million-dollar well-gated homes. I often caught glimpses between the hedges of what could be, but I liked Julsie's place. There was a lot of charm to it, little things other people wouldn't notice, like the sidewalk winding around her two front trees. I liked that.

I walked up the bricked walkway and to the well-lit white door, a huge contrast from my little, dark dwelling in Chicago.

"Well, sight for sore eyes," Julsie said as she opened the door. "It's my Addy girl. You look like a drowning kitten. Come in, girl. Come in. You couldn't wait to see me again," she laughed.

"Something like that." I came inside her house and accepted the peck on my cheek.

The inside was something out of a home magazine, perfectly placed but cozy.

"The crew is here, just around in the sunroom, if you want to say hello."

I choked. "Crew? Like this? Oh, please no. Really?"

"Oh, yes. It's my turn to host Wine night. I thought I told you."

I tried taking off the hoodie and got stuck somewhere inside. "You might have. I was distracted. I didn't think I would end up here tonight."

"Well, skinny minny," she said, lending me a hand by grabbing the arms and pulling up. "Take off those wet things and head on back here. I'll grab you a plate of food and a warm fuzzy blankie."

I smiled, though my stomach plummeted. The 'Crew' Julsie mentioned were all New York Times best sellers. Maybe I came to the wrong place to hide away. What in the world was I going to say to these people?

I slipped off my soaked shoes and walked through the front room to the parlor built on the side of the house. It was a room completely encased in windows, the rain spattering eerily on the panes, like a teen horror film. Four big, plush chairs had been arranged around. Three were occupied.

I nervously waved my hand stupidly. "Hey."

The room stopped their loud chatter and I received three different greetings.

"Hello there," the red-headed woman raised a glass to me. "Julsie said we might have company. I'm Mona. This is Robert and Charlie."

"Mona Blackwood." I clarified, still breathing, but hardly standing. "I know your work. You won't remember me, but I stood in line at C2E2 for you to sign Wonderlings. I was dressed as Crissha."

Mona laughed. "Of course I remember. You tweeted at me. That was a few years ago, right?"

"Yes," I breathed again. "That's so cool you remember." I addressed the other two in the room. "I'm sorry if I haven't read you guys' stuff."

Mona introduced again. "Charlie Pickner writes screenplays here and Robert Machete is a true crime novelist."

"Oh, I know the name. True crime scares me."

Robert had a barrel laugh, deep and throaty. I liked it.

"Here you go, my girl." Julsie came in with exactly what she promised, a plate of food and a warm blanket. She handed me the plate, then shook out the blanket and wrapped it around my shoulders. "There you go. Now, have a seat."

I checked around. "But where will you sit?" I asked Julsie.

"Right here." She pulled up a little cushion disguised as a table.

I quietly sat down in the puffy, red chair and munched on a carrot stick.

"Would you like a glass?" Charlie motioned to the elegant bottle of wine near to him. "Robert brought it back from Portugal."

"Bringing wine back on a plane from a different country," Robert mentioned raising a glass to me. "It's tricky business."

I waved it off. "Not at the moment," I said through the crunching. "I don't think I'd appreciate it as a delicate art like you fine folk. I'm more in the mood for a shot of whiskey."

The room laughed.

"I have that, too," Julsie mentioned.

"Nah, I'm good." I really wasn't. Emotions were coming, but I blinked them away and picked at the roll on my plate.

"Julsie mentioned your writing," Mona stated.

"Swe didge?" I said with a mouth full of roll. I quickly chewed. "To you guys? Why?"

"I think she believes in your talent."

I glared at Julsie, who wore a tight, white smile. "See? I'm not alone in my thinking."

I swallowed and rested the plate on the arm of the chair. "I always have a few ideas floating around in my head. I've been playing with romance, but lately, I suck at it. I think maybe romance comes better when you're in a relationship."

Mona laughed. "I'm not much for romance either. It's not magical enough."

"Oh, honey, wait." Julsie waved her hands in defense. "My writing is magical. You've met my husband. He is nothing to my imagination."

We all laughed. "Is Gerald here?"

"Of course," Julsie answered. "In the den. Basketball playoffs are happening. I won't see him for a while."

Mona leaned toward Charlie. "It was about time travel. Right?"

"Yes," Charlie piped up. "It's just a short story, but Julsie explained the plot. I think it has screenplay potential."

"But I think it has the concept of a series," Robert added.

"Wait." I took in these accomplished writers in the room. "You were having an argument about me?"

Julsie patted my arm. "Well, when I got your email, I thought I would tell them a little about you."

"And we like to encourage young writers," Mona added. "There is nothing better than inspiring others. I think that is part of my job, part of my young adult genre."

"But you haven't read it?" I returned.

"Not yet." Mona put down her glass. "But Julsie told me where to find it. It's published, right?"

My eyes grew wide. "But only in an online magazine."

"It's a good start." Mona laughed. "My first story was my worst story. It won some little award in small town Georgia and that was how I got my agent. Funny thing, she signed me with that story, but didn't know about all the other projects I would give her. Wonderlings has been my best seller. It's my first series and the first book in that series is my seventh novel. It doesn't happen overnight."

I laughed. "Yeah. Finding time is also a problem."

"But you'll find it." Mona smiled and went back to sipping from her glass.

"Julsie?" a voice from the stairs yelled. Gerald stood near the parlor holding a phone. "Your phone keeps buzzing. I guess it's important."

"Well, my stars." Julsie went over to her husband while the gentle conversation of creativity and first starts filled in the room. I listened until Julsie tapped me on the shoulder.

"Addy? Pauline is trying to find you. I guess some guy is at your apartment wanting to talk with you."

I rolled my eyes. "It's Miah. Do me a favor and don't mention I'm here. Say you haven't seen me. I'll go home tomorrow. I just need some time away."

Julsie nodded and started messaging Pauline back.

Sixteen

"Adri!" Simon yells from the side of the field. The wind picks up, but still no sign of her. He walks to the tree and sits, leaning against the names grown into the wood. "Adrianna," he whispers. "Where are you? I'm here. I'm here."

He sits for what feels like hours staring in the distance, resting his back on the carved names.

Adri emerges on the opposite end.

"Adri?" Simon's heart jumps. He waves. "Adri!"

Adri sees him and waves back.

Simon starts to race toward her. "You're here. We connected."

"What's wrong?" Adri worries. "Why are you running?"

"Adri," Simon pants as he gets closer. "Adri. I found you."

"Yes, right where you always find me—"

"No, you don't get it." Simon grabs her wrist. "Adri. I'm here. Me. I'm here in Chicago."

"You're where?"

"Here. I found you. I'm here."

Adri pulls free, thinking. She grabs her head. "Ugh, stop brain. Stop thinking things."

Simon reaches for her. "I'm here, Adri. It's true."

"Simon, I had a really hard day today." Adri presses at her temples. "Seeing you is all I want. But my stupid brain is trying to make things how I want them. Make me feel better—"

"No. Adri. Stop."

Adri rocks back and forth. "I'm dreaming again. And this is a stupid dream right now."

Simon grips her shoulders, preventing her from rocking. "Please. I've waited for you all night. I talked with Pauline. I was at your apartment. What proof do you need to know I'm real?"

"Simon, this isn't fair. I want this to be real so badly, I don't want to wake up."

Simon grows more animated, more impatient. "The dream is real. I know where you work. I brought my sister here. You talked to her today. The girl in the cafe. You talked with her. I found your green dress in the garbage. You have Frankenberry in your pantry. Hell, there was a hand-drawn picture of me on your bed, staring at me."

Adri takes in his words. "You saw that?" She fidgets with her hands. "What did you think?"

Simon huffs and laughs. "It's good. Really, really good." He smirks, "I think you made my nose a little too big."

Adri slaps him playfully. "It took me a long time to draw you from memory."

Simon rubs the slap away. "It's incredible. I always knew you could draw. Seeing it with my eyes was extraordinary. Do you believe me now?"

Adri looks around her. "I might be persuaded."

Simon slinks in exasperation. "Just tell me where you are. Please. I miss you. I need to see you."

Adri leans her head to the side, considering. "I'm safe."

"Are you still in Chicago?"

Adri squints. "Mostly. I didn't fly off to California, if you were worried about that."

Simon pats his chest in relief. "I was, actually. No one has heard from you. This is the only way I could think to contact you."

"I told Julsie not to say anything to Pauline."

"Who's Julsie?"

"She's a friend."

Simon moves close. "I don't have much time. I want to see you. I want to meet you. I'm so freakin' ready to kiss you, it's an overwhelming thought."

Adri stepped back. "You're serious?"

"Of course," Simon reaches for her hand. "I promised never to lie to you. I'm here. I'm real. Please believe me."

Adri took his hand. "I believe you. I believe you, Simon."

Simon tightens his grip and brings her fingers to his lips and kisses them. "I leave today. I fly back to Portland. I need to find you."

Adri breathes hard. "You're not kidding?"

"No. Not at all." Simon bends his knees feeling the exhaustion drain from him. "I found you. Finally."

The fingers disappear from his hands. Adri has vanished.

"No," he exhales. "No." Simon looks around, knowing Adri had woken up. "Adri!"

My eyes shot open.

"Adri!" His voice ran around in my head.

The pounding in my chest couldn't quiet. Details ran through my head, so many I couldn't keep track.

Simon.

I lay on a foreign pillow, my feet rubbing against incredibly soft sheets. I wasn't at home, not with this much luxury cocooning me. I rolled over to see the old digital clock reading 5:30. Orange from the streetlight filtered quietly through the blinds. The rain had stopped and only the soft drips from the gutters kept the reminder it had rained at all. I curled back into the pillow but didn't close my eyes. I couldn't.

Simon.

This dream felt different, a different kind of dream. Everything was the same, but Simon was different. He was insistent, urgent, no playful flirting, no sarcasm.

I tried to rethink the entire dream, but as I did little things started to float away.

"I'm real," I said out loud. "I'm here. Believe me."

And I did in the dream, I absolutely believed him. The realness was sticking to me, like deep dreaming does.

And he was in my apartment. And that's where I feel my brain took some liberties. How on earth would he be able to find my apartment? I couldn't recall ever mentioning to him where I lived. Why was it important to a fictional character?

But real Simon didn't know I liked Frankenberry. Why would he? Something else I would never have told him. But, come on. Frankenberry. Everyone loves Frankenberry.

And the picture I drew of him. He was right. The nose isn't right.

I straightened on the pillow and stared at the frilly canopy near the ceiling.

I hated how my brain made up things to make me happy. Cruel brain.

He's real. I promised to believe him. Why was I doubting my promise? I closed my eyes, hoping he was still there. I kept running over the details again.

I don't know when I fell back asleep.

I woke and looked at the clock – 8:27. I blinked a few times. I hadn't dreamed. I lay there until the smell of bacon got me up and I tumbled downstairs.

"Morning, sleepyhead." It was Gerald, Julsie's husband. He was obviously much more of a morning person than Julsie. He even had the pancakes stacked nicely and the bacon perfectly crisped. That takes talent and time. I always liked Gerald. I'd met him a few times before. He reminded me of Shephard from Firefly, which made him cooler somehow. "You all had a late night last night."

"Well, I went to bed around midnight. And wrote a little before falling asleep." I took a piece of bacon and let the savory smokiness fill my tired with satisfaction. "When did people leave?"

"No idea," Gerald flipped another pancake. "I was in bed right after the game."

"So good of you." The bacon was heavenly and I stole another one. Soon, Gerald had found me a plate with a pancake on it. Before I knew it, I was drowning it in buttermilk syrup.

Julsie appeared like a ringwraith, poured a small glass of milk, popped a few pills in her mouth and downed them in a ritual habit. Her dark sunglasses told me enough about how she felt this morning. Julsie didn't say a word but grabbed a piece of bacon. She took a bite, then leaned in and kissed her husband on the cheek.

"Hell of a cook," she muttered a few bites in.

"I know what gets you up in the morning."

"You," she pointed a finger at me, "shouldn't have mentioned whiskey."

I looked around me, all innocent. "You can't blame me for your headache. I didn't tell you to get it out."

Julsie leaned on the counter. "What I didn't mention is that bottle, my girl, costs three-hundred dollars. It's for special occasions. I don't get that out for everyone, just you."

My jaw dropped. "My little shot cost like thirty-five bucks."

Julsie went to laugh but grabbed at her temples.

"The headache will pass," Gerald mentioned, cleaning the last of the pancake mix from the bowl. "But the memories will stay."

Julsie giggled. "Or not. Right? I've never seen Robert lose it like that. He's always so composed."

I laughed with her. "I hope you don't change it to Whiskey night, instead of Wine night."

Julsie waved her bacon at me. "I just might." She giggled again then rubbed the bridge of her nose. "And you, young lady, need to let your roommate in on where you're hiding out."

"Oh, right."

"My phone has been buzzing all morning. I think she is worried sick."

"Fine," I said through the pancake. "Let her know I'm here with you and that I'm fine."

Julsie walked about to her bedroom. When she came back, she was typing one-handed while still holding her bacon with the other. She set her phone on the ledge of the island and made her a plate of food.

The sunlight in the kitchen was breathtaking. The high windows let light scatter tiny rainbows from the etched glass. The blue sky of morning slowly began drying the leaves. I could see Julsie's garden from my seat at the island, already full of color and life.

"I didn't know you had a green thumb," I commented to Julsie.

Julsie sniggered. "I don't. That's also Gerald." She started pouring coffee into a mug. "I have something else to occupy my time, it's called a deadline."

Oh, right. Not that I forgot Julsie was a writer, but it wasn't who I knew her as. "How is it going?"

"Not well." Julsie dumped sugar into her coffee and stirred. "I just received my edits back." She lifted her eyebrow and sighed before she took a sip. "I like my editor, but sometimes she doesn't see my vision."

I shrugged. "I wish I had an editor to complain about."

Julsie grinned. "You will, honey. Have you decided what to do with your story yet?"

"My time traveler story?"

"Yes. I thought we gave you good ideas last night."

I smiled. "Oh yes, I really like Charlie's idea, but as you said, it's hard to get others to see the vision."

"Not if you construct it well."

"The idea is these two people exist on the same plane, but at different times, living at the same time, but differently. Only they know, right? At those times they meet, it's so important to write it well. I'm afraid I'll screw it up."

Julsie gave my hand a motherly pat. "You will never know if you don't try."

She had a point. I felt feverish with creativity, with the bacon and the sunshine. "What's out that way?" I pointed toward the garden window.

"There is a park with a beautiful forest and this tree my kids used to climb when they were younger. You should take a walk up there."

I pulled my hair up into a sloppy ponytail. "I think I will. I like trees."

Julsie's phone buzzed next to me. I glanced at the number and didn't recognize it as Pauline.

Julsie learned over. "That's no Illinois area code I recognize. I'll let it go to voicemail." She gave a hearty laugh and I could tell she was starting to feel like herself again.

My eyes opened. "Dammit." I punched the pillow and rolled over on the couch. It was late, or early. I didn't know. I had tried for hours to go to sleep, but the excitement of Adri being here, being so close activated every brain cell and it wouldn't calm no matter what I tried.

I sat up and stared. A rush of frustration came over me and I picked up the pillow and hit it repeatedly against the couch. "Stupid. Stupid. Stupid." I kept whacking the pillow until Liane came out of the bedroom.

"What are you doing?" She pulled the pillow from my hand. "This isn't our stuff."

I put my hands to my head. "She was there, Lee. She was there. I dreamed and she was there, and I told her I was here, and she believes me, I know it. But—"

"But?" Liane sat sideways on the couch toward me.

"I didn't get to tell her where I was. She disappeared too quickly. I think I startled her. I—" I forgot where I was going.

Liane tried rubbing the sleep from her face. It had been a rough night for us both. Brody took us around to all the places we could think of to find Adri. I couldn't ask for any more time from the guy and had him drop us off at midnight. I tried several times to get to sleep.

Back in Colorado, Liane's daughter Lily had a fever and my brother-in-law didn't know exactly what to do. She was up and down talking with him, trying to get the right medicine for her. I think she crashed around 2 AM.

And here I was, waking her for such a stupid reason.

Liane rubbed my arm and simply asked in a scratchy morning voice, "Is there coffee?"

I didn't know where this was leading. "Umm, there's a Keurig."

"That's a start," she grumbled. "Give me a minute."

Liane stood, pulling her mop of bed hair into a knot on the top of her head, and went to the kitchen, clanking around until I heard sizzles of steam.

I lay my head back on the pillow I had previously whipped around. Details were slipping the more awake I became.

"Kay, tell me Sy," Liane called from the kitchen. "What can you remember? What did she say?"

I stared in the direction of the kitchen. "I'm so glad you believe me"

"Of course," her voice carried. She came in with a steaming mug and a handful of sugar packets. "This one's for you. It's all single cup. Keep talking. Tell me details. I'll go make one for me."

I didn't want coffee. I didn't want to be awake. But there was no one in my dream to find. She was still here, in Chicago, somewhere. "She didn't leave," I blurted out. "She said she was thinking about vanishing to California. That's where her sister lives."

"Write it down," she stated from the other room. "Oh," she came back in and rummaged through her bag. "Write it in here."

She handed me my own spiral notebook and then winked before heading back to the kitchen.

I stared at the beat-up journal, got nostalgic for a moment, but sighed and flipped to the blank pages in the back.

Liane came back in and sat on the floor at the coffee table with a fresh mug of her own. She had the bag of snacks we grabbed at CVS while searching last night. She took herself out a Redvine, bit the ends and started stirring her coffee with it like a straw. "Maybe start from the beginning."

So I did. I tried to run through all the conversation I could. The rushed conversation. The promise. Her friend Julie? The disappearance. Everything I could think of. "She didn't tell me where she was," I concluded.

"But who is Julie?" Liane asked, slurping her coffee through her makeshift straw.

"I have no idea. Julie or Joyce. It started with a J."

"Has she mentioned her before?"

"I don't know. Maybe?" And a memory flashed into my brain. "Did Pauline give you her number?"

"Yes."

"Maybe she knows where this Julie lives." I started thumbing through the notebook looking for the name anywhere. "I asked her if she was still here and she said 'Mostly'. You think she's outside of Chicago?"

Liane hummed in agreement, the Redvine hanging from her mouth. She reached slowly to the side of the chair where she had plugged in her phone. "I'll text her now."

I watched my sister crawl slowly around. "Do you regret coming?"

Liane's eyes brightened up her face. "You don't need to ask that. Of course I don't. Why even ask?"

"Lily's sick." My hands waved animated. "Ian needs you. This is such a ridiculous idea."

"It's called Parenting." She kept texting. "We do it together. We're a team. I can spare a day for my brother to find the girl he has dreamt about for years."

I rested my head back on the couch. "I still feel bad."

"You can feel bad about my girl being sick, but don't ever feel bad about this trip. I miss you and any time with you is time well spent. So shut up already."

Liane hit Send.

"It's early," I worried. "She won't answer."

"Pauline told us to contact her. It's a text." Liane yawned like a lion. "Plus, at this point, I don't much care about being polite."

I pulled up Google maps and stared at Chicago. My eyes glanced around at all the little neighborhoods in and around Chicago. The problem, there were so many little places, everywhere. "This place is huge. There is no way I'm going to find her."

Liane laughed. "Maybe we're trying too hard. We accidentally followed her around all day yesterday." She put her head on a couch pillow she had placed on the rug. "I'm optimistic."

I continued to scroll around the map with my finger. It was too small. I sat up and grabbed my laptop I had resting next to the chair, placed it on the coffee table and opened it.

I glanced at Liane, her eyes closed with her phone in her hand.

My computer warmed and I casually checked the emails Adam sent from work. He wasn't handling me leaving as well as he had made it seem. Now was not the time and I moved on to find the maps on my search engine. It found my location easily and I pulled in closer, casually scrolling through the different neighborhoods near Chicago. There were a lot of churches and a lot of baseball fields. I got lost in the virtual map. When I checked the clock, it was near 6:30 AM, which was 4:30 my time. Liane had fallen back asleep still clutching her phone, which lay still and quiet, no message blinking at her. I drank my cooling coffee and grabbed a red vine.

I don't remember closing my eyes.

The theme to Harry Potter startled me awake. I looked around to find where the sound had come from to see Liane answering her phone.

"Hello? Hey, yeah, sorry. I knew it was early."

I glanced at the clock. It was now 8:37 AM.

"Ah geez." I sat up, my computer still on my lap. The notebook now lay in a crumpled heap on the floor.

"You think?" Liane talked on the phone. She snapped at me wanting my attention.

My heart answered. "Is she there?"

Liane wiggled her 'no' and kept snapping and pointing. I wasn't getting it. What did she want? I picked up a red vine.

"Hold on, Pauline." She pulled her ear away. "Your notebook."

"Oh." I grabbed the heap and threw it to her, the different pages catching air before she snatched it.

She clicked the pen in her hand and started jotting down something on a random page. "Say that again? Okay. Right, I got it. But what would you do? Uber? Train?"

Liane has some solid information. I sat up straight, waiting to hear.

"Oh, fun. I always wanted to do that. Okay. No. Sure. I will. Thank you so much. Bye."

Liane's eyes were huge as she pressed the end button.

"Where is she?"

"Julsie, not Julie, lives in Lake Forest," she said with a silly grin. "I don't have her address, but I do have her phone number." She waved the notebook in her hand.

My adrenaline kept me from staying still.

"Call it." She handed me the notebook.

"You call it."

"No, Simon. This is not my phone call."

"Could I just text?"

"Try calling first. I'm going to go get dressed." She stood up. "Do it now while you have the nerve."

"I . . ." stood with the notebook. I rubbed my thumb over the freshly written number. "I can't believe I'm doing this."

Liane had disappeared into the bathroom. I sat back down and grabbed where I had laid my phone.

I kept muttering to myself. I put the number in and stared at it. "I can't believe I am doing this," and pressed Call.

The phone began to ring and my heart leapt into my throat. Two rings. Three rings. Maybe she went by the 'Do not call before 9 AM rule.' A voicemail picked up and I felt sweat building up on my chest and under my arms. Should I leave a message? I quickly hung up.

"She didn't answer," I yelled toward Liane and went to change my own shirt. "I'll text her in a minute."

In my bag, at the bottom of the backpack, lay my crumpled tee shirt, the only clothing I brought with me. I switched it out and put on some deodorant. I went to the kitchen and warmed up my coffee in the microwave when some memory thumped me on the back of the head. "Lake Forest?"

I ran back to the couch where I had left the notebook open.

"She lives in Lake Forest?"

Liane emerged from the bathroom, dressed in something comfortable, with her hair wrapped in a ponytail. "Hey," she said investigating what I was doing.

"You said Lake Forest, right?"

"Yeah." She grabbed her cold coffee and drank it through her Redvine straw. "Pauline said there is a train not far from here that will take us straight there."

I anxiously flipped through the pages. "I know Lake Forest. Adri mentioned Lake Forest before. I thought it was a joke. I mean, who'd name a place that? Is a lake or a forest?"

"I don't know," Liane remarked stuffing her bag. "It seems like a very practical place with a forest and a lake."

"Exactly." My computer screen blinked. I went back and typed in Lake Forest. A suburb north of Chicago reoriented on my screen. My hand came to my mouth. "Let's go. Now."

"Hold on. We have to gather all of our stuff."

I shoved everything into my backpack, zipping it mostly closed.

Liane rubbed around the bridge of her nose. "I've only washed my face."

"You look great," I stated. She did. "Really. You look fine."

She gathered her cords and odds and ends. "I need breakfast."

I threw on my jacket and checked my breath. Not minty fresh, but workable. "I'm sure there's a donut place on the way."

"We don't even know where we're going."

"I have an idea." The image rushed to my vision. "I know where to go."

Liane tailed after me as we rushed from the coffee shop to the train. I hadn't said much to her about all the feelings running around from my head to my stomach to my feet. I would tell her on the train, if she asked, but she followed me faithfully, thoughtfully eating her cinnamon roll.

"Why don't you take a bite?" I asked.

"What fun would that be?" She pulled off another piece, frosting covering her fingers. "And unlike you, I don't have a big mouth. Ever since I wore braces, I've been afraid to bite into anything doughy."

"Braces? You haven't had braces since you were sixteen."

She lifted her eyebrow. "Teenage years leave scars."

"You're weird."

She laughed. "I'm weird, daydreamer?"

"Fair." I went over to the kiosk and studied the train map. "Where do we need to go?"

Liane's finger traced over the notes she made. "UPN. Lake Forest is on that line."

"Got it." I fumbled with the kiosk until I finally got us both tickets to get on the train. "Kay. Let's figure this out."

I tore off in what I figured was the direction, but Liane grabbed my arm and forced me another way.

We found a seat and my knees bounced incessantly.

Liane, wiping the frosting from her fingers with a napkin, placed a hand on my knee to stop the vibration. "You gotta tell me where we're headed."

I tried to collect myself. "I know where to go, I think."

"What do you mean? Did you even text to get the address?"

I shook my head. "Nope. But we aren't going there. To Julsie's."

Liane sputtered. "But that's where she'll be. Pauline told us to—"

"I need to find the tree," I broke in.

She looked more confused than ever. "The tree?"

"Yes. The tree."

"What tree?"

My hands rubbed through my hair again, making everything stick up. "Our tree. Adri and me. It's been our connection. If we find it, I know we will find Adri. I know she'll be there. I feel it."

"I'm still not getting it. A tree connects you guys?"

"Our connect has always been about this tree." My mind went back in memory and filled the air with energy. "It's always been about the tree. I never knew it as a real place, besides in our dreams." I pulled out a notebook and found a scribbled note, oddly on the same page Liane had used to write the phone number. "It's right here. I didn't believe Lake Forest was a real place. She mentioned she had found this tree. Regardless of whether it's our real tree or not, she's drawn to it, just as I am. I'm being pulled to this tree. I can't explain it. I can't explain any of this."

The train stalled forward and then shot out on the track. I watched the world move faster and faster, just as my heart did. "How many stops? I don't know if I can sit here."

In the quick rumble, I rested my head on the headrest and closed my eyes.

Be there, I said quietly in my mind, alone in my thoughts. *Find me at the tree.*

As we traveled, I kept my sights on the scenery around. I couldn't sit still. I kept looking and watching for any sign.

"Do you know where to stop?" Liane asked at the side of me.

"Besides Lake Forest? Not a clue." I opened up my phone again, clicked on my map but couldn't bear to look at it. "Here." I handed it to her before staring back out the window. "Check around Lake Forest."

"What am I looking for?"

"Grass," I said, really thinking about it. "A meadow with a tree. I don't know."

"I don't think Google street view will give you that," Liane remarked. "It's of streets."

I felt the frustration but kept it down. "I'll know it when I see it. Where the grassy parts are?"

Liane was quiet as I took in the passing buildings. Our task felt impossible.

"Wow, there are a lot of grass areas."

I turned. "What do you mean?"

"Big mansions up there. Lots of acres."

"No," I argued. "That doesn't sound right." At least I hoped it wasn't right. If the tree was on private property, I would never find it.

"What's this place?" Liane zoomed in. "Fort Sheridan Nature Pres—"

I held out my arms stopping her dead. "Sheridan?"

"Yes."

I yanked my head back in disbelief. "She wasn't making it up. I cannot believe this." I grabbed Liane by the shoulders. "I know where to go."

I mushed my pancakes with my fork until the syrup was no longer recognizable. I licked it off the utensil, but it was obvious I was done.

"Would you like some more coffee," Julsie asked. "I'm ready to drain the last of it."

"I'm good." I continued to swirl the mushy mess. "I think I'll shower, if that's okay."

Julsie laughed. "Honey, that's the last thing you need to ask me. You go ahead and enjoy yourself. When will you be heading back?" She put down the coffee pot. "But by all means, stay as long as you need. I enjoy the company."

I smiled. "I'll think about it in the shower." I hopped up and cleaned my plate like a good guest.

I slinked back to my room and checked my skimpy packing. I didn't pack any clean underwear, which muted the cleanliness. But a shower would feel good.

I headed in the bathroom and let the steam rise from the showerhead. Her bathroom was much nicer than mine. Everything was shiny and well kept. Mine was well used by countless people before me. Julsie probably renovated this when they bought it, I thought. It didn't fit the style of the home.

I stripped and hopped in, letting the warm water soak into my skin and through my thoughts. I often did my best thinking in the shower, alone and vulnerable, relaxed and carefree, where I opened my mind and let all the emotion out.

My strange dream came back. The look on Simon's face was peculiar, something I had never seen in him. It was panic and delight at the same time.

But I had promised to believe him. I had made a promise to believe he was real.

He said he was at my apartment. What a ridiculous idea. Of course I would want him there. How many times had I daydreamed him knocking on my door and whisking me away?

I picked whatever shampoo was on the ledge and massaged the lather around my dripping hair.

I began to entertain the idea. What if he was real and he was in my apartment and my messy bedroom. I cringed at the thought. Would Simon really fly to find me? Chicago is a big place. He would get swallowed up.

But, yes. I knew it. Yes, Simon would fly to find me. He was impulsive and would drop anything for me.

I moved my head under the hot water, enjoying the soft massage from a proper showerhead, unlike the inconsistent dripping of my crusty apartment shower. It felt luxurious, clearing worry and reconnecting to my soul.

The meadow looked truly lovely. It breathed life into my tired, weary mind. How many days would I need to hide? When would I feel like myself again? In some ways I was glad for the shake up, the change from my ordinary existence. Public, or even global humiliation, weighed a lot on my spirit.

It broke me. And to be sold out by one I used to be in love with hurt more than I wanted to admit, or even think about.

Just wash all the feelings away. I spread out my arms like an eagle, forgetting I was trapped in a glass box. The water now splashed on my face and made me smile.

Meet me at the tree.

I popped open my eyes. Was someone there? I wiped my hand on the steamed glass, but no one had entered.

My heart began racing. I had heard him. It was Simon. The shower suddenly felt stuffy. I couldn't breathe and sat down on the tile, opening the glass door a crack to let in some cooler air.

Simon.

I began to tremble. Why was I trembling? I watched my hands shake as the water still flowed freely down the drain. My fingers combed through my hair, still sticky with shampoo I hadn't washed out.

Simon.

I had fought the idea for so long. Why not have a little faith? Maybe Simon was real?

My heart swelled and pumped at the idea. It was the first time I genuinely considered it to be a possibility. If he was real, the whole thing was real. Was I prepared for the idea?

I pressed my temples with the palms of my hands as I contemplated everything he said. He was there. He met my roommate. He came from Portland to find me. He didn't have much time.

And here I was wasting time naked and sobbing on the shower tile floor.

My hands reached up and turned off the shower. And I breathed, breathed in the first air I had in such a long time.

Meet me at the tree.

I fumbled out the door, my wet body slipping on the cool, slick floor, barely looking through the still steamy room.

"Where is a towel?" I found the cupboard holding the crisp, folded towels and wiped my face. I patted myself dry and wrapped the towel around me. I wiped the mirror with my hand, my red face blinking through the dripping from my soaked head. But something sparkled in my eyes. It was belief.

"Simon," I stated to my reflection. "Simon is waiting for me."

I drew a heart on the steamed-up mirror and a smiley face, hoping whoever used the shower next would see it, and rushed out of the bathroom.

My clothes were strewn about the room. I found what I could and started dressing. My body was still wet as I threw on my underwear. My shirt clung uncomfortably to my skin, so I quickly rubbed it dry with my tee.

My hair dripped everywhere. I hadn't properly rinsed it either. It didn't even have conditioner in it. I shook it a bit with my towel hoping for an improvement.

My face had nothing on it. I had packed nothing. Would he care? I thought. My gut told me no, but my skin told me yes. I put my glasses on. He had never seen me in my glasses either. And the state of my hair was too much. I fingered through it again and waved it back and forth like a rock star.

"Good enough. Maybe he likes the sassy Rockstar look." I took one more look in the bedroom vanity and grabbed a hair tie, just in case.

I checked around the room. My shoes. Where were they? By the door? What else should I bring? Nothing. There was nothing.

I dashed downstairs.

"Julsie?" I called.

"What on earth?" Her voice came from the back room. Julsie slowly began walking forward. "Shouldn't you be in the sh—"

"I need to go, but I'll be back. Probably. I mean, I know I will. I'm leaving my stuff here. I gotta meet someone."

"Have you now?" she asked. "You meeting someone here?"

I eased on my shoes without my hands and grabbed my hoodie. Did I need my hoodie? "Around, I hope. Not far, well kinda far. Fort Sheridan."

"Fort Sheridan? Gerald could give you a ride—"

"No. I'd like the walk."

"And you just remembered?" Julsie's eyes grew skeptical.

"I think this was what Pauline was trying to tell me."

"Would you like me to call her?"

"Yes." I held out my hands. "No, wait. Maybe. I don't know."

"I think I'll call her." Julsie winked. "Well, don't let my yapping stop you. You better get." She waved her hands.

"Kay." I held up my sweatshirt. "Yes, hoodie?"

"Take the sweatshirt, sweetie. The wind by the lake can be deceiving."

I halfway put it on and opened the door. "Kay. I'll be back." I fumbled down the walkway while putting the rest of my hoodie on.

"You be careful, ya hear?"

I saluted and started skipping down the rest of the steps. "Oh, wait!' I turned. "My purse."

Something came flying through the air. I caught it before it hit me in the face. Julsie waved at me from the door. "Don't want to forget that."

I smiled and wrapped the bag sideways around me. I was back down Sunset, heading toward the UPN. I started jogging, and then started running. My bag continually whacked me in the back as I moved. At the corner, I grabbed the ponytail holder from around my wrist and bunched my hair up in a quick bun before continuing across the street.

I jogged a little more, until I felt the stitch in my side.

What am I doing? I kept thinking to myself. *Adri, you are freaking crazy.* I was chasing a ghost, a figment of my imagination. He may not even be there. But I knew he would be. I knew Simon would be there in our meadow. I started to hop again, wanting to get to the station as fast as I could.

Market Square was still very quiet this early in the morning. A few shops were just starting to open. I passed through heading to the station. The train schedule said the next southbound train would be passing toward Fort Sheridan in fifteen minutes. I took it. My hand shook at the kiosk. I couldn't think. I fidgeted around on the platform watching and waiting like a nervous cat. I'd be on the train for only a few minutes.

I finally watched the steady silver bullet approach. I could hardly breathe.

When I stepped on the train a swelling started in my chest and completely overwhelmed me. The tears would not stop. I quickly sat near the exit. The poor lady sitting across from me sidled her legs away.

I took off my glasses and wiped my eyes. "Sorry," I said, though it was to no one but me. I continued to cry.

The train began to move and I let out a squeal. Other people on the train turned at my audible excitement. I couldn't care. It didn't matter.

"Oh my," a voice from behind me said. "No way. You're her."

I placed back my glasses to see a young guy with headphones.

"You're the girl, right?"

"The girl?" and then it hit me. "Oh, right. The video. I forgot about that." I wiped my eyes again. "Would you like a picture?"

The young man stared. "What? No. But check this out." He flipped his phone over and showed me a Twitter gif of me going off the rail and then back over and over. "I just used it."

I watched it and a little giggle came to my throat. "Hey, that's pretty good."

"I would be appalled," another voice came in. It was the lady across from me. "I didn't think it was funny at all. My grandson sent it to me."

"I'm a gif." I laughed harder, still the tears streaming. "I never dreamed I would be a gif. Achievement unlocked."

The train grew silent as everyone in the car rocked and shook watching me as quiet tears streamed my face.

"You know what? It doesn't matter." I patted the lady's leg but then thought better of it and removed my hand. "I'm glad it happened. I'm going to meet the man I have been dreaming about for years. Right now. This guy I pretended didn't exist, but I always knew he did."

The lady looked at me like I was crazy. Maybe I was. "If it was meant to be—"

"It was," I said. "It was meant for me, I guess. Fate must have a great sense of humor." I laughed a little insanely, like Harley Quinn. "Kissing my ex and getting slugged by his wife, pushing my mistake in front of a global audience . . ." I wiped my tears with the back of my hand, "Simon saw it. He saw it. I wonder what he thought. If he laughed like everyone else. And I suspect if I hadn't have fallen over that stupid rail, he wouldn't have found me. How can I be upset at that?"

I now had the attention of everyone on the train. I stood as the stop came closer.

"Enjoy your morning, everyone." I sniffed and used my sleeve for my nose. "I hope I've made your morning. Go talk to your family about the crazy girl on the train who once upon a time fell ass up over a rail and exposed her black lace, and may I add very expensive panties from Victoria's Secret that cost eighteen freaking dollars a pair to the whole stinking world. And I'm so glad I bought them and decided to wear them, so everyone would think I am more high class than I actually am, not the puddling mess of a human in front of you."

The whole car was silent as we approached the stop.

I looked at a little girl with her mom. "You know, she's right. Always wear clean underwear because you never know what might happen. You might fall over into some bushes."

I bowed a Shakespearian theatrical bow as the door opened. As I rose, I took in everyone's bewildered expressions.

"Well, I guess that's all," and stepped out of the train.

There I was on the Fort Sheridan platform. A few people exited from other doors, but for the most part the platform was empty. The train quickly continued down the line and soon left me without a care in the world. Across from me was the entrance to the Fort Sheridan Forest Preserve. I sprinted toward the crossing at the light. My heart and head were running a mile a minute. I didn't exactly remember where to go, but I knew I would know when I found it.

My feet glided, like I had wings carrying me down grassy paths and shady lanes. The spring sun sent streams of light guiding my feet where they should head. Each leaf glistened from the night rain, not yet evaporated. It matched my wet, bundle of hair.

My eyes kept a keen look out for any rise in the ground. I had to find a hill, a slope of some kind. I knew what I was looking for in my dream, but searching real trees and hills seemed silly. But I would know my tree anywhere. I would know.

A patch of sun stopped me in my race. Glittering beams lit my path. Two tall trees opened to a magnificent meadow, guarding the entrance like sentinels. I froze completely.

I no longer wanted to run. I closed my eyes and breathed. "It's okay, Adri," I told myself. "He may not be there. And even if he's not, which is most likely he's not, at least you came and saw it for yourself." I grunted out my breath as I opened back my lids. "Nice pep talk, weirdo in the woods. Talking to yourself. Freaking out on a train full of strangers. I'm completely losing it. Be there. Please, Simon. I need you here."

I shook my shoulders and took a deep breath. My stomach fluttered unlike it had before. A pulse of energy stung all the nerves in my body with each step. I felt as if I were about to walk on stage of a play. I let out a little laugh as I strolled forward.

"I am completely crazy." Talking to myself made it easier to walk. "He's not going to be there. I am going crazy. Hearing voices."

My muttering kept me company until I hit the treeline and walked into the meadow. I stumbled backward forgetting how beautiful it was. It was perfect, breathtakingly perfect.

I scanned over the green lush until I spotted the tree. I couldn't help it. I started to run. I let my feet and heart rush me forward. I didn't see anyone or anything near the hill, but I kept running.

A stitch came in my side, pulling at me in every stride. The tree crept before me and I slowed evaluating the canopy, checking all the detail. It was lonely, no one was there. I grabbed at my side, rubbing away the sore as I stepped closer and closer.

Despair hit me like a wave. I searched around again, but the clearing was empty, not even a passerby.

My feet felt heavier with every step until at last I stood right before it.

"Hello, friend," I said to the tree before I crumbled to my knees and began sobbing. Not the pretty, delicate sobs, but the ugly cry sobs, the ones bursting from the soul. I brushed my hands against the trunk and felt its rough bark connecting me to a world of make-believe. I wrapped my arms around it like hugging an old friend. Why did I think he would be here? I absolutely believed it with all my heart. I had hoped for something so foolish, so whimsical. I got carried away in the fantasy of it.

"I heard his voice," I said to the tree with its listening ear and wisdom. "Why isn't he here?" I sobbed harder. I was the silly dreamer who lived in a dreamworld I created. It felt real to me. The real world was hard. It hurt, it stabbed at all my flaws and insecurities. It made me feel like a dreamwalker all the time. "How could Simon not be here?"

Gravity caved in on me and I sank into the wood, pressing every hope, every emotion I had left into this one moment. The tree knew everything. It had witnessed everything, every dream. It knew me, and it was as if it was holding me, cradling me in the crook of its roots.

There, there, dream child.

"Adri?"

"No more voices." I couldn't handle hearing his voice again. "No more, please," I whispered to the tree. "I hurt enough."

"Adrianna."

My full name. Why are you using my full name, tree? I thought we were friends. I pulled back to scowl when an image appeared a small distance away. I sat up right and wiped my tears. My eyes stung from the swelling sobs. The image became clearer.

"I am dreaming. Did I cry myself to sleep?"

The image of Simon stood still, his chest heaving either from running or from emotion. "You're here."

"I am." I straightened more and wiped my eyes again. The startling reality of Simon standing where I wanted him was alarming. I was dreaming. I had to be. It was too perfect to be real.

Simon's image cleared in my vision. He looked very troubled, not sad, but relieved and confused. And there was someone else standing around fifty feet away from him, a girl.

"I think that I'm seeing things. There's someone else here. It's usually just us. No one else has ever been in the dream before."

"Oh my . . ." He covered his mouth like in shock. "Adri. It's you. Really you?"

I climbed on my knees. "Yes. And you've come at the right time too. It's been a hell of a week."

"Yes." He grinned. "Yes, it really has. I can't believe. . ." He wiped his eye.

I felt my hair. It was still wet. "Sorry. Usually in my dreams I'm a little more put together. Reality doesn't play a huge part. I was in the shower before I fell asleep."

Simon walked forward. "You wear glasses too." His grin was growing bigger on his face. "I don't care about your hair. That's the last thing I could care about right now."

"Is my face red, too?" I asked.

"Yes. But who cares? I don't care. It's perfect." He laughed uncomfortably and wiped his other eye. "You look perfect. I'm sure mine will be all red soon, too."

I stood and dusted off my pants. I pressed my palm against the tree for balance feeling drained for running and sobbing. Simon's steps toward me were hesitant, cautious. I evaluated his expression. "You're crying too."

"I know. I know." He laughed again, nervous, different. "That's my. . ." He drew in a breath, pointing. "That's my sister. She came with me."

I waved sheepishly. She looked familiar. Maybe I had run into her while I was awake, my subconscious bringing in a fresh face. "How did you get her here?"

"We flew here."

"You flew?"

"Adri." Simon stared at me with a look of bemused admiration. He thumbed his hands through his hair like I had seen him do before, but somehow it was different. His ruffled hair slid around like I hadn't seen. It wasn't in perfect shape; it went a bit mad science. "I can't believe I'm standing before you. I can't believe this is real."

"What are you talking about? Simon. It's a dream. We are dreaming. I'm asleep. I mean, I thought you would come, or hoped you would, but it's impossible. I kept hearing your voice. It kept echoing around or it might have been the bathroom tile."

Simon hitched. "Adri. I'm here. This isn't a dream."

So many questions flooded my mind. "It can't be real. There is no way that you would have ended up here. How did you end up at this tree?"

"You brought me here. Remember? I wrote it down." He threw off the backpack he was wearing. He had never brought a backpack in the dream before. Unzipping the top, Simon grabbed a notebook. "I kept track. I'm so glad I did. I would have never found you."

The breath went out of me when I saw the notebook. "Wait. No. This has to be a dream. It can't be possible."

"Everything's possible." Simon threw up his hands. "Don't you get that? How was it even possible for us to share our dreams? And you came when I needed you. You were listening."

I stumbled again. The tree caught me. Simon rushed forward and caught my arm. The shock of the warmth in his touch, the smooth skin, and the little details like the little freckles in his forearm sent my heart pumping. He pulled me up and didn't let go. I couldn't tear my eyes from his.

It was the same with him. "You're real." I wasn't talking to him, but to myself.

A strong surge of wind quickly wrapped around the tree, sending the branches rustling.

"Look," Simon motioned toward the tree. "No initials."

I glanced where the initials had always been, but the bark was smooth and unmarred. I gazed at Simon, my Simon, standing as real as I had always imagined right before me. "I think we should change that."

Simon pulled me close into an embrace electrifying every cell in my body. The pull of years without each other, and the years built together, knitted every stitch that made us undone. I clung to him tighter not understanding the connection. Not understanding anything, and not caring anymore. I felt his arms wrapped around me completely, real hands bringing the sleepy me to life. His fingers worked their way to my wet cheeks and brushed the tears gently from my face.

I pulled back to see his eyes, brilliant brown eyes glistening wet. Had they always been this color? He had tiny freckles on his nose too. Neither one of us spoke, just stared. His fingers still traced my cheek until he cupped my jaw and pulled me closer.

Our lips touched and the world vanished, lightly brushing until the pulse rushed through me and I wrapped hard around him, breathing him in for the first time. His caress parted softly, still fragile and experimental. The softest whisper escaped his mouth. "My dream girl."

I smiled. I couldn't help it. "I don't know what I could possibly dream about now."

He kissed me again before answering, "I'm sure we could figure out something."

Seventeen

Adri smooths out a blanket. "How long have you had this thing?"

"My mother made it." Simon places the basket on top. "She fixed the hole near the bottom. I used to bite it when I was little. You can see the patch work here." He points to a corner.

Adri examines the cartoonish fabric. "How thoughtful. I don't think I kept my baby blankies."

"Too bad." Simon says opening the picnic basket and grabbing a few small sandwiches. "They make great picnic blankets."

Adri absently rubs the gentle shell she wears on a chain around her neck. "My mom is not a saver. She got rid of a lot of my stuff when I moved out." Adri sits down next to him, placing a hand on his arm. "I won't be the same way. I'll probably keep stuff around." She absently caresses the shell placed on a chain which sits around her neck.

Simon smiles and winks. "When that time comes. Here." He throws her a sandwich.

Adri laughs and grabs the turkey and cheese.

Simon attempts to open a can of soda. It slips from his grip and sprays over his hands, but he recovers. They both laugh now as Simon sips a little. "Would you like some?"

Adri takes a tiny sip and hands the can back. "Still not a fan of Dr. Pepper."

"I'll get you there." Simon places the can in the grass.

Adri lays down looking up at the canopy of branches. "You know, no one would believe our story."

Simon lays his head next to hers. "I don't know. I think it's believable."

Adri laughs. "How?"

Simon lifts his head, can't help himself and kisses her deep on the mouth. He pulls back and stares at his beautiful bride. "Sometimes cosmic forces need to intervene." He brushes her neck with his fingers, making her blush. "It's like the only prank fate can play. When it sees two people so obviously perfect for each other, regardless of distance, what do you think it would do?"

Adri squints, looking up at Simon. "I'll have to thank fate someday."

Simon leans in again and kisses Adri sweetly. They lean back and enjoy the view, each taking a bite of their sandwiches. The names etched in the tree now linked with a plus sign.

"Nice touch," Adri states through her mouthful.

Simon grins. "Looks pretty good right there. Right?"

Adri wraps her hand in his hair before kissing his cheek. "Perfect."

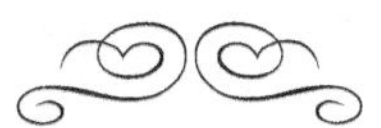

Acknowledgements

To all those that have helped me on this journey with "Daydreamers," my sincerest thank you, especially to my nieces who leant their names, completely without permission, to a few of the characters.

My incredible editor, Talysa Sainz, has been a fan and champion this entire, difficult time. Her guidance has brought a light to Simon and Adri I didn't know was there. To her, my deepest gratitude for her inspiration and clear vision that shaped this beautiful book.

Huge thank you to Liz Christensen and Todd Wente for bringing my characters to life, and for Liz's eagle eye.

My deepest appreciation to Becky Adams for the last-minute shaping and J T Moore for wisdom in character development and creation.

Aly, thank you for helping me experience your Chicago, with the surprising fireflies and winding sidewalks. Your input on the dreams was invaluable and I will forever be grateful.

Christine and Jen, you are the best for taking me to Portland and giving me a taste of the beautiful details and eccentricities that envelop that wondrous place.

To the Bens: thank you Ben I. for your honesty when pinpointing the relationship problem from the beginning; and thank you Ben V. for understanding my vision and creating a perfect backdrop.

Love to my family and writing community for always being there.

And to all those who dream in daylight seeking impossibilities beyond your sight . . . It is to you that our dreams become reality. Never stop dreaming.

About the Author

CANDACE J. THOMAS was raised by the wild, among the high peaks and winter snow of the mountains of Utah.

She is author of the award-winning VIVATERA series, VAMPIRE-ISH: A HYPOCHONDRIAC'S TALE, and several short fictions and poetry.

Candace is an ethereal thinker and often stands too close to the fire. She resides in Salt Lake City, Utah where you can find her in a hammock listening to fairy bells.

candacejthomas.com

Facebook.com/candacejthomas.author

Twitter: @cjtwrites

Instagram: @candacejthomas

OTHER BOOKS BY
Candace J. Thomas

Young Adult Fantasy

THE VIVATERA SERIES

Vivatera

Conjectrix

Everstar

Paranormal Romantic Comedy

Vampire-ish: A Hypochondriac's Tale

Short Stories and Poetry

Of Snow and Moonlight

Wandering Beautiful

The Hawkweed

Non-Fiction

Six Simple Steps: Build A World

www.ingramcontent.com/pod-product-compliance
Lightning Source LLC
Chambersburg PA
CBHW021101110726
47900CB00007B/1971